BELLOCQ'S WOMEN

Peter Everett

JONATHAN CAPE
LONDON

Published by Jonathan Cape 2000

2 4 6 8 10 9 7 5 3 1

First published in Great Britain in 2000 by
Jonathan Cape
Random House, 20 Vauxhall Bridge Road,
London SW1V 2SA

Random House Australia (Pty) Limited
20 Alfred Street, Milsons Point, Sydney,
New South Wales 2061, Australia

Random House New Zealand Limited
18 Poland Road, Glenfield,
Auckland 10, New Zealand

Random House (Pty) Limited
Endulini, 5A Jubilee Road, Parktown 2193, South Africa

The Random House Group Limited Reg. No. 954009
www.randomhouse.co.uk

A CIP catalogue record for this book is available from the British Library

ISBN 0–224–05988–2

Papers used by Random House are natural,
recyclable products made from wood grown in sustainable forests;
the manufacturing processes conform to the environmental
regulations of the country of origin

Typeset in Bembo by Palimpsest Book Production Limited,
Polmont, Stirlingshire

Printed and bound in Great Britain by
Mackays of Chatham PLC, Chatham, Kent

To Dan Franklin

1

In New Orleans, on 18 February 1889, officers led Étienne Deschamps into court to face Judge R. H. Marr. He was charged with the murder of a schoolgirl, Juliette Deitsch. Deschamps being E. J. Bellocq's mother's dentist, she sent her son to tell her every slander they were making against the good man. Easier said than done; Deschamps ranted and raved so loudly that he came near being ejected from the court. He was a well-born Frenchman, he shouted, and ought to be tried by a French-speaking judge and jury.

Unmoved, Marr set a trial date in April. Madame Bellocq insisted that her son attend.

'Why can't you read about it in the papers, *maman*?'

'There'll be things the *Picayune* won't print.'

'How do you know that?'

'Just do as you are told.'

Bellocq saw his face in the mirror, and looked away quickly. Often he would force himself to stare, else he would stop as a sob burst out of his mouth. He looked older than his fifteen years. Old enough to pass muster and get into the courtroom. He did not tell his mother that the heat sometimes sent him to sleep.

'Were many women there?' His mother put down her fork to stare at him.

If she were so curious, why not go in person?

Only women of a certain kind went to trials of that nature.

'What sort are those, *maman*?'

Lowdown women, avid to squeeze the last bit of juice out of every sensation. 'How many were there?'

'I don't know; ought I to have counted them? A dozen, maybe.'

'Of what class were they?'

'They must have leisure time on their hands.'

'Well-to-do, then? And you had no idea who any of them were?'

Bellocq shook his head. Apart from his mother, the women he had seen damned Étienne Deschamps as being guilty as sin.

'It's this city!' Madame Bellocq shook her fan. 'Before you know it, a crass chit can ruin any man of taste and culture.'

'Are you sure that's how it was?'

Things went on in New Orleans that he would not believe.

'What things, *maman*?'

If Bellocq had hated the idea of going to the trial at first, he was soon primed to learn more about Étienne Deschamps. The dentist had come to New Orleans in 1884, in time for the Cotton Exposition. He rented lodgings in St Peter Street and went to Jackson Square every day. Bellocq used to see him handing out pink cards that read:

> *Let us look for the truth!*
> *Let us do good!*
> *Let us be magnetized!*

DR EUGENE ÉTIENNE
68, rue St Pierre

He would treat any patient in the comfort of his or her own home. Magnetism could heal all ills. If he resorted to the use of chloroform at times, it was to help them submit to his will. Women, including Bellocq's mother, enjoyed his cures. A few left his house after the treatment so dazed that they threw up on his doorstep.

Deschamps had made no friends in the city except for Jules Deitsch. Deitsch, a widower with two daughters, was a carpenter from Paris, a lover of books and culture. Deitsch had not been long in America. His rooms were round the corner from Deschamps, in the rue Chartres, and there the doctor would go to reminisce about Paris and the life they'd once lived. Deitsch learnt that Eugene Étienne's real name was Étienne Deschamps, and that he had been born at Rennes of a wealthy family. In Paris he graduated from a course in dentistry with honours, but had then gone in for the fast life. His family drew the line: he would change his life or they would cut him off without a penny piece. When the Crimean War broke out he joined the cavalry, narrowly escaping death from a Russian lance at Sebastopol. Shipped home, he went into politics until left-wing forces drove him out. He sailed for Brazil but found it impossible to make his mark there either. Back in Paris, he set up as a dentist but spent too much time dabbling in the occult. Soon he came to realize that he had magnetic powers. Why, asked Deitsch, had Deschamps made the same mistake as he and come to New Orleans?

It was no mistake. Surely Deitsch had heard of Jean Lafitte? Deschamps was seeking the pirate's lost treasure. It was buried somewhere in the swamps and islands of Barataria. So far, Deschamps had found a few gold coins in the sand, but he hoped soon to dig up the bulk

3

of it. What he had to find first was a young girl, still a virgin, who could act as a medium. Deitsch was sure at once that his daughter Juliette could fit the bill. She was a plump twelve-year-old and, if she proved suitable, he would deem it an honour to let her help Deschamps.

So, last summer, the doctor had signed Juliette in as his daughter at Grand Isle and Barataria hotels. Never mind what else they got up to treasure-hunting in the swamps. But there were hints enough to set shifty images moving in Bellocq's imagination.

In October, Deschamps went to Barataria alone. Deitsch, to his horror, found Juliette in an alley with a boy. He had her up against a wall with one of her legs around his waist. That precious maidenhead was under threat until the carpenter beat him off with a stick.

Mon Dieu, it would never do! Dr Deschamps had to have a pure virgin. She could have thrown away a treasure in more senses than one. Deschamps, too, was beside himself.

Juliette and her sister were pupils at Miss Roux's, a private school two doors away from Deschamps' lodgings. Late afternoon, he'd go up to his room, a girl on each arm, where he fed them candy. Most people assumed that they were his own children.

Miss Roux agreed with the handwriting expert: Juliette's letters to Deschamps had to be forgeries. They were from his 'little mistress', but the whole world said the doctor wrote them. Miss Roux thought the girl was too backward for such grown-up sentiments, but yes, certainly, she was bright enough to have copied them. The man she named in them was a happily married jeweller who lived in the Garden District. He had never met Juliette, and it was a damned lie if she said he had.

4

He had not seduced her before she got into bed with Deschamps.

After the inquest, the poor carpenter went round the Old Quarter to raise cash by subscription to bury his daughter. In the cemetery forty thousand people fought to get near the coffin. Bellocq was one. The chief topic at the funeral, he told his mother, was how Deschamps had stuck a dental tool in his chest. He bled a lot – but, if he had been set on killing himself, a toothpick was no use. Two days later he left the Charity Hospital for the parish prison, where he made a mess of hanging himself from the bars of his cell. He had used his belt but made sure the buckle was under his chin. Hearing his groans the guards came running. They cut Deschamps down, him swearing the whole time they had to let him die.

'They had his photograph in the paper today,' Madame Bellocq said. 'You didn't say that he had shaved off his beard.'

'How was I to know you were interested in his looks?'

'He left only that straggly moustache. He looks like your father now.'

'He has made his own bed, *maman*.'

'I don't want to hear that.'

'He says that Juliette was no virgin,' said Bellocq. 'She was fast but, yes, they were in love. He did not mean to kill her: an experiment got out of hand.'

His mother could find no excuse for the doctor. But there were houses auctioned twelve-year-old virgins every other night of the week, she said. It was unjust to hang a man for a maidenhead.

'Your mama ought to hush up with all that, Mr Ernest,' said Louella, the maid, sure that Madame Bellocq was out of earshot, 'that son of a bitch did it for sure – and you,

5

nor anybody else, is going to prove otherwise. The man is grease-slippery in every way, and guilty as hell.'

On 29 April, Judge Marr heard that Deschamps had no counsel and appointed James Dowling. Dowling asked for thirty days to prepare the accused's defence. The judge gave him two, setting a new trial date for 1 May.

Three men talked about the case in the courthouse passageway. One was looking out for Mrs Elizabeth Hilroy, Deschamps' landlady. She was a witness, all set to tell how Deschamps had been her tenant for some years, but that she did not know him well at all. He had precious little to say and kept his door locked going out. Any cleaning he did himself. Sure, she knew the girls; they were up to his room most every day.

Another man, Joe, said, 'You couldn't get it up, you went to see the dentist. A magnetic trick or two got your dick stiff as a poker.'

'Well, by all accounts, and you can tell by her picture, that girl was some looker,' said Mrs Hilroy's friend. 'Wouldn't you fall off your perch to give her one? Twelve she may have been, but you'll never persuade me she didn't know what it was for.'

'So, why the chloroform before he got down to it?' This was from Charlie Serra, who had been with Deitsch when he found his daughter dead in bed with Deschamps.

Serra was a nightwatchman. He was asleep in the room next door when Daddy Deitsch came knocking. The dentist had told his daughter Laurence that her sister Juliette had gone to sleep and was going to die. She had run home in tears with a bundle of Dr Deschamps' books to weigh her down.

Deitsch, getting no reply from the doctor, had knocked

at Serra's door. 'I'd heard a moaning,' said Serra. 'Daddy Deitsch was dancing up and down. I had to bust the door with my shoulder! You never know where that might lead. I said we better get the police.

'Three cops ran back with us and got the key from Mrs Hilroy. The shutters were closed, so the room was dim. My eyes got used to it by the light of a candle on the mantelshelf.' Papers smouldered in the grate and the air was full of fumes. Both Deschamps and the girl were bare-ass in the bed. She was dead but still warm. Deschamps let out a groan when one of the cops touched him. He had four wounds in his chest.

In court, Jules Deitsch took the stand first. He spoke as little English as Deschamps; Deputy Sheriff Villeré was on hand to translate. District Attorney Charles Luzenberg led Deitsch to tell how Juliette's sister had run home on the day in question. Deitsch said he had known Dr Deschamps for almost a year and, yes, he knew exactly what the dentist had been trying to do with his daughter. It was innocent, and had to do with trances, with finding Lafitte's treasure. No, he had never for a moment suspected anything else was going on. Luzenberg held up a glass disc set in ebony. Bellocq saw the flash, but it was no mirror.

Yes, it was Deschamps', or he had one very like it; it was a device he used to put a person into a trance. Deitsch knew it because the doctor had tried it on him. Luzenberg gave it in evidence that the police had found the instrument beside the dead girl in the accused's bed.

Cross-examining Deitsch, Dowling got him to admit that he did not know the cause of his daughter's death. So far as he could tell it was the chloroform. But,

7

surely, Deschamps had put him under with that, too, several times?

Luzenberg had the policemen up next: Captain John Journée, and Officers Fernand Rance and George Legendre, the three who had gone into the room with Deitsch and Serra. Their picture was of Juliette Deitsch and the doctor naked, a blanket up to their waists. There were empty bottles of chloroform and handkerchiefs soaked in the stuff, fumes everywhere.

On the next day, the last of the trial, Juliette's sister sat, pale in her black dress. James Dowling said she was too young to testify, but Marr overruled. The judge asked Laurence, did she understand what an oath was? She said she went to mass every Sunday and she knew not to lie. So they swore her in.

Madame Bellocq leant forward. 'What did she say?'

'She had not got a word out before Dowling was on his feet to object that Deschamps was not on trial for sexual misconduct; he was on trial for murder, with his life as forfeit.'

'Well?'

Luzenberg excused Laurence and called Coroner LeMonnier to the stand.

LeMonnier related the autopsy findings. The victim's lips were blue and burnt by chloroform; it had been an overdose of that anaesthetic which killed the child. It must have been administered by the same fiend that abused her body over a long period. There were scratches and bite marks on her breasts, and her anus was torn.

Dowling called Laurence to the stand again. How often had Laurence seen Juliette take her clothes off and get into bed with the dentist? She could not answer for sobbing.

8

'They had gone to his rooms after school that day. He gave them candy and they sat talking. The doctor went for wood to make a fire, and her sister said he would put her to sleep again. With the fire alight, the doctor closed the shutters and told Juliette to undress and hop into bed. He was naked, too, which had not upset Laurence at all. She had the candy. Yes, she could remember the smell of the stuff he poured onto the handkerchief that he put on Juliette's face.'

Madame Bellocq gave a sharp tut of reproof, before urging her son to go on.

'Deschamps asked if she could see anything. Juliette said she could see God and the Holy Virgin in Jackson Square.'

His mother shook her head. 'How ridiculous!'

'She did, according to Laurence. Next thing Deschamps told Juliette to hold the chloroform bottle to her nose. Her eyes closed. After a while, he got up to burn papers in the grate. Laurence didn't know what those were; then he dressed and told her not to touch her sister but to keep an eye on her. He left, locking the door, but was not gone long. He came back with two bottles of chloroform. He undressed again, soaking more of the liquid on a cloth to hold over Juliette when he got into bed.'

Madame Bellocq leant forward. 'What did Laurence do?'

'She sat on a stool by the bed. It was going to be their most successful experiment, Deschamps had told her.'

'That poor child.'

Louella came in to clear the table, and the clatter she set up with plates on the tray said she would have no truck with any of that stuff.

It had been the last twist of the knife for Dr LeMonnier

to testify that Juliette Deitsch was not yet of an age to conceive or bear a child, Madame Bellocq said. Despite what the papers inferred she was not pregnant but, yes, it might have come about any time. 'Judge Marr ought not to have allowed that,' she said. 'That sort of thing sways juries.'

No doubt his mother was right. It took the jurors eighteen minutes to find Deschamps guilty.

Bellocq made no mention of Hermia Forbes in his account. She was going down the steps, talking in a loud voice to her friend. 'That poor worm is even less of a man now.'

'Looks dirty,' said her friend.

'So would you – that parish prison never sees a broom from one year to the next.' There was no answer.

'Eugene Étienne was a washout between the sheets,' said Hermia. Bellocq had her name pat before she reached the pavement, and knew that she was a Storyville whore. 'He'd drink himself stupid, hum along with the music and talk all kinds of crap. His magnetism was no help at all, but he could make you feel shivery when the moon was full. I never knew why.'

Hermia was there to see justice done. 'There was no call to kill a schoolkid just to get it up.'

Her friend said if she paid any mind to what most johns went on about she'd go crazy.

Bellocq had nowhere to flee as the car braked at the kerb. His father was at the wheel. How could he get back into the courthouse? He stood halfway down the steps, sure that his father would see him any minute.

'Why, Hermia, how is it that I know exactly where I'm

going to chance on you?' His father saw Bellocq. 'And who's that up there hiding behind your skirts?'

Bellocq blushed, coming down the steps.

'What are you doing here?'

His father got out of the car. Bellocq kept his eye on the parasol that the dark Mexican woman in the rear seat put up with a twirl. He knew that she was the loathsome Josune Baulaz, Señor Mezcua's secretary – his father's mistress.

Ought Bellocq to tell his father that *maman* had asked him to come? Living in the rift between estranged parents was not easy. As his mother said, 'Your father has so many balls in the air, no one can keep up with them all.'

'How did the day go for Deschamps?' his father asked Hermia.

'Not well, and that's all I want to say about that bastard,' she replied.

Madame Bellocq did not let up. She sent Bellocq to the prison with messages for the doctor. Hope was not lost. Deschamps must take heart. He had some friends in New Orleans still, and she would not desert him in his hour of need. Not that Bellocq got into the prison. The guard took his two dollars but would not be seen with him. 'There are times when all I want is to up and leave this place. I used to think this job had more to it than it has.'

'What's wrong with it?'

'What's right? It's no fun at all, boy, living with that stink of burnt nigger pig meat in there before we ship them up to the farm.'

Sure he had stories, information – but only if Bellocq took his photograph. After all, any bona fide reporter'd pay cash down for what he knew – take his picture too.

Bellocq met the guard in a deserted warehouse on the waterfront. Not a place he liked taking his camera. The man stood with his back to the river, talking all the while as Bellocq set about taking his picture. 'Deschamps is mad, or he wants us all to think he is,' he said. 'If you ask me, he's in a bad way. Would you believe he has us stew cigars to feed him? Don't ask why, 'cause that I can't tell you. Another thing we have to do is stay shut up when he's talking to the moon. You know some guy name of Voltaire?'

Bellocq nodded.

'Studies that monkey by the hour, or he'll read Anatole France aloud if you'll listen. Upset him, and he'll stick his ass in your face. He is in deep with Jean Lafitte all the time, and that girl he killed. The only living people he'll talk to are Sheriff White and Dr Hava. Hava visits all the time, trying to work out whether he's sane or not. Edgar, our sheriff, is a great one for books so he listens, never pays any mind to him going on about his innocence.'

They had two men on death row apart from the dentist. Henry Johnson shot a cop and a clerk, Philip Baker, cut the throat of the woman he worked for. 'Deschamps is something else. He says he'll live to see them hang. The guy he hates most is LeMonnier – the assassin, he calls him.

'In his own mind, if you can believe him, he's blameless – a scientist of the first water.

'His skull's sure thick, though. Tother day, two of us were walking him along the gallery over the courtyard and he went off, head first. How do you like that?'

'Was he hurt?'

'Not so as you'd know it. He didn't get a fair trial, he says. The judge and jury railroaded him in a language he didn't understand, now he's a fatted calf they're about to slaughter.'

Deschamps' appeal in March 1890 was a foregone conclusion. His new attorney appeared to be John G. McMahon, but Judge Roman said he was coming off the bench to act for Deschamps. He and McMahon came close to blows at this bombshell. Marr knocked that on the head by threatening a charge of contempt. McMahon left the courtroom in a huff. There was only the same ground for Roman to go over. He had to take the same tack Dowling had – that Daddy Deitsch had known all along what Deschamps was up to with Juliette. By then, the prosecution had the two St Peter Street drugstore keepers to put the lid on things; they told how the bottles of chloroform they'd sold the dentist never had a label. You could read whatever you liked into that.

Roman's address to the jury ought to have swung them. It was a fair and impartial balancing act that took a good three hours and a half to tease out. There were lots of quotes of the law on murder. The question they had to decide was whether Deschamps had slain the child in cold blood. He had not moved them at all. They trooped out and, thirteen minutes later, came back to confirm the verdict: guilty as charged. Mr Luzenberg seemed highly gratified; the monster would pay the price.

Judge Marr set the date of the hanging for the next January. The sentence was postponed while doctors locked horns over the question of Deschamps' sanity. That August, Judge Roman asked the Board of Pardons to commute the sentence, but was turned down. The new date for the execution was April 1891.

The French consul left for Baton Rouge to see Lieutenant-Governor Jeffries and Governor Nicholls. He did not get much joy. Deschamps would hang same time as Baker: 22 April 1891.

'LeMonnier says the autopsy he'll do after the hanging will prove the doctor is sane,' Bellocq told his mother.

Judge Buisson drew up the will. Deschamps left all his books, letters and newspaper clippings in his cell to Sheriff White; Dr Hava was to have his body.

Three days before the hanging, Judge Marr disappeared. He was last seen strolling near the river on Carrollton Avenue, going to vote in the election. Then he was gone – into the Big Muddy, people said, never mind that it was a hundred feet away. His body was never found.

'Good riddance,' said Madame Bellocq. 'If he could knot the noose around the doctor's neck he would.'

The disappearance brought a spate of rumours in the newspapers: dark influences were at work; Deschamps was a mason, and it was a known fact that any mason got away with murder.

The Freemasons struck back with letters to the paper. They said Deschamps was a Catholic; he had never been a member of their lodge.

'On the day, I had trouble to wake him; he was deep in sleep,' the guard told Bellocq. 'He ate breakfast – unusual for him – then we walked to the chapel. No, he wanted no truck with the priest. Baker was in the chapel, too, itching to say hello to the doctor before they stood side by side on the scaffold. Deschamps would have none of that either – told us to take him back to his cell, where he sat calmly to await his fate.'

However, it was Baker alone who Hangman Taylor stretched at ten minutes of one. Jeffries and Governor Nicholls had reprieved Deschamps.

'He will not die.' Madame Bellocq was sure.

That held true until 1892, with Deschamps getting crazier by the day. He stayed firm about some things, though, and that priest did not give up on him either. How could the doctor confess to a murder he did not commit? Walking to the gallows that day in May, he laid into LeMonnier again. The coroner had come to the yard to see justice done and heard the shout, 'Assassin! Assassin!' Deschamps had always sworn that LeMonnier had the power to save him but had refused! The man was a disgrace to France! Those words fell on deaf ears. Taylor put the noose round Deschamps' neck, and Deschamps stared him in the face and said adieu. He was not the criminal; no, the real criminal was – LeMonnier!

At ten past the hour, the trap fell. At half-past, they cut the body down for LeMonnier to start work. 'I saw him cut the skull open and take out the brain,' the guard told Bellocq. 'There was no sign of degeneration, he said, it was that of a normal, healthy man.'

A Creole boy came knocking at the door. He held his finger to his lips as he handed Bellocq a message. It was from his father, asking him to luncheon at Antoine's.

Bellocq had last eaten with his father at Mardi Gras. Nobody on feast days gave a damn, Father had said, amused by the crowds. Bellocq had felt then that something underlay his father's *bonhomie*, especially when he said, 'The ditch may be deep or shallow, but there is one with our name on it that waits for us to fall into.'

His son had no idea what ditch he was talking about.

Bellocq flinched at the sudden glare of a waiter's white apron; at a sign from Father, the man filled a glass for him to taste.

'Well?'

'How can I judge?'

'Say something. Jerome has to know whether it will pass muster. Other customers are waiting.'

'What is it?'

'A Sauterne, sir,' said Jerome, and Bellocq nodded.

'Jerome is very good; sage is a word that springs to mind,' said Father as the waiter left. 'They do their level best to make a man feel he has their total attention. Never mind their corns, of course.'

A man in shirtsleeves, pants and faded yellow suspenders came in out of the heat. He took off his panama and stared up at the fan, mopping his brow. His walk was silent; he wore greasy moccasins. The dark spots on them seemed to be blood, and they gave off a strong rancid smell. He helped himself to a peach off a salver and bit into it, heedless of the juice falling off his chin to moisten other stains on his shirt.

'What news from the bazaars, Priaulx?' Bellocq's father asked, as the man limped up on his cane to grip at the empty chair's back. Father's glance was taunting, openly daring him to sit. He swept an ant out of the glaring light of the table-cloth.

'Your ear was ever closer to the ground than mine,' said Priaulx. 'I did get along to see Deschamps stretched, though. You were absent.'

Bellocq's father gave a sigh for poor Deschamps. New

Orleans was a city like that. It led you to think you could get away with anything.

'Well, you're hale and hearty enough to know more about that than I,' said Priaulx. 'Too old to swing an axe, at my age, and this heat'll kill me soon, for sure. Who did keep you from waving Deschamps off? You were not in court, either.'

'No,' said Father. 'I thought Eugene had enough on his plate.'

'You take one step, the next comes easy,' said Priaulx. 'You know how it is. I hear you have troubles of your own.'

'What would those be?'

Priaulx merely smiled, raised his panama and limped on by to join a group at another table.

'Try, if you can, to avoid any dealings with that man,' said Father. 'You see that drawing on the wall. The artist who did it sat where you are now. He had relations in cotton before they went bankrupt.

'Paul Broca,' he went on, 'who was a neuroanatomist, proved that man had a dual brain; that was some thirty or more years ago. My left side is abler than my right, in that it controls the whole right side of my body.' He paused to reflect again. 'No matter what you hear, *mon fils*, I had my reasons; try not to think too badly of me. Your *maman* will try to tell you that I am – well, she doesn't know, her tales never ring as true as she'd like to believe they are.'

Bellocq felt that his father saw him as another failure, over which to make the best of a bad job. On his own side, those heroes he read about left him feeling he had been born into the wrong family.

His father smiled. He was reading Emerson. It was high

time he made a start on his memoirs. It was such a final business, though — and memories sapped a man. The truth was that he felt he had not yet begun to live.

Bellocq was left to wonder who Emerson was.

'See where she comes to brighten my life,' said Father, as Josune Baulaz came in the door. He went towards her, stumbled as they met and had to seize her arm. Steadying his head, he smiled and waved reassuringly to his son.

The next day, in a last parental flourish, Father bought his son a whore. He said it would stop him playing with himself, which he had to have started by now. The whole business only made things worse. Father and Mrs Johnson chose a thirteen-year-old. Her parents were trash from Minsk; they sent her out with flowers to sell in hotel lobbies so that she could meet men. The girl had kept them alive until they died of yellow fever. She spoke no more than a few words of English, said Mrs Johnson, but she was sharp and had soon picked things up. Ever afterwards, it was the girl's frail hands washing his penis that Bellocq brought to mind when playing with himself, relishing that exquisite pain as he came, too quickly to get inside her. Father was out on the landing talking with Mrs Johnson during his initiation. He was telling her that he was not yet sure when he would have to leave New Orleans, but go he must.

A month later, Bellocq's father ran off to Mexico with Josune Baulaz, leaving Bellocq deep in the maze. Things went on in New Orleans that he would never fathom. He thought of all those things that his father knew which he would never tell him now. He had gone missing with Emerson, having left rumours and promises not kept.

Bellocq had always felt he lived at the edge of nowhere. Now he had to endure the mystery behind his father's sudden departure, a mystery his mother felt she had to confess to *Père* Guersaint.

The priest came by after dark, since the house was in the wrong part of town now for him to be seen. The tide of fashion had turned, leaving it high and dry. Yet girls walking nearby streets went to the selfsame man. How did Guersaint keep going? His mind must be a bed of hot coals those women raked over night and day. He was serving God in the city, for which he had set himself up in Rome and the Holy Land. He had been to Jerusalem, trodden where the Saviour bore His cross. Yet his own approach was that of a sidelong scuttle, a crab's. He carried his solacing ritual in a portable black box of tricks; his breath reeked of dead scriptures. Bellocq was sure that his mother talked about him, too. She found more to say to the priest than to him, all that whispering. It would come as no surprise that *Père* Guersaint knew how long it took his left testicle to descend. As darkly close as lovers, his mother gave up her sins to him in the same breathy way that a girl's lips part for a kiss, fluttering her eyelashes. Not only did Guersaint hear of his father's crimes, he learnt the names of his mother's half-sisters, Fiddle and Faddle. How Fid died in childbirth of puerperal fever, and how Faddle, drunk at a party, fell backwards off a gallery and broke her neck. He would have heard the story of how Edgar Degas' portrait of her came to be destroyed.

The priest kept the secrets; but he was not someone you could ask about your father, in whose life Bellocq had lost any share now. Unhappiness was quite a normal feeling in his life. He did not know what he had done wrong; that he was alive seemed unforgivable. If he made a stand he was being stubborn or a dolt. Everything he did was wrong. He could not sleep that sleep of the just which his mother had after her confession, until those dreams began again.

The telegraph wire from Father came twelve years later; he was sick and coming home. Bellocq went down to the ship in the dead of night: they had to keep it quiet that Father was in New Orleans and staying in the house.

Armand Clouzot shared in the secret, having been the family doctor since Bellocq's birth. He came round to shake his head. 'You get away with the little things, then, before you know it, you want more,' he said. Bellocq's mother and Clouzot stood in the shadows on the landing, their heads turning each time Father coughed in the bedroom.

When Bellocq went in to see him his father smiled and said, 'I ought to be able to see the joke – why can't I?'

Not long after that, one rainy morning, Bellocq's mother took his arm and they set off behind the coffin for the cemetery.

Bellocq took photographs of the dead then. A bereaved woman's daughter had to look as if she had fallen asleep at play with her beloved doll. Often, the mother would want to stare at the face of her dead child. In another – one of his first customers – it was enough that she held a portrait of her dead son. He took the first picture to oblige. Then word got round and other families came.

He could have made a living doing those portraits until he died. Families lost loved ones every day of the week. The last straw was when the widow asked him to photograph her husband.

Bellocq set up his camera and signed for her brother

to lift the coffin lid. The corpse was naked, the eyes open wide, the flesh eaten up with lesions; scabs oozed everywhere on his body. He was a perfect illustration from the *syphilographe* Beaubien brought his mother when his father was sick. The brother said it was the parting gift of a whore in Jackson, where they had lived before.

Now Bellocq knew why each step he helped Father take down the gangplank was agony; his clothes had chafed such sores. He understood why his mother never put any crucifix other than her own to her lips for fear of contagion.

It was then that Bellocq knew he had to go. He told no one, simply boarded a train heading west, thinking about Mexico. He went in the hope of finding the woman his father had run off with.

2

S outh-west of Corpus Christi, on the road to Brownsville, Bellocq saw the outpost come into view. It grew darker in shape as he came nearer.

'You make a living where you can, *hombre*,' said Platt, as Bellocq set up the camera in the street.

Platt leant against a hitching-post under his new sign: 'U.S. Post Office and General Store – Dentist Horace F. Platt'. Every other building in the street was adobe, but the store was built of raw new lumber; it had an upper storey with a balcony, from which hung a limp 'Old Glory'. Platt wore a striped shirt and bow-tie, a white apron over plus-fours; his shirt bands glinted in the sun.

Bellocq could see earlier versions of Platt that the man had shed to find his destiny. Yet it was hard to imagine a childhood for him. About to uncap the lens, Bellocq stopped; the light struck Platt's mouth and chin in such a way as to suggest a penis, with the stained moustache as pubic hair.

'You were on foot all the way from Louisiana?'

'No, a train part of the way.'

'Has anyone told you you're mad, yet?' Platt laughed. 'You could have crossed the Gulf in a couple of days. What are you after here?'

'I set off for California,' Bellocq lied. 'They take a lot of pictures there now; I thought I might get work. I don't know what changed my mind. I headed south for Mexico. People say that Mexicans want to see themselves in photographs.'

'People?' Platt laughed. 'I'd think again, if I were you. That desert will soak up the blood of any young man who is tired of life.'

'I never had much of a life to throw away.'

'From what you say, I don't think you will find your Mexico on any map,' said Platt. 'Things there are hard, especially now, and they'll get worse. How is a man of your size and shape going to cope, if you don't mind my asking, Mr Bellocq?'

Platt said he was from Leytonstone, a suburb of London – that lair of moneylenders. 'I left a wife and child to make a go of it out here,' he said. 'I can't live in cities now – I'd miss the calm that nights have out here.'

'You've not been here long.'

'News travels fast, and no pain can equal that of a rotten

tooth. I've no rival here. Adam Smith has to be the patron saint of all dentists in the wild. All I need are satisfied customers and word of mouth. If I get no patients, I can get by on what I make in the post office and store. There are the Indians, never mind those yarns about their being stoical, and there are the Mexicans.'

An Apache rode up, hauling a travois on which lay a fat squaw with a swollen jaw. Platt could say a few words and used sign language well enough. He led the way through the store. Bellocq followed with his camera. Behind the counter hung a portrait of Abraham Lincoln flanked by two dusty Stars and Stripes. There were rifles, canteens, cheap calico dresses, canned food, oil lamps, shirts, bolts of cloth and barrels of salt meat and fish. Bellocq could also smell saddles and wine. He couldn't see much use for the two-handed saws hanging from the ceiling.

The black barbershop chair was in a small back room. Platt said he'd had it shipped from Baltimore. The squaw's eyes grew wide, but Platt and the Apache got her to lie down.

Outside the frame of Bellocq's viewfinder, the squaw gargled and moaned, as Platt probed her bad tooth. Using a metal spatula, he held down the corner of her mouth, then uncorked a bottle of chloroform. The Apache went over, shaking his head. Platt certified how safe the liquid was by dumb show. The Apache put the cork back and shook his head again with a grunt. Platt gave up. He took a bottle of whiskey off a shelf. Drinking a glass, he held it in his cheek to show the squaw that she had to do the same before swallowing. Both Indians were happy with the painkiller.

Bellocq had the brave in focus against the diplomas on the wall, copperplate proof of Platt's expertise. His dusty black hat lay on his lap, a dark blue cloth tied around long black hair. He was smoking a cigarette he'd rolled and sipping now and then at the whiskey that Platt had given him.

The squaw moaned again. Platt let the tooth fall into a dish and soaked cotton waste in spirit to poke into her gum. By then, Bellocq had captured the brave, who took a gold coin out of his pouch. Platt handed the coin to Bellocq. 'See, history: a Spanish doubloon.'

After the Indians left, Platt put on a white coat and posed standing with one hand on his chair. 'If I'd kept my old tails,' he said, 'I might look more imposing. Out here, you have to earn their respect.' He went out again to sit in the rocker on the front, where he had hailed Bellocq walking into town. By now the sun was low, a red disc the Apaches headed towards. The brave led the pony across the face of a dune in the afterglow. Their progress sent sand hazing away on the chill night air. They were a long time vanishing.

'You can sleep here, if you want,' said Platt. 'There's room, and I never let a chance to talk go by. When I saw you out there in that haze I felt maybe you had something to teach me. Why should I think that?'

'I have no idea.'

'You have a dark side to your soul?'

'I've never been in touch with it if I have.'

'I live with the dead a lot now,' said Platt. 'Any spare time I have, I spend in ruined pueblos digging up arrowheads, pots and beads. You can find all kinds of things: clay figurines, stone axes. The pots can be in one piece. Those things have a life of their own; you dust them off, you shiver. You come on charms in rotting leather that may have been a medicine pouch.

24

They choose them for their power, so you get a thrill from that force, be it healing or prophetic. The dead – well, their bones speak as well as their artefacts. It's only in such places that you get any true sense of time, or can feel the infinity of space. Often I ride up to Mesa Verde. There's a family up there that feels about the past as I do. You get down that isthmus you are going to see wonders, Mr Bellocq. Olmec remains, Aztec, too – my God, I'd give a lot to be going with you. If you get there, I would value any photographs. I'd pay for any prints, of course.'

A chosen one in the tribe had to keep track of the past – a woman, more often than not. She painted it on rocks and pots, or wove it into baskets. Nobody died unsung. There were gaps, of course, and Platt felt he had to fill those. He gave the flag a nod and a smile. 'I run that flag up every morning. If I don't, I feel I'm going downhill.' What he missed most about England, apart from his family, was the fishing – a shady stream where a pheasant would rattle by, a frog hop in the shallows. You could sit with a hatful of flies while white clouds massed high amid blue reflecting blue. It was a lost paradise.

For a man who said he was no more than a down-to-earth dentist, Bellocq thought he was up in the air.

Back inside, Platt rapped the table. 'Are you here, Mr Bellocq, or what? Maybe you don't need whiskey at all; maybe you're already in a trance.'

'What trance?'

The light came from behind Platt; it shone off the cloth he was using to polish the whiskey glasses. 'You won't believe it, but my brother works at the Library of Congress. He went to the right schools, read the Classics, knows Greek and Latin. He looks down his nose, of course; I'm a blemish, a rude mechanical. He disgusts me, too, that goes without saying. The last time I saw him was at Lord's Cricket Ground. I was drunk, and that was a great sin.' He stopped, suddenly exasperated. 'Damn it, what is that air of mystery about you?'

'I can't say,' Bellocq replied. 'I take photographs; nothing else.'

'Some people say I've got a screw loose,' Platt brooded. 'Can you believe that? I expect they say the same about you.'

'Never to my face.'

'You don't wear a ring.' Platt held up his hand to rub his ring. 'What you need is the love of a good woman. We all do. Only a woman can make us whole men. Take another whiskey, Mr Bellocq. It's the best cure; it softens us up for foolish laughter. It can also open your heart to the spirit.'

'*Un poco*,' said Bellocq.

'Never say die, Mr Bellocq.'

Bellocq nodded, without a clear idea of what Platt meant. He could hear the insects outside – then, distant, a low rattle of thunder. Platt leant over the oil lamp to light the cigarette he had rolled. 'The Paris gendarmes used newspaper photographs to track the Communards down,' he said. 'Scotland Yard took pictures of the eyes of those women Jack the Ripper cut up. They had the idea that his image might be there, on their eyeballs. Is that feasible, or newspaper stuff?'

'Do you leave your image in the mirror when you go?' Bellocq was drunk enough to giggle now.

'Try to imagine how that photographer felt, the one who took pictures of those five women,' said Platt. 'They were ritual murders, you know. Jack left their entrails in a heap on their shoulders. You're not a misogynist, are you?'

Bellocq shook his head. He did not know the word.

'A man who hates women. Ah, our women, Mr Bellocq!' Platt sighed. 'You are without one, I know, or you wouldn't be here, looking for God knows what. My wife is a goddess. I used to serenade her with my ukulele. There are some things I can't credit any more. If she were here, my life would take on the natural shape it's missing. Here's a postcard from her, see. She cuts things out of the papers all the time. What do you make of this?'

The local preacher had seduced a member of his flock. The husband had lain in wait for him after evensong, broken his leg and nose and left him out in the churchyard all night. At dawn an angel appeared and told him to spread the gospel in China. 'More tea, vicar?' Platt said, with a laugh.

There was a typewritten message pasted on the back. It said: 'I saw this. In case you forget, he was the minister who married us.'

'What did she mean by that?' Platt took the card. 'Am I reading something sinister into it?'

'About jealousy and pain, you mean?'

'Find the right woman, and you will never know those,' said Platt. Was that shrug meant to shake off his uncertainty? 'A good woman can bring a dead man to life again, Mr Bellocq.'

A herd of wild horses raced out of the night, their eyes flashing, their manes streaming in the moonlight. Bellocq stood at the door with Platt until the mustangs ran off, circling in the dark, then thundered into the light again.

Platt waved his arms and stamped. '*Vamos!*'

The hoofbeats came and went all night and kept

Bellocq awake. When he opened his eyes at first light, he saw a photograph of Platt in the shadow of a Mesa Verde cavern: a ghost above a mummified Indian and a skeleton propped against a rock, a line of skulls set below.

Over breakfast, Platt said it was the lightning spooked the mustangs. 'They go loco now and then. They come and frolic around the town, looking to have a little fun.'

Bellocq took the photographs out of the dish. 'You can see I spend more time making the prints.'

'What's that you wash them in?'

'Gold chloride. Let them lie in the sun for an hour until the image develops.'

'Listen, Mr Bellocq, look out down there unless I can get you to give up the idea,' said Platt. 'Come back this way again. You're always welcome. Steer clear of that albatross!'

'Albatross?'

'Never mind.'

After Platt paid him, the total in Bellocq's pocket came to one hundred and ten pesos and a few cents.

Sweating in one of his father's old white linen suits, Bellocq hauled his box camera and plates on a wheeled frame. A straw hat kept the sun off, and he wore tinted goggles against the glare and dust.

There was a fruit stall at the crossroads. Two women under a striped awning said they were sisters. They had peppers, beans, corn-cobs, root vegetables and sacks of cornflour. As he paid for three oranges, Bellocq watched a boy with a burro go by.

He put two in his pocket and walked on sucking the third until he saw the boy again, resting in the shade of the burro. It was some time before he realized from the way the boy moved his head that he was blind, or nearly so. Bellocq asked him how far was it to the next town. There was no sign of life among the Joshua trees and giant cacti except for Gila monsters, sidewinders and rattlesnakes. Yet even they no longer moved among the hot stones and dust. He gave the boy an orange, put up the umbrella, and set the camera to take his picture. When the boy asked what he was doing, Bellocq said 'Nada' and got him to take off his straw hat. The boy raised a hand to ward off what he thought was a blow when Bellocq brushed his hair off his brow. He said his name was Eladio Rubén Montoya.

The dirt track became a cobbled street. Bellocq walked in the shade of a walled graveyard. He passed a stone trough that the women used to wash clothes. He ran water from the brass tap over his face and neck; the scum of algae began to heave. A bell rang. It had to be three-thirty of a Sunday afternoon. Three black pigs rooted for scraps in the square by the church.

Bellocq sat outside the cantina across from a sheeted carousel. The four red folding-chairs had 'Coca-Cola' on their backs, and there were jars of pickles and hot sauces on a blue check table-cloth. A woman selling food held a basket up to the windows of a bus that was going to Mexico City. The child with her had a crateload of bottles. A couple of dogs nosed around. They took to yapping when the driver got out to crank the engine.

High above the ragged cornfield, snow shone on the mountain peaks. 'I'll die here, but not yet, *maman*,' Bellocq said, as he ate a taco with beans. 'What can you do if I bury myself alive? Dig my body up?'

29

The food made Bellocq drowsy. He fell asleep. When he woke, it was chill, almost night; the edges of the clouds shone brightly against a darkening blue sky. He went into the cantina. An old man in a sack apron was lighting the oil lamps; they stank until the flames steadied. In the corner was a stall with the sign '*Mijitorio*'. With all the lamps alight, Bellocq could see four old yellow banknotes stuck to the wall; they had what seemed to be bloodstains. Some bandits had left them to pay their bar bill. They had raided a bank in a nearby town. There was a photograph of evil *pistoleros*, faces lost in the dark shade of their sombreros, with bandoliers and machetes.

There were rooms to rent. Under the arch, Bellocq found a tiled counter with an ornamental metal grille. A cook came when he struck the bell. He slid a faded register under the barrier and gave Bellocq a key tied to a slab of wood burnt with the number '10'. Stone steps led up to a balcony with twelve or so rooms. Below, a fountain trickled in a small courtyard, and the light from an open door cast a woman's shadow.

Room 10 had whitewashed walls and a red tiled floor. It was cool; the night air was loud with cicadas. Above the bed, a saint rose to heaven offering his flaming heart in his hands. Bellocq's mother had dozens of such cards, of men with their eyes upturned to God. Men in the wilderness, waiting for Grace – cards she had collected over the years.

Beating dust off his clothes, he stripped for a shower. The faucet was so low he had to sit in the stall.

He knew he was a runaway who did not know where he was going – anywhere, so long as it was far from New Orleans and his mother. He lay naked on the bed and opened the only book he had with him, which he had won as a school prize.

Ah, happy, happy boughs! that cannot shed
    Your leaves, nor ever bid the spring adieu;
And, happy melodist, unwearied,
    For ever piping songs for ever new;
More happy love! more happy, happy love!
    For ever warm and still to be enjoy'd,
        For ever panting, and for ever young;
All breathing human passion far above,
    That leaves a heart high-sorrowful and cloy'd,
        A burning forehead, and a parching tongue.

After his earlier siesta, sleep would not come. Spectres
went to and fro in his mind such as those a camera often
creates: haloes, spirals of floating ectoplasm formed
faces all asking the same question – when are you
going home?

The sound of someone cranking a car woke Bellocq.
It would not start. He heard the clatter of the hood,
swearing, then the door slam. The big man stood at the
counter with his jacket under his arm. He held a beer.
His face was still red with the effort he had wasted. His tie
was loose. He was asking where he could find a mechanic.
'Say, are you an American?' He strode to grab Bellocq
by the shoulder. 'You can fix a car? Who knows where
you'll get a mechanic in this country.' When Bellocq said
he knew nothing, the man brushed him off to question
the owner again if there was anybody who had a car or
truck and would take him to a garage for a dollar.

The man was out of luck. He turned back to Bellocq.
'What brings you to these parts, *compadre*? Nothing hap-
pens here except a cactus blooms.' He gave his name as
Waldo Nordhal as they shook hands. Bellocq was not

keen to have anything to do with him. He sensed that he was not the sort of man to get involved with – yet, invariably too eager, he said bluffly, 'Who can answer that in Mexico?'

Nordhal said he had come there to sell, maybe win a few bucks playing poker. 'No *peón* knows fuck about cards. Do you play?'

Bellocq said no; he had no cash anyway. He took photographs to live. 'I earn a dollar, sometimes less, to eat.'

'Bully for you,' said Nordhal drily. 'Anybody can make money down here. All you need are guns.'

'Is that what you sell: guns?'

'Not too often.' Nordhal grinned. 'They get to know your face. Maybe next time. Fuck it, you can never tell how something will pan out in this country. Shit, I have to be in Mexico City the day after tomorrow. I'll lose money over this. Worse, my wife will not be happy.'

'She's here?'

Nordhal's nod implied that he ought to ask how long they had been married.

'A lifetime?' Nordhal laughed. 'Three years come Easter. She soon got bored. She begs to come on trips but she hates them. Who knows what she wants any more? She was a tramp when we met. Nothing has changed. I was a soft touch. One morning I'll wake up and find an empty bed.' Nordhal laughed again. 'You must be solo.' He looked at his watch. 'Pearl'll be down any minute now. Take my advice, you watch your step around her. The crazy thing is, I'll never be free of her.'

Bellocq had no answer.

Nordhal put on his hat and said he'd go ask around.

Bellocq stood by the swing doors and saw him shield

his eyes against the sun before striding off. He heard the thud and creak of crutches, one high heel click across the tiles as a woman came to the bar. She had to be Nordhal's wife. She asked the old man whether he had seen her husband as she lurched over to the door.

'He has gone to get your car fixed,' said Bellocq, turning away and going back to sit at the table.

'The car again, huh?'

'He left not long ago.'

'So I got to sit here with my fingers crossed.'

It was her right leg in a plaster. She limped back to get the drink she had ordered, then came over and sat down. She was blonde; the long braid was too young for her. She was probably thirty years old.

'You speak dago?'

'I understand more than I can say.'

'More than I do. I know "How much?", "when" and "where".'

Bellocq looked at his father's watch. 'I have to get my things together.'

'You're lost, is that it?' She laughed. 'Where you headed?'

'I don't know. South.'

'Terrific. There's a lot of nothing there.'

Bellocq spread his hands, a gesture meant to agree.

In his room, all power left his body. Sitting on the bed, the strength ran out of him in sweat. He had schooled himself to admit nothing about his state of mind. The everyday could vanish at any time. He was always afraid that people would start talking about him as if he weren't there. He feared that Pearl was doing that now; there was no one she could say it to, though. Not only did his strength go, but any sense of purpose died too. His sudden dread left him in need of a drink. He loaded his trailer and got it down the steps. The effort left him weak again. He sat outside in the chair he'd used the day before. The sweat made his crotch itch. Scratching it turned the itch into a sore, one more reason not to move. Every so often he could hear Pearl's crutches each time she went to the bar, her sighs growing more audible. He knew it would not be long before she came out to ask more questions.

When she did, the old man came after her. He put a bottle and two glasses down. 'You look as if you can use a whiskey,' she said. 'Is that okay?'

Bellocq nodded, sipping it slowly.

'Jesus, everything is so parched. Don't you thirst all the time?' She fanned her face with a bullfight programme. 'The fuck, it itches!' She clenched her fist to fight an urge to scratch, then let her head fall until her brow touched her hands. 'I'll dance when it comes off. I got a stick I practise with now. Looking forward to the day.'

'You have a lot of names on that plaster,' said Bellocq.

'One of my good qualities is I make friends easy. I got these in the hospital.'

'In Mexico?'

'No, thank God. Do you know Palm Springs? I broke it there — so I had a good doctor.'

'You live in California?'

'Sometimes. Walt is all over the place.'

'He's not back yet, then?'

'Sometimes I wish I'd never set eyes on him,' she said abruptly. 'He thinks I ought to get down on my knees night and day on account of him being such a white man when he found me as to give me his name.'

'Where was that?'

'At Veracruz. Ask him, and he'll tell you he saved me

34

from a fate worse than death.' She lit a cigarette and got out her compact. 'Where are you from?'

'New Orleans.'

'That's some haul. How long since you been there?'

Bellocq would not answer. Three years, he thought. Two, at least, since his mother's last letter.

'I lived with a guy from old New Orleans,' she recalled. She used her mirror again. 'He was crazy with big ideas. I fall hard for men with a tongue in their heads. When he took sick and died, I was without a dime in Veracruz.' She was brooding now. 'You do what you have to, if you want to stay alive. It's all sailors there; what they have in mind is to rent a boy, so they turn you over. Every port attracts shit, but you must know that, coming from Crescent City.'

'You met, I see,' said Nordhal, looming against the light. 'It's all *peóns* who can tell you fuck all except about the Virgin Mary. Christ, I need a drink.'

'Nothing doing, huh?' Pearl clicked her compact shut.

The swing doors rattled as Nordhal went into the cantina. He came out with a beer and sat down at the table. Bellocq could smell his rank sweat. 'They say there's a mechanic ten miles that way,' he said, pointing west. 'I can walk, or ride a mule. The fiesta tonight will bring people in. Maybe one of them will have a car. Sure, there was a burro, but the boy drove it a long way yesterday and the old woman thought it might drop.'

Bellocq said he had never cared for Mardi Gras. Fiestas were always about religion, nothing else but what people thought they could get away with.

'You moving on?' Nordhal lit a cigarette.

'I was, but I'm not up to it now. I'll stay on another night.'

As Bellocq paid for the room, the old man said it was the Feast of John the Baptist. He could drink the fermented juice of the yucca for free. Bellocq took the key and went to lie down. He could see Salome dancing naked for the prophet's head. He was asleep before the last veil fell. It was after sunset before he woke.

The cantina was almost empty except for the three men with Nordhal. Everybody was out to see the fireworks that now lit up the sky. When Nordhal went over to the stall his piss came with the force of a bull and rang round the bar.

Pearl came in, made up and dressed to go out. 'Getting ready, I see,' she said tartly.

Nordhal left the stall buttoning his flies.

'You take her,' he said to Bellocq.

'Where?'

'See the sights, the fiesta, dummy.'

Pearl rummaged in her white handbag then hung it round her neck. 'Suppose I don't want to go with Mr Bellocq?'

'You stay here and watch the game. You won't be doing any dancing, anyway.'

Nordahl sat at the table with the three men and nodded to the dealer.

'You have to do this tonight, you big shit?'

'You say such sweet things, sugar.'

Pearl took hold of Bellocq's arm. He held the saloon door. As she swung out into the street, she said, 'I've had it with him. If he's not cheating at poker, all he thinks about is selling! Last week he sold rusty rifles, this week he cooks up gallons of piss he calls perfume. I spent my honeymoon here so that he could have fun as well as do business. I'm sick of eating Mexican shit.' She spent half her life in and out the crapper, if they had one, screaming what white woman in her right mind would use such a thing.

An old man in a serape had taken the canvas off the merry-go-round. He sat at the hub, turning it by hand. Some girls were tossing flowers at the *mariachi* band strolling in the street. They were not local men; they wore silk shirts with big sleeves. There was the smell of a pig roasting on a spit. Two men on horseback rode slowly through the crowd. Boys ran a fiery bull's head on a wheel at women and girls. The fireworks were too loud for the music to matter much. A small grey man, some way below his partner's shoulder, danced with a fat woman. She had a flower in her hair and smiled as she clasped his head to her large breasts. Their rhythm was slow, scarcely a dance at all. Elsewhere, the women swung side to side, arms akimbo, while the men shuffled in front of them, their hands clasped behind.

There was a macabre sense of plenty. It was a false feeling; it said everything was possible, but it had nothing to do with reality, which was that these people had to wrest life from a desert. As so often with festivities, things went wrong. A sudden jealous quarrel flared, seemingly to foretell what was to come. Two women set about each other, screaming *puta* as they fought, tearing at their braids. Both of them had eyes for the same man. Pearl was amused. 'You ever see me do that, shoot me in the head.'

As they came back to the cantina, one of the poker players ran out covered in blood. He almost knocked them over. The swing doors rattled shut in the silence, broken only by a bottle rolling hollowly in the urinal.

Nordhal had been stabbed twice, in the face and neck; the other players stood staring at him as he lay with the knife in his throat, blood spurting in the greasy light. When Pearl limped over, the other players made for the door.

The bartender held a towel to Nordhal's throat. Unable to squat, Pearl had to lean sideways trying to reach his face. She tucked her dress around the cast so that the hem did not touch the blood. Bellocq helped Pearl upstairs, then went down to lend the old man a hand with Nordhal. They brought him back to the room, laid him with his head and shoulders in the shower and left the water running.

The old man had to go. It was sad, he said, but he was sure that Señor Nordhal would not see the sunrise. No, the nearest doctor lived thirty miles away. Bellocq and Pearl sat on the bed; neither knew what to do. Every so often she would ask him to wring the towel out. Pearl did know some of the words: each time the old man said *muerto* her eyes widened.

It took Nordhal some hours to die. Sometimes he made gurgling noises, working one leg as he tried to get up. Now and then a rocket burst with a far-off pop and crackle – the fiesta was over. When Nordhal died, Pearl began to cry. 'What am I going to do? I can't sleep, in this bed with him lying there,' she said. 'I knew it would happen some time, the way he had to cheat at cards. I'm going to have to take it in my stride.'

A cock was already crowing as Bellocq went down to the kitchen. The old man said they had better put Nordhal in the refrigerator. The Coca-Cola man was late with the delivery. The machine was low on ice and bottles, so there was room for him. Bellocq held Nordhal's ankles as they carried him down. Stumbling near the bottom, he let go and Nordhal's boot heels bounced down the last three steps. A girl wiped away the blood in the bar. '*No comprendo inglés,*' she said; then went on about the killer. He had gone; he would never be seen in the village again. He was a loner; nobody cared about him. She said his name was Montoya. Bellocq did not want to believe that he was Eladio's father, or was any relation to that family – and yet, why not? Bellocq knew the man would be back anyway, as soon as the gringos left. The only thing he or the señora could do would be to report Montoya to the Federales when one of their patrols rode through there.

A prim plaster Virgin set on a board inside an arch of flowers went at the head of the small procession. Two of the *mariachi* men from the fiesta and a bass drummer played during the funeral march. The trumpet was so close to Bellocq's ear that he wanted to walk faster than the mourners' pace allowed. People came out to watch; the men took off their hats, the women crossed themselves. Everything the priest wore was dusty and threadbare, apart from the purple silk brocade that shone on his shoulders. Two young gravediggers held their straw hats and rested on their spades. They had dug two graves: one for Nordhal and one for a baby the villagers were burying. There were peasant jars and ornaments with dead flowers on the other graves, or heart-shaped wicker bound with strips of red cloth. The other coffin was still open. The baby had a piece of black lace over its face. The mother knelt and took the lace away to kiss her child, biting a handkerchief that had blood spots on it. Bellocq thought she asked what God had done, and why. A woman helped her up and wiped the tears from her face, brushing a fly away. As the mother began to sway, the woman held her arm to strike her cheeks. Pearl's face was glum. She had a cigarette in the corner of her mouth she felt she ought not to light. 'I do not want any of this,' she said. 'Let's go!'

'We're here now.'

Pearl took the cigarette from her lips and threw it down. 'I have to go; I can't stand this.'

The mother fought with the relatives to keep the lid open. When she failed she could not be spoken to, or touched. As they put the coffin into the hole, she walked up and down some way off. Nobody wanted to go near her. She seemed to be listening but could hear nothing – nothing.

A gusting wind spun the sand, slapping photographs tied to the wooden crosses which the sun had baked into yellow tubes. A man was waiting by the gate. He held out a jug which the mother pushed away. She hit him twice in the face before turning on her heel. The man poured liquid out of the jug, then, head bowed, followed her.

The desert wind came stronger in the late afternoon. It made an unending drone as it rose and fell, rattling every loose thing and rolling the tumbleweed around. Pearl wept. 'I don't know what the fuck I'm going to do,' she said. 'You drive a car?'

'It won't go,' Bellocq pointed out, 'and I have no money.'

Pearl said the bartender had given her Nordhal's winnings, and she had money she had put by in case of trouble. 'You can't go alone, and leave me here with this leg. You've got no real place to go, so why don't we go together? You don't have it in you to say no, do you? Just one thing, though, I have to get out of Mexico. I can't bear this desert any more.'

They would get by. Nordhal had taught her tricks — how to tip him off to the cards a man had in his hand. Maybe they could use some of those. '*Non, merci,*' said Bellocq. 'I don't want a knife in my neck.'

'Don't say things like that! You close your eyes, you open them and people have gone.' She gave a shudder. 'They don't come back, no matter how often you try again.'

Images, silvery black and white, flickered on a sheet; moths' shadows hit the faces now and then. Pearl had drunk half a bottle of tequila she had with her, cutting a lemon slice to suck each time. Off to the left, far brighter than the screen, a nacreous moon hung low above the mountains. It was so close that Bellocq could see ridges on the crater rims as he tried to forget the funeral, the graves of Nordahl and the baby.

The film was about vampires. A girl in a trance turned her face away, offering her neck to his fangs. He sucked long enough to cover his face with blood, which must have made a mess of his big moustache. The titles were worn, hard to see for scratches. A crude plot had actors rush to and fro so that ramshackle scenery shook. If it fell, you'd see the studio in Mexico City, said Pearl; she had been to a party there once. Sections of the film had been lost; there was an abrupt cut to a monk, one hand raised to ward off evil and the other holding a crucifix to call down the wrath of God. The vampire's top hat made him stand out from the rest. The one bat hung limply on a highly visible wire. It had none of the taxidermist's art, but was a fake lump of fur with leather wings. The audience laughed most of the time, except when an old *dueña* turned into a vampire and got her fangs into the girl she was supposed

41

to protect. They liked the horses, the swordfights and the carriage racing through a storm. Most gratifying of all was the finale: a vengeful mob with torches chasing the vampire to drive a stake into his heart.

Pearl had fallen asleep with her head on his shoulder. Two men took the screen down, rolling the sheet over a pole. Pearl lost her temper when Bellocq woke her, striking out as she tried to get to her feet. When she was up she clung with her arm round his neck, giggling. Holding the crutches in his other hand, he helped her back to the car.

Pearl began to moan that they were a hundred miles from nowhere. Sure, the car was running fine now – but *she*'d had to get that *peón* to fix it. Coyotes howled in the arroyos. 'Jesus! That's a godawful noise!'

Bellocq lit the lantern. He could not imagine his mother's God, he told her. One thing he did know was that He craved submission. Yes, he may have many reasons for not liking himself, but he was marking time until he could start a real life.

That made her laugh. 'You don't seem to know too much about yours.' She shook her head. 'I think tomorrow's my birthday.'

'You mean you don't know?'

'Not everybody knows when they were born.' She finished the dregs of the tequila.

'I do, in 1873,' he said. 'Why don't you know?'

'There's no right and wrong about anything, only what you do at the time. Some john got it up my mother, and sure enough – nine months later, whenever that was, I came out wailing.' She lay back on the seat with a sigh. 'Jesus, those stars! Nothing up there bears thinking about either. What the fuck does any of it mean?' She began

42

to empty her suitcase, hanging dresses out of the window and hunting through her underwear until she found an envelope. 'See, that was another of Walt's big ideas.' She handed Bellocq a set of pornographic photographs; in some she was with another girl. 'He got a kick out of them, but they never sold. They were only good for calling cards when he was making a deal. Come to think of it, maybe that's where we ought to head for – New Orleans. They got that tenderloin there – what do they call it?'

'Storyville.'

'Eudie Thibeau, the guy I lived with, used to go on about what highfalutin ways the girls had there.'

'Then you must sell the car and go by train,' said Bellocq. 'I am not driving back there.'

'Nothing gets past you, does it?'

The sun was high. Bellocq woke to find Pearl reading one of his mother's letters, asking, 'Is the photograph of her? Did you take it?'

It was not something he wanted her to see.

'Whatever it was, you fucked up good, with your mama, I mean,' she said with scorn. 'No nest egg for you when she crosses the river, huh? *Are* you like your father? She sure seemed to know what you were both looking for in Mexico.'

'What was that?'

'You don't want to put a name to it.' Pearl laughed.

'All she made me feel was guilt,' he said. 'That will be her legacy. Quite a few parents, I believe, have that in their gift.'

'Don't come out with that shit. You're not deep as a well, more of a mudhole.' Pearl shook her head. 'I can see through you. The day we met, what did

43

you do? You had to look to see if your flies were open.'

After the gas station, the road improved. They reached the border at noon, and were in Nogales. The fat Navajo woman holding Pearl's arm began to push her, talking in a shrill voice, holding beads up as if to make an offering to the sun. Neither Pearl nor Bellocq had any idea what she was saying, but she forced bangles onto Pearl's arm. Pearl's shriek of childish pleasure gave way to alarm. '*Nada, nada,* no *dinero!*' The squaw shook her head, and held up three fingers to mean three dollars. Pearl took a five-dollar bill from her purse, which the Navajo folded neatly and put in her shirt pocket with a nod of finality. 'Don't I get change?'

The Navajo did not turn round.

'That was our last five dollars,' said Pearl.

Night fell. Bellocq did not open his eyes as one shoe hit the floor after the other. He heard her bracelets clatter on the bedside table. She was always there, insisting that he do something or other. His life drifted by and he had no record of it. He hated time passing, and he missed taking pictures.

Every morning two vultures circled lower until they came down to perch on the low wall encircling the Territorial Hotel. From there, with ungainly stealth, they dropped to hop to the trash bins. Bellocq could hear their claws, the thud of their wings, as he lay in bed. Spinks, the hotel's owner, came out early to empty his trash and shoo them away. 'How's it going? How's the wife treating you? She's not here, I know.'

Bellocq said she was not his wife.

'She's quite a picture when she's painted up. So your

name in my register is false. I guessed so.' Spinks's low laugh was dry, confiding. Did Bellocq know that Nogales was Spanish for walnuts? They used to call it Isaacstown, after some innkeeper here. It was the seat of Santa Cruz County; it had silver and lead mines, and cattle ranching, too. 'We get a lot of drifters,' he said. 'I had a guy called Sloan through here last week, going south to find his daughter. Some Mexican pimp had sweet-talked her into a fuck joint in Mexico City. All Sloan could go on about was her mouth, her lips. He was having fits imagining what men were making her do with that mouth. He got so excited, he began to pant for breath. I felt his heart; I thought he was going to die, right there in that chair you're in.' Spinks fixed his gaze on some far place. 'People turn a corner of a building and you never see them again.'

'What did you say?' Bellocq was unnerved – it echoed what Pearl had said.

'There are stories.' Spinks paused, then leant forward accusingly. 'You don't believe it?'

'How did he know she was in Mexico?'

'The girl got a letter out to the wife, it killed her dead. Sloan lit out for the border. He was going on sixty-five, if he was a day; looking for a way out, pure and simple, I thought. I knew I'd never see him again. He hit that rock painted white by the entrance when he left. You can still see the heap of rust there. That's how good his car was.'

When Bellocq told Pearl the story, she said, 'That's all horseshit, the stuff you read in the papers about knockout drops and gangs raping virgins out of their minds to turn them into whores. What those girls don't have, and what they want, is money. Would you drive yourself crazy working all week for six dollars when you can get two dollars a trick?'

'I'll say whatever I goddamn want – at least Waldo was a man,' said Pearl.

'I can't go on doing this,' Bellocq said.

'You can. You are looking out for me now.'

'You go out and steal food. When I ask you about it you lie; I have no self-respect any more.'

'Everybody eats, even saints,' said Pearl.

She was drinking, too, which was worse, and sometimes he had to go round the bars to find her. There, he sat watching the man paw her. 'Sugar, I know what you want, and I'm going to make damn sure you get every last bit of it.' When Bellocq went out to piss, the man followed. 'Are you that mama's pimp, or what? She brings home the bacon for you: is that it? I got a few bucks. Listen, I'm not so bad. All I want is to fuck her blind.' Cupping his groin, he jerked his hips. 'You get what I mean?'

Bellocq told Pearl he had to go to the hotel.

She was drunk when she got back, muttering as she creaked around on her crutches, a reechy smell of sweat in her armpits. She struck a match to light the oil lamp, humming the tune playing on the Pianola all night. She took a handful of dollar bills out of her bag and let them fall on the bed. 'Here's every last cent he had.' She laughed. Bellocq lay doggo, knowing she was not fooled. 'Is that a pipe dream you're having there? He never got it near me.' She pitched her voice high, a child. 'One squeeze, some quick handiwork, and he was off all down his leg.'

She shook his shoulder. 'Don't play games. I know you're awake.'

46

Bellocq opened his eyes and stared at her.

'What did you say to him?' she said.

'Nothing. He did all the talking.'

'He took you for my pimp. Where did he get that idea?'

Bellocq shook his head. 'Let me photograph you tomorrow.'

'No, fuck you, no goddamn pictures! You want a picture? I'll show you one!' She laughed and threw her skirt up, with a laugh and a shout, 'Which came first, the chicken or the egg?'

Bellocq had expected – well, he hadn't known what to expect. What he saw were thin shiny flaps she laid open with her bony fingers. It was the first time he had seen a grown woman close.

'Get down here, come on! Yes, like that.' She sighed. 'You know what to do. Somebody taught you, right? You're doing it good. Yes, just there, where you are now.' His ears were full of the sound, a dog lapping at a bowl. His jaws were aching as she cried out; then the spasm of pleasure left her face as she saw him in the mirror. 'Put that back in your pants! I wouldn't have that thing in me if you were the last man on earth,' she shrieked, using her fist. Tiring of that, she hit him with her crutch.

When he came round, she was not in the room. The cast lay on the bed, along with the crutches and the bangles the Navajo sold her. He could smell the salty odour of her body on the leather pads. He was relieved that she had left his plates in one piece. The camera was intact, too, except for a sliver that had split off when it hit the wall.

The car had gone. 'I knocked earlier, when I saw no sign of life,' said Spinks. 'Are you okay?'

Bellocq saw his face in the mirror. 'You should fix that cut – could turn poisonous. I knew right off that she was crazy.'

'She took all the money,' said Bellocq.

'Where does that leave you?'

'Unable to pay.'

'Not your fault. You can stay on another night, but you have to go tomorrow.' He paused. 'She had some guy to drive the car. You're better off without her.'

'You think so?'

'Well, the two of you weren't hitting it off.'

By the next morning, Bellocq was sure that Pearl would not come back. 'There's a bus for El Paso tomorrow,' said Spinks. 'I'll stand you the fare. Mail what you owe when you have it.' He knew how Bellocq must feel. His wife left seven years ago. 'These women, huh?'

In El Paso, without cash or anywhere to go, Bellocq slept in an alley. He spent the next day walking the streets until noon, when the sun drove him to seek shade, and he found Ethan Smithline's photographic studio.

Each step of the steep stairway had an enamel plate advertising 'Photography', 'Enlarging', 'Developing' and 'Printing' in black letters. He felt dizzy and weak hauling the camera up. He had to lean against the wall.

'Are you okay? You look set to keel over.'

'If I can sit down a moment, I'll be fine.'

'What's your name?'

'E. J. Bellocq.'

'What's the E for?'

'Ernest, but I prefer James.'

'That accent – you French? Where are you from?'

'New Orleans.'

Smithline's face lit up. That was the jazz he loved; there

48

was not much in El Paso and no Mardi Gras either. 'Could be providential you coming here. One thing I know: you take better pictures than I do. You have a real feel for faces and things, I can see that.'

Smithline went down to hang a closed sign on the door, then led Bellocq through a passageway into a messy dining room with a kitchen, where he served up two plates of chilli con carne and cut some bread. 'You were south of the border, you got used to this, huh?'

He said he came from a family of preachers. He had been a preacher himself for a time. 'Religion is always there, waiting in the wings, when reason fails,' he said.

Done eating, he wiped the blade of his knife, then tilted it to see his teeth.

'I'll show you round.'

There were the usual sepia backcloths, the stunted Corinthian pillars, and ferns in brass pots. Sweat had soaked into the brocade of the chairs. Some framed samples showed Confederate soldiers in the War Between the States. They came with the place when he bought it. There was a screen with a storm scene, a crude mass of bluish clouds with a bare tree. 'Some women have to feel they're heroines, Jane Eyres,' said Smithline, showing Bellocq upstairs to a room above the studio. Among the books were *The Count of Monte Cristo* and Fenimore Cooper's *Last of the Mohicans*, *Gulliver's Travels* and the works of Robert Louis Stevenson.

'Why not rest up here awhile, until you get your strength back.'

Bellocq said he was grateful, but he had to move on.

'Listen to yourself, James,' said Smithline. 'I don't want to pry, but you got nothing in mind except running away. You are crazy to think that you'll get anywhere doing that.

Things might look different after a good night's sleep. Why not lie down now?'

'If you wouldn't mind, I need a rest.'

Bellocq's dream was more of a nightmare. He was with Jacob Riis's outcasts in New York. One of the old hags had such a hold on him he could not escape. She gripped his hand so tight that the blood began to spurt from under his nails. He closed his eyes. When he opened them again he was looking at Pearl.

Smithline was sitting on his bed when he awoke. Daylight had almost gone. 'Is that night already?' Bellocq sat up.

'I left you. Come down and eat. You fell asleep so fast that you couldn't have had time to think over my offer – never mind that now. The wider you get from any centre, no matter how bad you thought it was, the worse the disorder seems.' Smithline stood in the doorway with his beer. 'Like when I got that mail-order bride. Soon as she got here, life took a strange turn. You have to read those letters she sent from Austria to know what I mean. I could not believe my luck.'

Later, at the table, Smithline showed him a photograph of Marta, a dark-haired woman in a large hat lifting a veil away from her face. 'I needed help around the place, a woman to cook, wash my shirts, sweep the studio. She had other ideas. Nothing was what she hoped for, and it got harder. She had moods. Didn't want to get out of bed. We had fights. She came at my face with a knife, and I knew that she was out to kill. I never drank; I do now, and how could anybody blame me?'

'What happened to her?'

'She ran out naked in the street one day, until the sheriff cornered her in a livery stable. That's why she's

in the local asylum. When I got to the jail and found
her wrapped in a blanket, she had nothing to say. Doc
Stratton had signed papers declaring her insane. Soon as
he took out a hypodermic she began to scream.'

A girl singing woke Bellocq. The door of Smithline's
room was open. He lay on his back in a torn vest;
his mouth was agape, showing two incisor rabbit teeth
glinting against the white bristles round his mouth. When
Bellocq came down, the girl was washing dishes in the
kitchen.

'Her name is Florrie,' Smithline told him later. 'She
used to help out at McClure's barbershop. She swept
the floor and lathered, then got to shave a few of the
customers. George has a piano she would play, so she got
tips to live on. McClure damned near lost his mind when
she came here to work. I don't go by his shop now. She
takes my linen home for her mother to launder. If there's
anything happening in town, a dance, a fair, I let her pass
out handbills. She's twelve; I don't ask much from her. I
give her a dollar or two, and I'm teaching her to read.'

Florence skipped. Her hair swung side to side in a hank;
there was a fleece of curls in her nape. Each swish of the
rope beat dust around her bare feet. Bellocq watched the
soft swell of her small breasts rise with every step.

'Mr Smithline says you can cut my hair for five
cents.'

She nodded. He sat down in the chair and she tucked
a blue sheet into his collar. 'You did this working for
McClure.'

'I hated that. I could never stand the smell of his
pomade. Folks around here call him the bog man. He

51

was not much of a hand at pulling teeth, but he was good at cutting off warts. Some of the men would try to get their hand up under my skirt. They used every trick.'

Bellocq held his head down as he muttered, 'I found a ballet dress in the studio the other day. Would you wear it?'

'What did you say?' She leant round to look up into his face.

'When you finish my hair.'

'You want to take a picture, is that right?'

Bellocq pinned a flower in her hair. She held one of her arms above her head – wrist limp, little finger upright – then set her other arm across her body at a right angle. He could not recall where he had seen the pose, but it felt right. She would not let go of the lollipop he had given her. He opened the lid of the musical box; the jangling might help. He was using the ballet dress as an excuse to touch her. He forced her head back until her throat was taut. Afterwards, he let her fall into that abandon of a Degas pastel, when *les Sylphes* slumped in weary postures, their underwear rank with effort.

'Florence? I don't know how my mother could saddle me with that!'

'You don't care for it?'

'No girl would.' She swung her legs as she sucked the lollipop. 'Flat shoes don't suit my legs at all. I look good in my mama's high heels, though.'

The costume showed off her breasts and the curve of her belly. Bellocq knew he would ask her next to pose in the nude. 'I won't touch you at all. No one would know. It would be a secret between the two of us.'

'How much would you pay?'

'A dollar?'

'Are you sure you can go to that?'

'Why? You think I can't?'

'Maybe you'd do better to spend it on clothes. Look at you! You never bought that jacket. It's too long in the sleeves.'

'Does that matter?'

'Not greatly, I guess.'

The low sun spread a red haze in the room, so that the fuzz between Florrie's slightly open legs blazed in scarlet fire. She reminded him of the girl his father bought for him.

Bellocq's legs shook long after she left. He sat in the wicker chair, so drained that he fell asleep.

'I'd not start after that girl. She's jailbait,' Smithline warned.

Weeks went by; there was not enough custom to afford the two of them a living. 'You'll know all about New Orleans,' said Smithline. 'You know we can do better there. I'm going to sell the studio, buy a truck and load up the stock in trade. Of course, it's up to you what you do with your life.'

Bellocq had to speak of his mother, knowing that Smithline would never understand the situation, or his feelings. He said he could never go back there.

'Don't tell me about mothers,' said Smithline. 'When we lived in Houston, mine spent every hour God sent playing the chapel organ. There's no reason at all why you should ever run into your mama, a town that size. If you didn't want to, that is.'

Bellocq felt he ought to warn the couple who came in reply to Smithline's advertisement. They were Jews from Odessa, the woman said. Her husband, Igor, was deaf and spoke very little English. He was a silversmith and

53

trader interested only in the right property. He held one hand cupped behind his ear, leaning forward as he tried to follow what was said. Bellocq held his tongue until it was too late: Smithline had found a buyer.

That night, thinking about packing to go, a vision of Florrie, naked in the scarlet light, kept him awake. As so often, he'd reach a certain point and come to a standstill, as if nothing lay beyond, and then have to retrace his steps.

Florrie hung around watching as Bellocq and Smithline loaded the truck. 'What's that sniffle about?' Smithline said, handing her five dollars. 'You can find your way there when you grow up. We'd take you with us, if we could.'

She was playing with the ebony yo-yo Bellocq left her, a toy his father had given him.

The red brick building had a grim iron fire-escape. It was on the desolate edge of town, facing every freak storm, the insects and the heat. The windows had bars and, despite the heat, smoke rose from an ornate chimney-stack. The guard wore a black uniform. He took a watch out of his vest pocket to check it against the wall clock before going through into another room lit by a bare bulb. Smithline knocked again and the guard came back to unlock the door. He led them along a wide corridor.

'Nobody is safe from some of the male degenerates we keep here – kids, animals, women old enough to be their grandmothers,' he said. 'Bath-times are the worst. You were here, you'd see things you wouldn't believe.'

A smell of urine came off a group of sullen women in striped pinafores, some in wheelchairs. The guard led Bellocq and Smithline through a large dining room with slabs of sour bread and bowls ready on the tables. Two girls tittering in the kitchen doorway ran when the guard shook his bunch of keys at them.

An old woman bounced a ball in a larger hall; another tried to master a skipping rope. A middle-aged woman hung on to the top of a stepladder, staring up into a corner of the ceiling. Two lopsided girls went by, crooked legs awry and hands drawn up under their armpit or chin, their mouths opening to snap this way and that. The walls were a pale sanitary green; a darker green paint was on each door. The guard took his cigar butt from his mouth to look through the peep-hole. Saliva ran down his chin. 'I guess you can see her. She looks calm, but better I make sure,' he said. He went into the cell. The door was ajar; Bellocq had a glimpse of the woman sitting on the bed. She put her arms into the straitjacket the guard held. He stood her up to fix each buckle before he led her out.

Marta kept her face averted, not wanting to see anything. She said nothing in reply to anything Smithline asked, her chin down on her shoulder, her mouth leaking saliva. His present lay untouched on the table.

Smithline did all the talking, but he could not find much to say. Bellocq stood by the window as he went on about leaving El Paso and writing her soon from New Orleans. She could join him whenever she felt better.

She started to scream the instant he kissed her cheek and rose to go.

'You saw that? She's been that way since the day they buckled that thing on.' Smithline paced up and down outside. 'Ask Stratton, ask anybody you care to. Don't you think I would take her if I thought there was any hope?'

'This place will never cure her.'

'I know, and I hate leaving her, but tell me what else I can do.'

Smithline set to humming a tune as he drove. When Bellocq asked him what it was, he said, 'I don't know the name. I heard a fella named Ned Bass sing it in a bar. Goes this way:

> Do you see that fly crawling up the wall?
> She's going up there to get her ashes hauled.
> I got a woman lives right back of the jail,
> She's got a sign on her window – Pussy for Sale.

I went to listen to Ned every night the three weeks he was in El Paso. He told me all about New Orleans. Marta used to hate that song.'

He said that the present he had left her was a Bible.

Bellocq had noticed the two arches of the firehouse. It was Smithline who pointed out the smoke. The fire wagon driver was too fat, phlegmatic as he waved an idle hand to warn off kids pestering him to let them ring the bell. Neighbours stood around, arms folded, waiting for whatever came next. A fireman emerged from the smoke on the fire-escape with a woman over his shoulder and got onto the ladder. He had an axe in his free hand. Some clapping broke out and a couple of men cheered. The three-storey building was well ablaze now. It was old, and the fire was undermining the front wall. Mr Pitt, the fire chief, spread his arms to usher people back; then the front fell suddenly, hurling bricks across the stream in the road.

Folks who had escaped from the building sat on the sidewalk, dazed and disbelieving, some on chairs brought out by residents across the road. They had lost only the paint from their doors and window frames. The horror was that one man had run screaming down the street with his clothes on fire until someone threw a tarpaulin over him and knocked him down.

The pharmacist, a Mr Murchison – his sign was only slightly scorched – brought some medication out to treat people's burns. His white coat was speckled with soot as he brushed aside the flying ash, prodding to keep his gold-rimmed glasses from sliding off his nose. Beside him, a doctor had his bag open and his stethoscope on a woman's chest. She lay back, holding a wet cloth to her face. In an open window of the house behind, a cat was stalking a canary; its shrill peep went unnoticed as it flew from side to side of the cage.

'Some crazy nigger walked in to rob the pharmacist, then set fire to the place,' said an old man.

'Sure did. They ran him to ground among those trees across the field there and strung him up,' a woman joined in.

'Let's walk over, take a look,' said Smithline. 'Go get your camera.'

'No,' said Bellocq.

'Let's go over there, anyway.'

Flames spread to a fence. That set the cornfield alight. People were helping the firemen, flailing sticks and coats. A telephone pole was burning; they were fighting to stop the fire reaching a large billboard. One of the firemen came out of the field, took his helmet off, wiped the sweat streaming down his face and bent over coughing. None of the pipes was long enough to reach the blaze. A fireman was rolling up the one they had tried.

'If we got some pictures,' said Smithline, 'the news-papers would pay.'

They set off across the field, where a burnt stretch still gave off heat and sparks. The threatened billboard was for Dr Worden's Female Pills, a product of the Seroco Chemical Laboratory, Chicago. It had been there for years; the woman's portrait on the lid was missing a nose.

As they came up to the body hanging from the tree, Bellocq felt sick. He did not want to look at Smithline, whose face was a blend of prurience and fear. Bellocq became angry. 'What do you want me to say?' He turned away. 'Even if I had my camera, I would not take a picture of that grisly thing. This is all sense-less.'

The mob had soaked the Negro with kerosene before torching his corpse. Bellocq had a whiff of roast pig from the fiesta. A man sat nearby, holding his bruised head. 'I took a knock,' he said, 'but we sure cooked that sonofabitch! The fucker screamed his head off – and, boy, did he sizzle!'

After the fire, Smithline seemed to drive faster. He did not need maps; he had driven to New Orleans so often in his mind. Bellocq had no sense of going anywhere, felt only sadness at losing subjects all the time – an old man on crutches, with nothing to think about, nothing to do except wait for somebody to take his picture. Bellocq was in no rush to get back to a place he never wanted to see again.

Coming into Houston, Smithline said they would stay in a hotel; he did not plan to see his brothers – one was a preacher there, the other a cop. He knew a bar, 'Harley's

Spring', around the corner from the chapel where his mother used to play.

The man who joined them at the bar gave his name as Aaron Hines. He had lank, fine blond hair hung over one eye, which he would lift off his brow with one finger. 'You can have no notion how demeaning it is for a man with my sensibility to prowl the bars of Houston hoping to find a spirit who is *simpático*,' he said. 'I spent six months in New Orleans. The boys there are angels, every one.'

Freedom was the vilest word in the language, Hines said, a snare and a delusion. He was free to catch a variety of diseases, and equally free to pass them on. To be at liberty meant always that others were not. The freedom he wanted he could never have. Freedom was a come-on to drive men to despair, including those who thought they were without chains – often the very ones who got others to go out and die in its defence.

'Some piker is free to tell you any lie he likes when he sells you something you don't want,' said Hines.

'Who is this guy?' Smithline whispered to Bellocq. 'Is he crazy, or what?'

Shaking his head, Smithline left to speak to the bartender.

'Your friend Mr Smithline thinks I'm talking horseshit. I can tell.'

A train wailed in the distance as Hines took out his watch. 'I'd like to get to know you better, Mr Bellocq,' he said. 'Tomorrow you'll be gone. Don't you hate it, too, a train makes that moan?'

Bellocq finished his beer and turned away.

'You're not going, are you?'

On the wall above the trough someone had drawn a naked man with a moustache, under whose livid erection was the caption: 'The Daring Young Man on the Flying Trapeze'. Bellocq half turned hearing the door close behind him. Hines got him in a stranglehold with a gun in his ear. 'This is the only way,' he whispered. 'Hold still, it won't take long. Forgive me, but I live alone, you understand? I have to do this. You're too stiff; give a little. All you need is a friend to show the way! If I didn't believe that, I wouldn't do this.'

All Bellocq could think of was the gun as he felt the man's mouth sucking at his neck. He heard the coyotes howl, and sank back in time, a spectator again as the vampire smiled. *'Je vous en prie –'* he began.

'Never mind my tears,' Hines pleaded. 'It's just the way I feel.' He held Bellocq tightly; the harsh sound of his breathing was deafening. Then the door burst open and hit the wall. Smithline blundered into Bellocq and Hines, knocking them to the ground. Hines lay with his head on Bellocq's belly until Smithline pulled him to his feet. The gun fired; a shower of plaster fell from the ceiling. There was a smell of burnt powder. Bellocq thought Smithline had kicked the gun across the floor, so that it hit the skirting-board. He had heard it that way, but when he spun round he saw that Smithline had the gun pressed to Hines's head. He was shouting. 'Right, now! It's your turn to break this fucker's face!'

Bellocq shook his head, blinking tears out of his eyes.

'Here! Take this.' Smithline handed him the gun, and hit Hines in the gut with a blow that forced the air out of him and left him gasping. Bellocq knew it would not stop there – that Smithline was going to beat Hines's face bloody. When Hines fell among the garbage in the passageway he lay on his back, staring up at them, croaking, 'Don't stop there! Goddamn right, I deserve it! Have you all done? Get back here and kill me, why don't you?' He touched Bellocq's ankle. 'Hey, it was nice meeting you,' he said, his mouth bloody. 'You may think you're free, but you better look over your shoulder.'

'Come on!' said Smithline, out of breath. 'He's crazy.' Bellocq could hear Hines's laughter, even with the door closed. 'Would you believe that shit? Are you okay? If I hadn't come in he'd have got into you in no time flat. He would. That goddamn jasper had his tongue in your ear, the dirty litle fucker!'

'He's bleeding,' Bellocq said. 'He has had to live with that all his life. Perhaps he gave in to it today.'

'For the first time?' Smithline sneered.

'He was frightened. I could feel his heartbeat.'

'Oh, sure. You heard him asking to be hurt! Don't give it another thought. Nobody is coming after us.'

Bellocq waited for Smithline, giving only half an ear to the barbershop talk about the riot in New Orleans.

How it had started was Robert Charles, a newspaper seller on the corner of Dryades and Melpomene, had a spat with his wife. She called the police. Charles lost his cap as they took him to the station. He asked to go back and pick it up. No, there was no time for that, and that was it. That nigger lost all self-control: the son of a bitch grabbed a Winchester off one of the cops and shot him dead. Did he stop there? Kill one, kill them all was a good idea – some say eighteen, others thirty-two – whichever it was, Wilson got clean away. The cops, being cops, then lock up his friend in the parish prison. A mob goes out there to take him, but the jailer won't give him up. So they run off to find any nigger to kill. All that night, and the next day, they go on a spree; they snuff niggers out in their houses, on the streets, in bed, and at their places of work. Sure, they had always had black and white in Crescent City, but no riots until Robert Charles set out to rake the coals over. Now nobody feels safe, even in the Garden District. The killing closes the city down; even the streetcars stop running. Calling in the National Guard did no good. There was killing going on for two days. B. A. Baldwin, a big dealer in ammunition, put the lid on it when he said he would arm the Negroes.

'You seem to think this Charles was standing on that street corner nursing an urge to kill a white cop,' one of the men said to his friend with the paper. 'I can't see that.'

'It's getting late,' said the barber. 'Light the lamp so's I can see what I'm doing here.'

The kid leant his broom in the doorway and did as he was told. Moths came flying in. The customer put the *Picayune* down, hawked and rang the spittoon, shifting on the bench as he cleared his throat.

As Smithline settled into the chair for his shave, Bellocq felt a wave of nausea, hating the futility of another night in the saloons that were open and waiting.

'I don't know what the South is coming to,' Bellocq heard.

'If we'd won that war none of these things would happen,' said the barber, lathering Smithline. The throat-clearing, inarticulate sigh that echoed around the room was a tacit assent.

A woman left the deepening shadows to stand pigeon-toed in the doorway. She wore a dress the colour of dried mustard that hung off her bony shoulders. The youngest of the men got up with a sigh to ask why had she come. She needed twenty-five cents. He was going to drink it else, and the kids were hungry. 'What'll you do if I don't?' Unwilling, he took a handful of change out of his pocket. 'I see your face here again, you'll wish I hadn't. You understand?' His tone was harsh. She went off into the street to stand at the edge of light from the shop. Bellocq knew that it was the last place on earth she wanted to be. Nor did he, so close to home.

3

Crossing the coastal plain, with New Orleans in sight, Smithline reeled off names from the world of jazz, men he hoped to meet. Buddy Bolden and others Bellocq hadn't heard of. His anxiety left him with a sinking feeling. It became harder to draw breath now. He could hear his mother's footsteps in the night. In his dream, the mirror was grey with the soap she had rubbed over it. The fear with mirrors was that people hid behind them and might appear unbidden at any moment. There was no longer an exit through the looking-glass.

Bellocq left Smithline in a bar on Perdido. The rain fell harder as a brewer's wagon went by. The driver had a sack hood over his head, and his team steamed under canvas covers. When the lantern on the tailgate died in the dark, Bellocq turned his collar up and made his way by sheltering in doorways.

He could hear the gaslight by the church front. There were the same notices on the board; the tacks were rustier in the humidity. The more recent sheets were white, on an older yellow base. 'You'll go home to your mother,' Pearl used to say, 'that's where you belong. You never got away.'

Bellocq stood by the cast-iron gate. What was Louella doing there so late at night, singing?

There was a black dog by the man holding a lantern. It ran up and began to bark and snarl. No dog ever barked at him in Mexico; there, the dogs had things to do – food to find – places to go. The man had been out in the rain some time. His wet clothes gave off a brackish smell of mud. He had some sort of buckle or brooch glinting above his hat brim, which was pulled down over his left eye. The mongrel shook its pelt in the rain, stopped barking to let the man stroke it as he crouched. He talked to the dog, but his remarks were for Bellocq. 'You were a boy lived in this house,' he said. 'I know you. Repent, and save your soul.'

'Save it from what?'

'What is the Book for, if you don't live by it?'

'Get away, you crazy old fool! Go on, go!' Bellocq thrust the old man away in fear and rage; the dog began to bark again.

'Who's out there?' Louella was at the window. 'What's that dog doing, creating so? Come out in the light where I can see the both of you.'

The man moved on; the dog stood its ground, barking again. Then it slunk off to its master's call. Bellocq's face brushed the ivy hung from the broken balustrade. The same tubs of hydrangeas stood each side of the door. He would wait there as a child while his mother went upstairs, in two minds about her gloves or forgetful of her rosary and missal. Behind the scrolled ironwork, pale amber flowers shone inside a maroon-bordered clear glass.

The colours had always been mystical; he did not know why he thought of the Valley of the Kings. Now, there was a crack. He saw the light from a candle Louella carried. 'Why, Mr Ernest, get on in here; you're soaked to the skin.'

Coming into the house, Bellocq suddenly recalled that it was his mother's birthday. How long had he been gone? Four years? He followed Louella along the passage lined with dark panels, past a tapestry of jaded courtiers fluttering handkerchiefs as they bowed to the Sun King in his garden.

'Sweet Jesus, I'm glad to see you,' Louella said, going into the kitchen. 'We got to get you out of those wet things right now.' She made him take off his jacket and hang it on a chair by the stove.

The air was sweet with the smell of apples she had been peeling. The table was full of them. Others lay on the flagstones and seemed to glow where they had fallen.

'Why? What's happened? Where's *maman*?'

'I had to stay here,' said Louella. 'Your mama's sick now. I got to be here all the time.' It all started when he left, his mama's mind going – at first no one hardly noticed but now Madame Bellocq could not remember what she did the day before. 'You don't fool me,' said Louella. 'Did you see what was going on? You always paid more heed to your mother than I did. Is that why you took off so fast?'

Bellocq sat down at the table and bit into an apple. The juice made his jaw ache.

'I had the sharp edge of her tongue all my life, but she rages so now,' Louella went on. 'Your mama did not have many friends to start with; those who put up with her stopped coming around when she got like this.

She's mean now. She is going to tell you I do some awful things to her. I know because that's what that old sourpuss tells everybody. Well, Mr Bellocq, none of it's true. You know me – how many years? I was your nurse, your cook, and your maid. I used to wipe your ass. Tell me, how could I beat your mama with a stick? You know I'm easygoing, and always was, but I swear to God, it's been so bad this week I thought I might run off.'

'What do you do about wages?'

'There's money in your pa's old roll-top,' said Louella. 'I took what was mine by right, and a few dollars to pay for food. I don't know how much she owes storekeepers. They deliver stuff and send the bills.'

'Is there anything left?'

'I don't keep count. She hides it. There's more squirrelled away someplace. I know why she does that. I do it myself; you never know what's coming round the next corner.'

'I better go up,' said Bellocq, squaring his shoulders.

Louella said she would come with him, then he would know.

Tiny candles glowed in red jars around the room. They had been burning there all his life. They gave the only light, apart from the candelabra Louella carried. It was difficult to make out the plaster statuette of Joan of Arc and the photogravure of the Last Supper. As a child, Bellocq used to dream that he was there, under the table when Jesus told Peter he would deny Him but become the Rock on which He would build the Church. He had seen Judas silent, his hands twisting like snakes in his lap, waiting for the soldiers to take Christ. But though he thought he had been there, he had never understood any of it, or felt much.

'Why did I hide there?' he said aloud, hoping to forget that, in those days, he'd had nowhere else to go and nothing better to do.

Bellocq looked over Louella's shoulder, and was forced to step back when she turned to face him. His mother was asleep. She had her nightdress on back to front.

'She smells. Why?'

'Ask her, why don't you?' Louella shook her head. 'I get her into the bathroom to get it done right, but she's some wildcat, scratching and biting. Reach me out that chamber; I better empty it.'

'What does Dr Clouzot say? Has he seen her?' Bellocq spoke in a whisper.

'That it's dementia. I sent for him the day the cop brought her home. She had no notion where she'd been, or how to get back. It was lucky the cop was old enough to know her. He found her sitting in Congo Square. After that, she puts one spoon of sugar in her cup she puts six. Dr Clouzot – what does he know? Maybe she has a tumour in her head. He says old people go that way, some faster than others. Who wants to know? I asked a couple of nuns to see her. They took one look and ran.'

A fly hummed across the ceiling. 'I got fly-papers up there,' said Louella. 'It'll hit one soon.'

His mother stirred but did not open her eyes. Bellocq asked Louella if she had given her some drug to make her sleep.

'It's that or strap her down,' Louella replied. 'She'll ramble 'less I do. She goes crazy, cutting up her dresses or changing everything around in the kitchen. I come down one morning and find her in an unholy mess, fast asleep, sucking her thumb.'

Someone was knocking on the front door. Louella

went to the window, asking who could be there at that hour.

Bellocq knew that it was Smithline. He had a girl with him. He was maudlinly apologetic, but Bellocq knew his plan had been to come there all along. 'You can't stay here,' he said. 'My mother is sick.'

'She would never know, she's dead to the world now,' said Louella, coming behind.

Smithline had nowhere else to go. 'You can't leave us out in this,' he said.

'They can sleep in the box room,' Louella said. 'The bed is narrow but they won't notice that.'

When she came back from lighting them upstairs, Louella was tired. 'A floozie like that is mischief. She will bring your friend nothing but grief.'

'What sort of floozie is that?'

'Out of some bayou by way of the District, I'd say.'

Bellocq did not want to see his mother. He rose early and set off for Dr Clouzot's. As he left, Louella was busy in the kitchen. 'I feel sorry for you, coming home to this,' she said. 'Maybe it can teach you something that'll help you both.' Bellocq knew he could not, and did not want to, cope; yet how could he walk away? There was nothing he could learn from his mother's plight. 'I got to get home, Mr Ernest, now you're back,' she said. 'I've not seen hair nor hide of my family in months. Just about this time last week, I met Joyboy off the prison bus.'

'Again? How long did he get this time?'

'Six months. Not paying a fine.'

Joyboy had lived with Louella on and off for years.

'I'll cook and clean daytimes, as usual,' she said, 'so I won't put it all on you, but I just can't stay here nights.

68

I'm not cut out for this, Mr Ernest. It'd be easier for the two of you if you put your mama in a home.'

Dr Clouzot did not agree. 'I have other patients in the same state,' he said. 'Some worse off than your mother is. I read somewhere that there is a name for it now, but I can't call to mind what it is.'

'She won't improve, then?

'No. There is no cure, and there is nothing I can do.'

'Louella has gone through a hard time.'

'Your mother was better off at home, in familiar surroundings. If you put her away somewhere she'll fade fast.'

'How long will it go on?'

Clouzot shrugged. 'I can't say with any certainty. How long is a piece of –' he stopped with a dry cough; 'you know what I mean.'

'She does it all, shits herself and wets the bed.'

'You get a nurse in who can cope. I can give you the names of a couple.'

'I can't afford that.'

'I don't know what else to suggest. You were in Mexico, you say – not the healthiest of places. Are you all right? Nothing you need?'

Bellocq said he had dreams.

'Nightmares?' Clouzot scribbled a prescription. 'No, there's nothing I can give your mother except sleeping draughts. She's best off asleep; you look as if you could do with them, too.'

Bellocq loitered, walking back. He wanted to be going somewhere else, but no other destination came to mind. The girl had gone by the time he got home. Smithline was eating the breakfast Louella had cooked before she left. He wore underpants, socks and a grubby vest. He

69

handed Bellocq his mother's bedroom door key and said that Louella had locked her up.

'You can see what the situation is here,' said Bellocq. 'I told you last night.' Yet he could not give vent to his rage against Smithline for bringing him back.

'What will happen to our plan to set up shop together?'

'That was *your* plan. I can't even think about it now. Not with the way things are.'

'When will you be able to?'

'I can't say.'

After Smithline left, Louella came back and let his mother out of her room. Bellocq heard them shuffling down the stairs. When he went into the parlour, his mother's first words were: 'Get away from me, I know what you are. I know your name is Satan.'

'No, *maman*.'

'I don't know about that; my children are not here.'

She was sitting at the piano she used to play; her sole interest now was in the metronome, which Louella had set ticking. Soon, there was a ghastly, nowhere smile on her face.

'Best when you talk to her you speak low,' Louella had said. 'Anything can spook her into a tantrum. I made her this wire hoop. You want to keep her out of mischief, soapy water does the trick. She'll blow bubbles for hours. Read her fairy stories; she likes those. Sit her by the window so she can see a bird now and then.'

It might be a real blessing if she could see that God of hers she'd mislaid, Louella said.

Scabs of distemper fell everywhere, making a mess round all the skirting-boards. Bellocq could hear scratchings behind the walls, the click of seed pods falling from dead plants. Spider webs hung in corners. There were all kinds of insects now, and the damp sheets on furniture in unused rooms lent a feeling of absence and death. 'What time is it?' his mother asked again. Why ask that? Habit? Did time have any meaning for her now?

'I told you ten minutes ago.'

'What time is it?'

'The same as when I told you.'

His mother had smoked cheroots before his father died. Now that Louella hid the matches she could not light them. She chewed them until the juice ran down her chin, asking 'Do I live here?' She did not remember. She would start out for somewhere, then stop halfway just frozen, turn around and come back, still going nowhere.

Bellocq put on a long black glove that lay on his mother's missal in the chest of drawers. Sniffing old scent in the palm, he gazed at the stuffed flamingo, a pink sentinel guarding the book cabinet and prie-dieu. Its pink plumage had faded chalky white. Her tropical shells and netsuke carvings were dusty now. She no longer read books: *Madame Bovary*, Renan's *Vie de Jésus*. He sat numbly, hands limp on his thighs, palms upward. He could not shake off the feeling of how ephemeral things were; nothing, not even the marble hands – a pious keepsake – had any weight worth holding on to.

His mother had ruled with an iron will, the sound of her heels alone would strike fear; now she was a dubious shadow in doorways. Bellocq kept finding her stalled in odd corners she had no reason to be.

Louella had made efforts, cleaned the silver, but, with his mother's fall from power, she felt no urge to do anything much, not even sweep the courtyard where most of the flowers his mother used to tend had died.

A few, such as the night-scented jasmine, hung on to pierce the air with their fragrance. 'I got *Père* Guersaint to write to your brother,' Louella had said. 'So far, he's not seen fit to answer. So I just did what I had to do, got on with things needing to be done.'

After more dreams, Bellocq was unsure where he was – until he saw his mother's dead eyes staring. Anything she said that he could make sense of lost all meaning. Most days she said nothing. Her silence was stoical, as if she knew how bad things were with her. She had always made him feel that he had failed her. She had never had any time for human frailty. Suddenly she asked, 'Where are the children?' He did not know whether she meant him and Leo. They were alive only in that part of her mind where he had never lived. Then she said, 'Where was it that the two men came out to strike the bell with hammers?' How could he tell her? He had no idea what country she was in. Trying to reach her, he showed photographs he had taken of her when he was twelve. They were those of a stranger she did not recognize, and did not care about. The only ones that had any interest for her were of his brother Leo as a child. 'Too many babies,' she said, as if she had in mind every birth since time began.

As the days went by, Bellocq began to see what Louella had to put up with. He wrote to Leo at the seminary:

'I say my name every time I speak to her and get her to repeat it, but I know it means nothing. Your name is a dead letter, too. I showed her your picture, but she did not look at it. Often she calls me by her brother's name; so at least I am part of the family. I think if you came home, you might do more good than I. You share her beliefs;

you can speak that language she understood once. When I asked her why she was crying the other day, she said she had not seen her mother for so long. She said she wanted to go home. I did not know where that was, when she sat on her own bed. You can catch a flash, a look, thinking that something will follow, but it does not. Now she will never go anywhere without one of her old dolls, which, she says, is the Baby Jesus. Sometimes she does not need a doll, but will rock in such a way as if she holds a baby. Is that child you, or I?'

Bellocq did not tell Leo of the stab of pain that brought him close to tears on finding the doll abandoned. Nor could he say anything of the day he came into her room and she had her shoes on the wrong feet, her hand jerking under her skirt. It took him a moment to realize with horror that she was masturbating.

She told him she could not find her way in the dark. She let go with whoops with no rhyme or reason, jabbering sometimes until she cried or gave up with a low growl out of some nowhere. Never mind how strong and stern her face still was, her gestures were those of a baby, as were her tears.

Leo wrote that he would come soon. But he was not to turn up until it was all over, in time for the funeral.

The ringing was from the belfry of Our Lady of Guadalupe. He had used to brush his mother's hair as a child, but she took no pleasure in it now. He edged the comb down her frail skull to make a centre-parting in her white girlish waves. He could see her in a fur hat and muff in the snow. The photograph was taken in Paris the winter his mother met Paul Claudel. The photographer had caught the hauteur which came with being born rich, the assurance that lent things a spurious meaning that was such a waste of time. All this went through his mind as he set up the camera to take her picture.

After taking three photographs he could not face doing more. He saw his reflection in her eyeball and had to burn the prints.

Bellocq was tired after another night vigil; he boiled up water to fill the tub and lay drifting near sleep. Ivy grew through the top of the open window; a tendril hid the Victorian jug's rustic scene. He tried to imagine climbing the steep path towards the flock of sheep, their fleeces lit by an orange sunset. The air smelt of lemon-scented soap laced with menstrual blood.

Startled, Bellocq came to, and saw his mother's apparition in the mirror, a wraith in the dusk, before it flitted away. The water was cold. He dried himself quickly, dressed and went to her bedroom. She was not there. He found her in the kitchen, sitting on the floor. She had eaten half a jar of honey, and had started to empty the sugar bowl.

He tried to take her back over things they had shared – Is that it? I'm right, yes, I'm right? What about the day he broke her string of freshwater pearls? She beat him with her stick as he went around on his hands and knees picking them up, could she remember? – trying to force the past out of her, to make her talk about things that she alone knew. He cut pictures out of magazines, anything, showed her books and asked her to name things, but every day she was slipping further away. All that was left was her anger. 'I don't want you near me,' she said; 'I don't want to hear your voice! Go and talk to someone else!'

*　　*　　*

Bellocq knew there was two hundred dollars in the house. He had hidden the money when he left for Mexico. Finding more cash his mother had salted away, he went to buy a car, thinking that to get her out in the country might help her.

'Choose a Ford Model T,' the dealer advised. 'A new make, sir, but less trouble than any other, I guarantee. Believe me, my business only thrives if I satisfy my customers. Owning a car will change your life, sir. I'll just give the handle a turn and take you for a spin. You'll get the hang of it in no time.'

Bellocq went right at Krauss's department store on the corner of Canal. Leaving the shadow of the Regency Shoe Company's chimney smoke, he drove along Basin Street past Marcet's shooting gallery. On the corner of Iberville, the lights were still on in Anderson's bar. It had been the Fair Play Saloon until Anderson bought it in 1897. Ahead, the sun lit the bright awnings on the sporting houses, Hilma Burt's and The Arlington, going on by Martha Clarke's and Mahogany Hall. There, the dealer raised his hat in mock salute to Lulu White, who was coming down the steps. 'Look at that old black sow, will you? Would you believe that I don't make enough to afford a fuck in that bitch's crib?'

'I can't listen and drive at the same time,' said Bellocq.

They came to the firehouse and Barrera's. Then Bellocq swung onto Conti. With the St Louis Cemetery on one side and Groshell's Dance Hall on the other, he turned onto Franklin then went left to go as far as Bienville. There, on the right, he was heading for Claiborne. 'You are a natural, if I do say so,' said the dealer, looking at his watch. 'Well, what about this vehicle? Don't it beat all? It sure is everything I said.'

Bellocq could only wonder whether the aura of confidence he felt around his body was visible to the dealer.

Bellocq lowered the veil on his mother's hat and sat her stiffly upright. Louella had got her into a black silk dress and hung jet beads round her neck. She made no complaint about the dust flying, as she used to in the old carriage days; he was heading out toward Barataria, he shouted, tooting the horn.

Seeing an ideal spot for a picnic, he pulled over. The dust haze hung in the trees long after he came to a stop. With the cloth spread, he set out every dish he could recall his mother relishing. Beaubien, for years the family grocer, was happy to provide the wine and cheeses. He hoped Madame Bellocq would enjoy her day out, and said he would have come too, but the business did not run itself. He supplied fine wines to all the high-class restaurants – Fabacher's, Antoine's and the rest.

Everything done, Bellocq realized he was alone. A thrush and a warbler set up a piercing trill. Noting that, he got his mother to repeat his words. She forgot them a moment later. She took the sandwich he gave her, ate a mouthful, and laid it in her lap.

He wondered idly how near they were to Barataria, and tried to envisage Deschamps there with Juliette – and yes, those anal lacerations – that 'abuse over a long period' to which the dentist had subjected the girl. But they had surely had such dreamy afternoons, time for idylls in such a glade.

The frogs' chorus set off the bleating of the goats Bellocq had seen on the road. He saw a girl fleet swiftly between the tree trunks to the pool, a solid mat of red and yellow leaves. She sent a blizzard of white seeds flying as she strode singing to the water's edge. She knelt to haul a line in, unhooking the fish one by one into a pail.

The faded blue dress she wore was a tatter of holes. Her bare feet were pasted with yellow leaves. 'Say, mister, can I sell you one of these catfish at all?' She tilted the pail slightly.

Bellocq said no. Flies droned by; the goats were hot, panting a faint bleat now and then, with scarcely a clank of their bells. Three butterflies flew across the glade.

'I see you go by in your car.'

Bellocq nodded. The girl bent low to peer at his mother. 'She's a sick lady. Is she your mama? My auntie is a *bokor*, and she can do good for her.'

'A *bokor*?' Bellocq did not know the word.

'A *houdou* woman. You want I take you to see to her?'

The girl said her name was Ashanti, and that she had never been in a car before. 'What's that?' It was the rosary he had looped around the rear-view mirror. 'You don't know? Leave it there; it calms my mother.'

Soon, the track began to narrow and Bellocq had to stop the car. Ashanti said it was not far to walk the rest of the way. Bellocq heard the squealing of piglets first. Two of them ran at him from behind the hut; they were tied to a rope that he almost fell over. The hut was roofed with palm leaves that made it impossible to detect in the cane-brake. There was a vegetable plot with a stained frock-coat hung on a cross by the entrance. Ashanti spoke Baron Samedi's name in a hushed tone and said her aunt talked to him all the time. Bellocq saw his own image, a wraith in the mirrors around the door as he crouched by a shrine adorned with bits of a broken glass. On it were two dolls – one was a black Virgin Mary with a gilt

77

coronet and tribal marks cut into her cheeks, the other was white, with imitation pearls around her neck.

Candles lighting the hut were just bright enough to see pots and pans on makeshift shelves, a cutlass standing in a corner next to a heap of sticks. The roof and walls were lined with woven matting. There were paintings of animals – Aunt Cybele made the paints from berries and powders, and got her brushes off the pigs. Another girl – Ashanti's twin, Magalie – sat plaiting the old woman's hair while a kettle sang on the fire.

Some acrid herb burnt in Aunt Cybele's pipe, not tobacco. Bellocq could not guess how old she was. The rings on her fingers were costly. She laughed, saying, 'Yours is the first white face I've seen in many a year.' Bellocq said how could that be, with the city only an hour's drive away?

'Sure, if I had a car, that is – I went by there when I came from Haiti as a girl. No good would have come my way if I had spent any time in that city. I know you sometimes see yourself that night, watch them carry your daddy down the gangplank. I remember those dark and terrible ships, sleeping head to toe in that stinking darkness. My name then was Cybele Louima, and I didn't see much for that fog after I got ashore. You need eyes to see.' They had torn her from her mother whose powers were greater than hers, and she'd had to learn nature all over again in that swamp.

There were six lemons in a dish and an osier basket full of fish heads, some of their eyes milky with decay, floating in entrails and blood from the livers. Only gradually could Bellocq make out that there were newspapers lining the walls; one front page was about the carnage at Antietam.

'What you doing out here?'

Bellocq said he had brought his mother for a picnic. To wear a suit was a bad idea; he could feel the sweat running down his side from his armpits.

'Or maybe not; maybe a spirit led you here. How would you know what power called you home from Mexico? Maybe that same demon bewitched this woman.' She touched his mother's knee, sitting beside Bellocq on the low wooden stool.

'She is not under a spell,' said Bellocq, nervous now.

'You sure about that? Invisible spirits fly everywhere; they fill the air with that evil pollen to blind us. Your mama has to have some help from the *loas*.'

Bellocq knew that Louella would have heard if there had been any *houdou* cure such as Aunt Cybele was about to offer, yet he felt the hairs rise on the back of his neck.

'Get my coat, Ashanti,' the old woman ordered, tying a red bandanna round her head. The girl took the frock-coat off the cross and held it out for Aunt Cybele to put on. 'You got three dollars, I can treat your mama good,' she said, going outside.

After some thrashing in the bushes, some squealing that became throaty screams, she was back with one of the black piglets in her arms. Its eyes rolled in terror; it shot its feet out stiffly as she threw it on its side and knelt to tie its legs. 'Unless you feed the spirits, you get nowhere,' she said. 'They are pretty rogues, my piglets, and they are angels; they are life, they are mothers of mothers.'

Magalie left the fire to go into the dark at the back of the hut. She came back with two tall drums. The sky clouded over as the girls began to rattle them with their fingers. Neither of them wore knickers; they let their knees open, grinning at Bellocq. As the darkness in the hut deepened, the signs Aunt Cybele daubed on the piglet's side shone, luminous. The animal was quiet now; it lay still enough for her to stand a burning candle on its flank.

Magalie knelt, offering the cutlass. Aunt Cybele took it and began to strike sparks from a stone with the handle in time to the drums.

His mother began to tremble; her rigid body shook with spasms as Aunt Cybele waved a bunch of feathers in her face. The feathers were a signal for the girls to stop drumming. Crossing herself, Aunt Cybele was ready to sacrifice the pig. The dark air was close now; it smelt of pepper and was so hot it parched the lungs to breathe. Aunt Cybele thrust the sword into the pig's throat, edging a bowl with her foot to catch the blood. An instant after the pig squealed, his mother spoke fluently with the old woman.

They used French to say that the spirits of the fathers had all the power, and they were taking some of that. Aunt Cybele told his mother that she must not forget her joys along with her sorrows. By the great power and strength of Yaphet, the husband she loved those years ago, she was releasing her from her spell: she was no longer a zombie. She took his mother's hand, stroking a feather up towards her elbow. His mother swayed on the edge of sleep. Bellocq looked away. Forced to face them again, Aunt Cybele had a lapful of snakes. Some were crawling onto his mother's leg, which he had no strength to prevent. His mother held her hand by her ear with a lost smile, hearing voices, while her lips made a suckling noise as if she had lost her mother's nipple.

It took no longer than ten to fifteen minutes, then

Aunt Cybele brought a bunch of dried leaves out of a corner of the roof. Her voice came from far away. 'You put these to soak three minutes in hot water, then make sure your mama drinks the potion.'

Deep in a dream, from which he could not wake, Bellocq heard a voice assign him the lead in a play he did not know, had never read. His tongue was cold; it cleft to the roof of his mouth as the girls shook his arm. It seemed as though he stood afar seeing himself lift his mother into the car. When he came to his senses, he saw the lights of New Orleans growing brighter as night fell. Afraid to nod off at the wheel, Bellocq stopped the car and laid his mother down in the rear seat, covering her with a rug. Looking in his wallet, he found that his brush with the supernatural had cost him five dollars. He got his head down on his folded coat and drifted off into uneasy sleep, waking whenever some animal or bird cried out. He was hoping that his mother might get up and wander off into the bayou, and he would never see her again. She did not. When he woke at first light, her eyes were staring as if she knew what he'd had in mind. Her brief sanity had gone.

Bellocq pulled over at Ahrens' Filling Station. Ahrens' wife came out, tying the strings of her apron. 'Lady, you don't look good at all,' she said. 'You could use a coffee and some of that nice ice-cream I made first thing this morning.'

His mother ate the ice-cream as though it were the first she had ever tasted.

When Bellocq spoke of Aunt Cybele and the girls, Ahrens said no, so far as he knew nobody lived out there. Some weird things went on, though. 'I don't venture far into that swamp,' he said. 'I'm too old a slowpoke to go now. You need all your wits about you – even then, you're courting grief.'

Outside again, the old man held up a glass jar to show Bellocq the two cottonmouths. 'Everything in that swamp is poison; things strike fast at you out of nowhere; one of these bite you in the foot, or the ass, and you'd know about that. The sun will bake them to death before nightfall.'

Bellocq hung over a pan of water until it began to boil, as if close attention to every move were part of the spell. Then he sprinkled the leaves into the pan and took out his father's watch. Louella soon smelt the brew and came in, disgust on her face. 'What's that poison you got there?'

Bellocq told her of meeting Aunt Cybele.

'Can't you smell how bad that stuff is? It will surely kill her dead!'

'What else can I do?'

'Your mama is just not there any more,' said Louella. 'Better you get used to that. No conjure woman without any decent place to live than a mudhole is going to help that.'

'I wonder you didn't go to one yourself, Louella.'

'I been with this family too many years for that kind of talk.'

That night, his mother spoke fluently enough in her sleep, often with squealing cries of pain, but had little to say in the morning. She had periods of clarity all day. She was alive then, and hideously girlish, even piteously so. It pained him to hear her say, 'Don't let *papa* whip me.' He knew now that she had tried to fight off her pain by inflicting it on others. As Louella said, 'Your mama built her whole life on grudges. I had to respect her because she had the whip. Now I can't, that's all.'

After dark, any clarity went. His mother showed no sense of prior existence, and all he wanted for her was to die. She had not meant anything to him for so long, and he hated everything he had to do for her, from picking up a cup she broke to brushing her hair. It was taking too long, with no let–up day after day. She stank badly again, and he had to overcome disgust to give her a bath.

He was unlacing her shoes when she got hold of his hair. She pulled it. 'Stop that, *maman*, don't do it; it hurts!'

After a quick scrub, he sat her down to soak until the water was cold. He hated having to see her naked, so frail and thin. The bizarre thing was a faded tattoo of a blue rose on her thigh. What did it mean? It was impossible to imagine why she had let anyone do that to her. Yet it was too artistic to be self-inflicted.

Her ears were still dirty; she refused to let him remove the long, heavy earrings she had worn all her life. They had torn long slits in her earlobes. If she were not a living corpse, she was somewhere else, living a life he did not know about.

Bellocq told Louella he was taking his mother to visit relatives in St Louis.

'How come I never heard about those?' Louella was suspicious. 'Why in the world would you want to do that, in her state?'

Bellocq's plan was to go leave her in some St Louis hotel – maybe one that was holding a convention. He would make sure somebody found her, then board the next train for New Orleans.

Everything went smoothly until the train reached Baton Rouge. There, his mother said she had to get home; the children were hungry and had to be fed. When Bellocq said she had no children, she lashed out and screamed. He realized then he could not go through with it and got her off the train.

They sat on one of the station's big mahogany benches while he tried to think what to do. Should he book into a hotel for the night? Unable to decide, he walked up and down. When he came back he could smell that she had shat herself. He was angry; twice he had taken her to the toilet, shut her in, and waited to hear the flush. They could not board the train with her like that. He took her arm and set off to find a place to clean her up. They came to some waste ground beside the tracks. He sat her on a plank between some bricks and told her to stay there. Leaving, he turned to look back and saw her as someone he might glimpse from a train, a lone, well-dressed old lady sitting on a plank who sometimes shook her arm to warn of her displeasure.

The railyards seemed to have no end; then he came across the hole in the wall and found a street of cabins.

He gave a barefoot black woman two cents for a pail of water, which he carried back along the track.

His mother had brought the long black dress she'd worn half a century ago. He made her hold it around her waist as he unpinned the towel. Using his handkerchief, he washed her shrivelled buttocks. '*Maman*, you have dirtied yourself again. I shall have to give you a talking-to,' he heard himself say. He could barely see what he was doing for tears. The journey was over. He walked back arm in arm with her to the station.

The preacher's white, short-sleeved shirt cut into his

biceps as he bit a frankfurter. Then his hand fell slackly on his fat thigh. His snack over, he tipped his hat off his brow to wipe the sweat, then took another swig of beer. His hat tilted down again as he eased himself against the handle of the truck he sat on. He put his paper over his face.

The signal arm cast a dark, diagonal shadow in the glare of the sun. Tar oozed out of the ties. The tang of it lay a sharp fur on Bellocq's tongue as the sweat ran down his back. Would the train never come?

Either she could not, or refused to, control her bowels. Each time he took the towel off, her body had grown more shrunken. Nor would she eat, but shut her lips tight against any food. Her breathing was soon a painful wheeze. Clouzot came and diagnosed pneumonia; he said she was not long for this world. The sound of her breathing got on Bellocq's nerves, trying to sleep on the floor beside her bed. The flesh hung on her bones, now as fragile as a bird's. She had to go, or she would pull him down into the same hole she was in. Early on the morning of the third day, as he put a pillow over her face, she looked at him in what he saw as a kindly way, almost with gratitude. She did not fight, did not lift her frail arms. When he took the pillow away, she was no longer breathing. A thin trickle of blood ran out of her nose. He did not know why his hand felt numb until he realized that she had seized his wrist. She was holding it so tightly that he had to force her fingers open.

He did not know why he had done it. He told himself it was for her, in reply to some mute appeal he had seen in her face. He knew that was a lie; he had killed her because he was unable to take any more. He had her

85

in his power and had revenged himself for her cruelty over the years. Having done it, he felt he had shared her death. He held on to that, staring numbly at the food she had left on the plate, and would never eat now. Her feet were cold already; his filial impulse was to rub them. The sob hurt his chest, and made him feel an ache in his ribs. He lay down on the bed beside her, able at last to talk to her. She smelt as sickly sweet as violets already. Did flesh corrupt so fast?

He closed his eyes. When he awoke, it was dark. Someone was knocking at the front door. He went down to find Louella, a coat over her nightdress. 'I hear a whippoorwill last night before I slept,' she said. 'In my dream, there was black, muddy water everywhere I go, and that stream ran slow. I had to wake up and come. I could feel it in my bones. I had lost my purse. So many things go missing. I looked everywhere. Something was not right about that. I had the feeling something bad would happen.'

'Well, it has, Louella.'

'Sweet Jesus, I know, Mr Ernest, but I mean something bad. You look awful. What's going on here?'

Bellocq felt the tears start and run chill on his cheeks. He could not see Louella. She put her hands on his shoulders, then stroked down his arms to the elbows, saying, 'You were never able to fake it, Mr Bellocq.'

'*Maman* is dead, Louella,' he said.

'Well then, that's for the best,' she said.

'I'll call Dr Clouzot.'

'Not at this hour – he'll have a fit. There's nothing he can do about anything.'

'I think I had better.'

Bellocq took the car and telephoned from a bar that

was still open. Clouzot said he would be over first thing in the morning. Louella knew how to do the usual things, the routine. She had done it enough times.

Arriving home, Bellocq sat in the car. Louella came out to ask him to eat something. 'What you plan to do? Drive out to the bayou and talk to that conjure woman who was maybe never there in the first place? Come on in. It'll be light soon.'

Bellocq let her lead him into the house.

'I can't believe what I heard happened,' Louella sighed. 'Unless I had my eye on her all the time, I knowed she would do herself harm.' She sighed again. 'She sure was some bitch, your mother, if I do say so. She never let a day pass without she put it across somebody, and maybe she did it to the wrong person along the line. Not that I want to speak ill of the dead.'

'What are you trying to say?'

'You live in a city where souls get stolen, I hope you know.'

Louella had always had the power to chill Bellocq's blood. He hated her going round the house, turning mirrors to the wall. She said she was afraid of what she might see in them. She said she had been up to wash and lay out the corpse. His mother was stiffening fast, and not to worry about that. He better get some rest.

'I shall have to let Beaubien know tomorrow.'

It was noon; the shade was drawn. A dusty, faded green awning said 'Augustin Beaubien, Groceries'. Bellocq could smell the fruit under the grey canvas that covered the boxes outside; wasps were humming under there. The driver of a buckboard at the kerb slept with reins in hand. Bellocq would come there as a child; Beaubien had Delphine ladling milk at a wooden tub, a hose running over the tiled floor, her face spectral in the reflected bluish light. She had gone – married long ago, he supposed. Bellocq stood gazing at the shop's bell. It had rung so often it had beaten a scar into the wood as it lost its twang. He had always hated the smell of mildew that lay under the odour of cheeses, garlic and spices. The bell had not woken Beaubien. He was asleep with his head on the table in front of the matchstick replica of St Louis Cathedral it was taking him years to build. It was the same impulse, he used to say, drove his father's brother to make ships from slivers of animal bones when he was a prisoner aboard a hulk moored off Chatham in the Thames. The book on the table was Guy de Maupassant's *Bel-Ami*.

Beaubien woke, taking off his dusty blue beret to rub his baldness. Bellocq had no need to say why he had come. 'The best I could do was make sure she did not starve to death,' said Beaubien sadly.

'You leave your door unlocked, anyone could walk in one of these days and take advantage.'

'There is not a lot to rob, unless they are hungry.'

'Like *maman*? Did she pay you lately?'

Beaubien had never given that a thought; it didn't matter. As Bellocq knew, his son spent his days making corpses look lifelike. 'I don't say that because you might need his services, you understand.' He shook his head. 'I don't see that as any sort of work for a man. Mind you, he did well with *his* mother; I'll say that. She looked better than she did in life. When will you bury her?'

'As soon as I can arrange things; I'll let you know, of course.'

Bellocq knew of Beaubien's high regard for his mother. He knew the grocer would soon bring out the postcards she sent him from Florence. She had gone there the year after her crush on Claudel. Beaubien had read a great deal into those meagre messages, too much for his own good, perhaps. How was she to hear herself speak for the rush of pigeons? She was going now, out of a bright noon, to enter a dark church, built by faith, to see the memorial to Dante Alighieri.

'I have a sour taste in my mouth all the time now,' said Beaubien. 'My body soaks up poison all night. The onset of old age, I suppose. Everything is shot through with sadness. We talk about time; I have no time for anything! At least, I feel that I don't. Leo knows, of course? He'll come home for the funeral?'

The sheets on the washline picked up the afterlight of sunset. The dead Negro lay on a wagon beside a broken watermelon. 'Threw himself under a train,' a porter said. 'Nobody around here can think what to do with him. The police came, then left. You think they'll come back. Who knows?'

'Some drunkard with no idea what he was doing,' said Leo, passing the corpse.

Bellocq took his suitcase. 'You travel light.'

Worldly goods were a burden now.

'Do I call you Father?'

'Leo will do fine.' Leo took off his glasses to clean them.

Two Negroes and a policeman came along the platform. They hauled a rough packing case on a station wagon.

Leo asked whether *maman* had died in a state of grace. Bellocq laughed. 'A state of grace? She had gone far beyond any idea of that.'

'At least you were here for her.'

'You knew. I asked you to come.'

'Yes, you did, and I ought to have heeded that call. Sadly, I thought I had time.'

'Never mind; there is no right and wrong about these things.'

'Wrong? Is that what you think?'

'You have your burden, I have mine.'

'Ah, you know about those.' Leo was silent awhile, then said, 'Is there any money?' He looked away before facing his brother in all seriousness. 'She has to have the whole thing, the hearse, the horses with plumes.'

'How will we pay for those?'

Leo's case was open on the bed, a copy of the *Confessions* of St Augustine in view. Did Leo aspire so high? He had a photograph of himself and Leo, taken when they were altar boys. He was smaller and weaker than Leo and, even then, evasive − not looking ahead at the camera as they had been told to do, but darting sideways into a dream, trance even. Leo's gaze was steadfast and true, all the way to heaven's gate. They had never been close. The jar of salts for constipation said it all about Leo. It stood next to an opulent cope that had red fleur-de-lis at the top and on both arms of a gold cross. Finding the scourge came as a shock. Did priests still use those, or was it peculiar to Leo? Leo had always let it be known that he spent his nights fighting demons, but Bellocq had seen no evidence of that.

'I am to stay here now, to serve God in New Orleans,' said Leo. 'I shall have to seek an advance to cover my share of the funeral expenses.'

Bellocq let out a long sigh; he realized that he had been

holding his breath too long. He did not say that it was just as well that *maman* died when she did. Leo went on about the vow of obedience he had taken, and said he had given up his life to serve God. 'If you can root out that unholy taste for worldly pleasure, those paradisal tastes are the sweeter.'

'Yes, *maman* would know that too,' said Bellocq.

'Chastity was your great stumbling block, Ernest, as I recall. Has that changed? Have you met anyone yet to whom you can bare your soul?'

Bellocq shook his head.

Leo looked at his watch.

'I must go round to Beaubien's and phone the bishop to let him know I'm here,' he said.

Bellocq took the coins away from his mother's eyes. Her watch lay beside her lapis lazuli rosary. He wound it tight and pinned it to her bodice. Only her nails, the hair he combed out of her hairbrush, had any life in them.

The postman had left a packet from a cousin living now in Atlanta. She enclosed photographs of relatives killed in the War Between the States, officers and other ranks. Bellocq sat by the coffin and read the letter aloud; he looked at his mother's watch to check the time for the funeral, then rewound it. The cousin said the older she got, the more she seemed to need old photographs and the solace they gave. She had made these copies for his mother to keep, and went on to say how she hated Atlanta. She ought to have stayed in New Orleans, and not run off with those other women when the Union army took it.

They followed the hearse to the tomb in No. 1 Cemetery where his father's body lay. Smithline was nursing a hangover; Beaubien blowing his nose. Next to Leo, deep in conversation, stood Albert Jomy, Bellocq's oldest friend. Jomy was now a cabinet-maker. There had been three of them at school. The third, Chenault, was in Memphis on union business. He worked in the slaughterhouses, organizing every one. Bellocq had put a notice in the *Picayune*, but none of his mother's friends turned up. They had to live in fear of the cemetery now.

Louella's Joyboy stood off to one side, raking a finger inside his tight collar. Louella, decked out in her best finery, shook a fan to waft away smoke from a fire that hung a blue haze over the tombs.

If Bellocq thought he was rid of his mother, he was wrong. Where was she going now, her dark parasol moving off between the tombs? Bellocq had no ready answer. He looked over at Louella. Her face was blank as Cybele Louima and the girls went to meet his mother.

Aunt Cybele leant on a stick. She had a bundle on her head, as though she had come there on foot. Both girls took his mother's hands and led her away. Bellocq stared at Leo, then at Louella again; neither had seen anything. His senses whirled, as if he were having a bout of malaria. He had to follow, and did so as far as Marie Laveau's tomb, with all those pleas to the voodoo queen chalked on the wall. Turning from those, he found his mother and the others had vanished. Had she found a way into a tomb? Marie Laveau's? He felt relief not to have caught up with them.

He took his place again, pretending he had not been anywhere, but their faces showed they saw his behaviour as odd.

They left the cemetery and came out onto Conti, across from the cheap cribs. Smithline said, 'This has to be a sight for sore sinners' eyes of a morning.' At the corner of Marais, Louella told Joyboy that wild horses would not drag her into the house. 'If I never see that place again, it'll be too soon,' Bellocq heard her say bluntly.

Bellocq moved aside to join Jomy, who greeted him oddly. 'How can life ever satisfy all our desires?'

'How is your sister doing?'

'Not well,' said Jomy. '"Enervated" is her favourite word.'

She had reread Flaubert of late. His great news – and he was full to bursting with it – was that he had fallen under the spell of Nietzsche. He was *the* philosopher who had answers to those painful feelings that had beset him since childhood. He would lend Bellocq a copy of *Thus Spake Zarathustra*, which he had to read. It might help him in his present state.

Bellocq had to feel the same way, born to swelter in that city, his blood overheating nightly. Some days, said Jomy, he had no will to move his limbs. Nietzsche was of another order, from another world; he led him up along high trails to feel joy on the cold heights of snowy mountaintops. Through him, he could summon up strength to overcome his sloth; he could root out cheap, everyday sensations and achieve a higher state.

Jomy opened his wallet to hand Bellocq a creased photograph, folded and unfolded many doting times. The philosopher's deep-set eyes glinted darkly bright in their black pits. He reminded Bellocq of Platt.

It was tragic, said Jomy, that having endured the burden of this world for so long he had gone insane before he died in Weimar.

Leo stole an envious look at them. Suspicious, he could

93

only bear to step close to overhear a word or two before shying away again to rejoin Beaubien.

'That's a quality both you and Chenault have, Albert,' said Bellocq. 'Neither of you could ever accept your lot. I admire you for it.'

'You say that, but I've let years waste away waiting for things to happen. All I can do is chip away at wood – I'm no use for anything else, and it doesn't answer.'

Bellocq said he knew how his friend felt, he felt the same, and what was he going to do now?

'Do what you do best – take photographs.'

When Leo could bring himself to say something, it was, 'Nietzsche is not the man for you, Ernest. You would come apart under the pressure of such depths of pessimism.'

What fate lay in store for Jomy? Leo knew exactly – he would meet with a very bad death. He would go out like a candle with a sense of his own futility. Hideous!

At the house, Bellocq filled a jug and went out into the courtyard to water those plants that were still alive. No sooner did he step out the door than the cloudburst brought rain on with a rush.

Bellocq had gone there as a child with his mother, fearful of the purple wart on Amateau's nose. There was the same smell of hot sealing wax and old parchments filling the room. The lawyer kept the city's secrets locked in his archives, in private agreements, settlements and dowries. He was a tactful go-between, courteous and masterful. No one called him anything other than *Maître* Amateau. 'Her will dates back some years,' he said. 'Not that it matters. You are poor. There is no money. I kept it from your mother. I've held creditors off for years. The house is

94

mortgaged twice over, and you'll have to sell it to pay off debts. I doubt that you'll even own the furniture, you and Leo. But there is nothing else.'

It was only a short way from Amateau's to the dealer who had sold him the Ford. 'My mother died; I have no more use for a car,' he said. The dealer was sad to hear that, but not unhappy enough to give him anything in line with what he had paid. His best advice was to hold on to it. 'You can never tell when you might need it. That vehicle will last you a lifetime.'

Bellocq opened his mother's diary. He had to use a magnifying glass to read her writing. It dealt mostly with the weather, until he came on a picture of Paul Claudel, cut from a magazine, to mark the entry about their meeting. Bellocq had always thought his mother's pathetic secret was illusory – but there was a letter Claudel had written. As a married woman she had to see that she had no more than a crush. He did not want to hurt her feelings, but it was a truism that some women felt life had passed them by unless they fell in love with a poet. He had made himself plain when he spoke to her husband.

His mother's perfume seemed to cling to everything, strong as the old cigar smoke in his father's desk when he rolled up the lid. He had seen his father do that countless times, palming his hands flat on the green leather inlay. Leaning over, he tried to sniff those dark stains made by writing letters; or was he brooding over bills and debts? He saw his father as he had last seen him, on the stairs, nightshirt open with sweat streaming down his body. He was babbling something intended for no one to hear. He came to a halt with a harsh cough, and blood ran out of his mouth until he hid his face in the crook of his arm.

95

There were early photographs of Bellocq as a child. He wore a plaid dress and his legs were dangling as he sat with ankles crossed, a sailor's cap on his head and a large bow under his chin. How hard he fought to keep that cap when he lost the rest of the uniform! He found other letters from his mother, damning his father for showering money on whores. Then his father had run off to Mexico with Josune. There was a photograph of her pasted inside the lid of a box, a braid over her left shoulder. Younger than when Bellocq saw her. Tiny silver crucifixes hung from each ear that had to be anathema to his mother. Her name, along with a faded date, was written on the back of the photograph. There were postcards, too: tinted views of Mexico City, each a lost image from his father's life. Something about which he would never know the truth now. His father had been sick when he came home, tail between his legs, a suffering sinner who had to be cared for as a Christian duty. His mother had let her son understand that his father's illness was punishment for fornication with some fallen woman riddled with a sexual disease.

Having put the house up for auction, Bellocq sold the furniture. He could not let his father's roll-top go, so he put it in store – now it was a question of finding a job and somewhere to live.

There were two gilt-fringed flags on the long rosewood table: 'Old Glory' and the flag of the Confederacy. On the wall behind the brothers was a Japanese woodcut of Matthew Perry's warships in Tokyo Bay. A framed Medal of Honor was on display; one of them had won it fighting in the 1st Volunteer Cavalry with Roosevelt in Cuba.

'We've studied your work with interest,' said the

younger, dark one. 'This iron bridge took our eye. You must understand that if we take you on you will have to be very down to earth. Light must bring out form and detail, never blur. We need a man who can work to order on his own, out in all weathers. You'll photograph our ships, their engines, other parts and machinery. My brother says he sees a touch too much of art in your work – you'd need to subdue that. You'll have to travel – to Memphis, St Louis, wherever on the river. You are to bear witness to mechanical failure. Yes, above all, your photographs must be exceedingly sharp, always precise, in order for us to assess the damage.'

Having found a job with the Foundation Ship Company, Bellocq went to see Beaubien again. Beaubien was full of advice: 'You need a place to live? Go to Hermann Hecht's house; maybe you've seen his card in my window? One of his rooms is vacant he told me the other day. He has commercial travellers stay there mostly, also captains and river pilots. Hecht's wife is a good cook, he said. They have three daughters: one married recently, the other helps in the house; and there is a younger sister. Write down his address.'

'Hermann was a salesman in the old country; he went all over Alsace selling agricultural tools,' said Mrs Hecht, bringing in a tray with wine and glasses. 'So, who to know better what a man seeks in a lodging-house? We serve breakfast from six onwards in the dining room. This wine is to welcome Mr Bellocq, Hermann – so don't go crazy.'

Mr Hecht smiled, took up a glass and raised it. '*Prosit!*'

They asked about his work. Bellocq spoke of the Foundation Company, saying how happy he was to be paid for taking photographs, which gave him great satisfaction.

It was almost four o'clock; if Mr Bellocq had a spare five minutes he could meet her daughter Miriam, who was bringing Flis, her youngest, home from school.

The front door opened to shrill girlish laughter. Mrs Hecht went out into the hallway and had a *sotto voce* conversation. 'They will be down shortly,' she said, on her return.

Miriam had changed quickly into a dress and necklace that were meant to impress. Still flighty, she was ready for inspection. At Mrs Hecht's urging she sat at the piano to play a duet with Flis. They were soon knocking into each other with the effort they put into the piece. Miriam said it had taken her some time to overlook his being a Pole, but her great hero was Chopin.

Apart from the girl from Minsk, Pearl was the only flesh and blood woman with whom Bellocq could compare Miriam. Her youthful blush gave her an aura so very different from that of Pearl.

When both girls came to sit beside him on the sofa, Flis twirled a finger idly around Miriam's ear and neck. Her smile said she knew that Bellocq would like to do the same.

4

It did not take Bellocq long to fall in with the routine of the house. He learnt what the other roomers did, knew their footfalls and voices on the stairs as they went out to work. He met the maid, Violet, and would listen to her tread as she swept and dusted on the landing. Then Mrs Hecht would knock, come with her feather duster and stand in one place chatting, flicking at the same spot, usually the top of the chest of drawers. 'You keep your own company too much,' she would chide. 'You know you're welcome any evening in the sitting room. Miss Faulkner knocks out some merry tunes on the piano, or we make do with Miriam's repertoire. It can get quite jolly.'

When he did venture there, it was as convivial as Mrs Hecht had said.

Miriam, her face flushed after three glasses of wine, got up suddenly from the piano stool, blushing hotly at the applause. Losing her balance, she steadied herself by catching at Bellocq's shoulder. Then, sitting across from him, she leant forward to press his knee in gratitude, a gesture that moved him to speak of it to Jomy. 'It was light enough, friendly and confiding, I thought. She gave it a full stop with a jab of her finger.'

'Playful, then?'

'Yes, I suppose that was the word for it. Flis was all smiles.'

'Flis?'

'Her sister – a child, but very sharp. Say something, Albert, anything.'

Jomy thought the wisest course would be to stay calm. Take things as they came. In lodging-houses there was bound to be a fine line between what was nice and not nice. Any girl had the power to make convex and concave as much a mystery as stage magicians. He had to give up any idea that she might sit stitching samplers – few girls did that now in this day and age.

When Miriam came into the room, Bellocq told her that he had kept his word; he showed her the photograph. 'Who does she remind you of?'

Nobody for the life of her that she could imagine.

She did not see herself?

Bellocq's flattery was quite the end! 'I'm not that pretty, sir.'

She was more beautiful than the girl in the photograph. Her calling him 'sir' again made him wince. Surely they had left all that behind long ago?

'Her hair is fair; mine is auburn,' Miriam argued.

'Let it down; I know it falls below your shoulders. Step over here, into the light. How can I tell you apart? This girl is mulish, too, saying, "No, never!" – the same way you set your mouth when you stand your ground.'

'So that's how I look when I say no,' Miriam laughed.

Bellocq said he had only heard that 'no' once, with that frown and wilful toss of her head. 'You don't know the pain you can give doing that.'

'Don't say that word! I don't want to hear anything about hurting you.'

'You know just when that was. You had made a vow

never to marry, you said. You took the light out of the room; I was alone in the dark.'

Miriam left the window. What right did he have to say such a thing? And just who was that girl? Did he take the photograph? Did he have some fool notion or hope that she might take her place? 'Home truths, Mr Bellocq, those are what we deal in here.'

'I did not know her name,' he lied. 'I met her in Hot Springs. I used to see her go up and down in the hotel lift.'

It was an old dream he was about to serve up, an old tale he often told himself. She was with him in the park again, his mouth atremble on her cheek, under her eye. When she turned away he saw her lips were open. She could spare a kiss. The skin on her lips was dry, she said, although she oiled them last thing at night. He tasted the rough flakes, then licked the smoothness of his own. Gently urging her face round to his, he felt her hot breath. In the dark of their kiss, her tongue darted into his mouth; it was as rough as a cat's. She put his hand to the buttons of her blouse. As soon as he felt her breast she drew back crying rape and struck him. A man ran out of hiding in the bushes. He came at Bellocq with his fist clenched. It was about extorting money. Of course Bellocq would pay anything to stop a charge of rape being read out in court and printed in the papers for his mother to read. Had it not been for the sheriff, he might be on a prison farm now. He said that the sheriff had known the couple, lying again. He had been just another victim of the old badger game. They shook men down all over the county.

'I photographed her only the one time,' said Bellocq.

'You'd have liked to know her better, though, I can see by her smile.'

'Some smiles are not all they seem.'

What did he mean?

He meant nothing. With her looks, he said, Miriam could be a star for Vitagraph. Light made those beauties – without light there would be no stars.

She stared at him now – which would look away first? If she could see herself, so pale, she would know that she put the Hot Springs girl in the shade. He had to take her picture.

'You won't stop there,' she said; 'but if that's what you want, I don't see how I can refuse. When?'

Bellocq said early sunlight was best. Unable to sleep all night for rehearsing the morning, he went out at daybreak to find a white rose for her to hold. That done he could lie down and close his eyes.

Miriam came early and woke him with her knock. She had a parcel of shirts Violet had picked up from the Chinese laundry. He had not had time to ready the camera. He did it swiftly while she sighed, going round the room, trailing her finger along his books. 'Are you free of chores?' What if she had those? They could wait. He planned to take more than one, he said.

'That looks old; how long have you had it?'

It was the camera his mother bought him when he was seven years old.

'Any brothers or sisters?'

Bellocq said he had a brother, but would rather not talk about him. That intrigued her to ask why. He was a priest – to talk to him, even about him, was the same as going to confession. If his mother had got her way, he might have been a priest, too. No respect for her wishes, of course, as she often said. He spoke French until the age of seven. Could read English but not speak it. For years his mother hoped to find him a suitable girl from a good French family.

'Is she alive, this mother of yours?'

No. And she ought to be glad about that; she would have found her too stern.

'So stern she could never let you marry, then.'

'I would not wish a strong mother on anyone. *Hélas*, I was not the son she hoped for.'

From all he said, she got the feeling that he did not care much for New Orleans.

Perhaps she was right, but how could he hate it now? It was the city where she had been born. It might have meant more to him, perhaps, if his studies had paid off. They had not, and it was that which had made him unhappy.

'You never found anything to admire in those girls your mother brought home?'

Bellocq looked up from under the cloth, shaking his head with a smile.

'Why does it take so long?' She went to the door as she heard her mother's voice in the stairwell, and stood there listening.

'I had my mother pose when I was a child,' he said. 'She never minded then what I did; it was no threat to her. In those days, her friends came with those dogs they pampered. They brought them round for me to photograph. I was a child. When we went on outings, a black manservant carried the camera and plates. I had no aim other than to record.' He told her about coating the glass plate with gun-cotton, ether and alcohol, then sensitizing it in silver nitrate solution. He had a yellow glass let into the top of the camera so that he could see to mix the chemicals under the cloth. He had to treat the plate with ferro-sulphate; then, the easy part over, there was all the rigmarole of rinsing and fixing it in hypo before drying and varnishing. It took no time at all now using gelatin plates.

He went over and took Miriam by the arm to lead her into the light. 'Turn your head slightly; look out the window. Who is coming? Who are you waiting for? Say what you see.'

'Is this all?'

He did not want to make a study, as they were called. So, when he asked her to face the camera, she must do so without thinking.

'I can hear the iceman.'

'Right. That's the plate in now. Look this way; smile for thirty seconds when I uncap the lens.'

He took the picture, venturing to say that he wanted her to pose naked some other time.

'What?' Miriam gave a laugh.

He had seen her in the bathroom when Flis brought her a towel. Her image was in the mirror behind the half-open door.

'You never did spy!'

Bellocq had not seen it as spying. He saw only what he knew already, that she was perfect.

'You ogled, drooling on your chin, you beast! Not a thought in your head about what I might feel!'

Miriam ran her nails down the windowpane, a cat that wanted out.

What would she have felt?

She was silent, smiling, in full mocking flow now. Better he asked Flis about taking her clothes off, if that was what he was keen on. No nymph could be happier naked.

Bellocq blushed.

'You better not mind, though, that she can't keep a straight face any longer than a minute at a time, or that she's not too bright.'

'Why do you tease? You know your mother would be up in arms.'

'But not if I did it!'

'What are you trying to say?'

'I know what I mean; it's for you to find out.'

He knew then that she would have posed naked had he put it another way. Quite how he might have broached it, he did not know. His breath came faster; his balls felt heavy. She was smiling. He faced away, uncomfortably stiff.

'Near you, I can get out what I want to say.'

'Take care, then. Your words may shrivel in your mouth one day.'

'If I let go your hand I am walking a cliff edge, a blind man,' he said. 'I shall stifle in Memphis. Away from you, I am hollow.'

'I go nowhere,' she said, with a sigh.

If she would agree, he would take her to Paris! She would soon learn French.

Her face had a sad air. 'The awful thing is that people never age in photographs,' she said. Bellocq tried to lift her spirits, babbling on about needing a good reason to take a picture. It had nothing to do with the Kodak ad: 'You press the button, we do the rest.'

She had gone; he was talking to himself.

The boy was from the Foundation Company to pick up some photographs, said Miriam. Bellocq was sure he could wait a while, now that he had her to himself. She said she hated dresses with short sleeves; all they were good for was housework.

Her long sleeves were what kept men from going blind in the light from her flawless skin, he said.

She had no such power to dazzle, and he had no right to laugh and make her blush so.

Bellocq said how like a dream girl she was, moving in and out of the light. Other men ought never to see her. He was jealous even of the boy. She ought to wear dresses that veiled her – like those Muslim women. Even then, every stride would drive men mad.

She would not hear such things! There was nothing she could do about any of that. The boy had been waiting long enough. Ought she to send him away?

Only if she stayed! He did not want her to go. Her blushes spoke of hot flesh, warm and human. He longed for her as Miss Hecht; but he would adore her as Madame Bellocq.

Miriam went to the window. 'He's over there across the road now. He knows you're in; his eye is on the window.'

Bellocq joined her. He was not the usual boy they sent. His scowling face was blunt; his big elfin ears stuck out. He chewed strands of his hair. The taut bruised skin under his eyes spoke of a life in some drab hole-in-a-corner existence. 'Here, give him this envelope,' Bellocq said. 'Step near him when you do, he'll squirm as I do. Just one kiss first! Ah! I am the happiest man in New Orleans, *Mon ange!*'

The jeweller had a black girl braid Miriam's hair tight into a heart shape to fit the locket Bellocq had bought. He had crept around the house combing it out of Miriam's hairbrush whenever she was out. So he had always to be sure of her whereabouts.

Where had she been that took so long?

To see her aunt, who was not feeling well, Miriam replied.

Bellocq hoped that such a long visit had left her aunt feeling better.

She had smiled and waved enough when they parted.

Bellocq said she looked pale, *triste*. Did her offhand treatment of him give her sleepless nights? Each twist, each refusal, could only forge another link in the chain binding him to her.

Her shiver made him tremble; his throat was parched. His heart beat faster. How could any man who had her love ever leave her?

'No man did, that I know of.'

'Flis says one did ditch you.'

'She used that word?' Miriam's laugh was bitter. 'Flis has a genius for nailing the cat to the barn door.'

'Why did he go? I never could. I want only to please you. Tell me what you want – say what I have to do, and I'll do it. Am I your pet monkey? Feed me titbits, only don't lock my cage.'

'Not you, nor any other man,' she said, turning away. Flis was at the piano in the parlour now, patiently picking her way through her Schubert.

'Must you go?'

'I'm late; my mother will wonder where I am.'

'She knows where you are! Let me ask you about the necklace you wore the day I took these rooms.'

'What could you want to know?'

'Can I see it again?'

'Why?'

He needed to be sure it was unlike the one he had seen in a jeweller's on Canal. With Christmas near, he planned to buy the necklace then, later, when he had the money, a sapphire ring, which was the blue of her eyes.

She had to go. She said she would wear it in the morning.

When she came with his breakfast, she put the tray down. She said that Flis had forgotten the coffee, and she went to fetch it. When she flounced back with the pot she was wearing the necklace.

A police patrol wagon went by below, the horses giving off a cloud of steam. The rain had been falling since first light and there was no sign of it easing. Miriam was moody, saying she hated the wet so and wished it would go away. Bellocq went over to her and put his hand on her shoulder. She had to be pining for her other lover.

'How long ago was it?'

'Almost two years.'

'Two years – and you have to lie about it? Maybe you see him. Is that it?'

Not all feeling for him had gone. He lived up north now, with an aunt in Boston, and had been there since the Christmas before last.

'He loved you?'

'I felt he did.'

If that was true, then why did he go?

Miriam turned away. 'He had to walk the line his family laid down. I wasn't good enough for him.'

'You were trying to get something you couldn't have.'

That was a nasty way to put it, but yes that was how it was.

'Were you free with him, too?'

'He was a gentleman, and never behaved in any other way!'

'He'd have good looks; his breeding would dazzle you. He had money, education!'

She grew restless and walked up and down. 'I felt I was to blame. I fell to missing him soon as he left the room. I was over the edge before I saw it.'

What did her mother and family make of it? Did they know?

'No. You're the only one I've told, or wanted to, aside from Flis. Why? I'd rather you heard it from me. There's nothing I want to hide from you.'

'Do you write?'

No. She felt, though, that they might meet again one day as friends.

'You've got by on hope since then.'

It sounded stupid now to say it, but at first she did not want to live. Could not escape a sense of doom. It had been hard to shake off.

'You will never forget him?'

There were times when she would go down, lost under a wave of feeling.

Bellocq was glad she had told him. She was loyal in love, and it had taught him a lesson, he said.

'I want you to be my friend, sir,' she said.

'Is a friend only "sir", to you?'

Things were as usual until midweek, when Mr Bold moved in. It was then that it all went wrong. Soon as he came, Miriam ran hotfoot upstairs to wait for him. Bellocq would come on them on landings, in passageways, whispering together.

★   ★   ★

It was March. He was to go to Memphis again.

'I hoped I might have found a way to be sure of you before I left,' he told her. 'Surely my state of mind is proof that I had that at heart; I adore you.'

It was the wrong word, and the last straw. No man should ever start the idea that she was some saint! Unless he swore not to use that word again, she would never speak to him. 'Men are always after trying to prove something,' she said, going briskly towards the door. 'The hell you say you are in is of your own making. I'm not the first woman in the world to change her mind.'

'You're keeping something back? What? What is it?'

By then, he could have struck her, stung by each fresh dodge and denial.

No, she had no tie! No, she did not plan to marry. No. She had told him so already!

'Can't we be the way we used to be?'

It was beastly of him to wheedle any such promise.

She glittered yet was pale and deadly as a creature out of a Poe story. He had drowned in the depths of her spell. Spaces between a table, a chair, when she left fell lifeless and empty. The voids that sprang open between everyday things were fit only for ghosts.

'You have no qualms about the way you treat men.'

'Well, quite frankly, Mr Bellocq, maltreating men comes easy,' she said, smiling. 'Don't they all warrant it? Some take delight in making a girl do it, I swear.'

He heard himself beg – saying that she could make her own terms.

She said nothing to this; dodging his every attempt to bar her way, she ran out of the room. Bellocq sat, choking with rage, skin crawling, fighting hard to get his breath.

*　　*　　*

Although he left early for Memphis he had to wait till three o'clock for the steamboats to make smoke along the landing. Miriam had been cold until the morning he left. Why had she been so tender the first months? If her early warmth had not sprung from true feeling, then she had to start out the same way with all the roomers. Flouncing to the door, she said she was glad to learn his real opinion of her. As she turned away, he was afraid she would be another person when he saw her face again. Then she ran back and held his hand, standing at the window where she had posed for her photograph.

Going over this again as he left, he imagined he saw the curtain move in her window.

He had booked a steamboat passage feeling he needed time to think. He crossed the gangplank numbly, deaf to the clatter of baggage vans, and sat on deck. His vain hope was that Miriam would relent before cast-off.

The gongs sounded for non-passengers to go ashore. A Negro staggered up the plank with the pilot's trunk. The red-headed man came strutting behind, smoking a cheroot. He got the steamboat quickly in line, heading upriver, where Bellocq had a melancholy view of derelict mansions on dead plantations between New Orleans and Baton Rouge.

He felt as if were running a high fever. He did not want to speak, and cut people who thought they had anything to say to him. He knew nothing either of the islands they skirted, beyond the fact that they had a number. Sometimes they overtook a trading scow heading for some lonely hamlet or a skiff ferrying kerosene to navigation lights. For four days he saw little to dwell on apart from the vicissitudes of river life, the echoing cries of a leadsman's 'Quarter less three!', the threat from coal barges hurtling down from Pittsburgh, the great forces in nature on that river.

On the fifth day, bells rang to cut speed. The stern wheel hit the trees with a clatter of twigs. The boat was on a sandbar. The crew ran about shouting, every pipe and gauge gave vent to steam with a great hissing. Then the smokestack burst into flame. What with the fire, soot falling everywhere, people went on about it hammer and tongs. One was a Pinkerton agent who offered Bellocq a swig from his hip flask. He was soon boasting how he had served as Harry Houdini's bodyguard.

Houdini was a kid when the circus came to Appleton, Wisconsin. He saw a Mephisto magician that day. He stole the name Houdini right out of a French magazine, for his real one was Erich Weiss. He was a Hungarian Jew with a rabbi for a father. The bodyguard had been with him in Moscow, in 1903, where he busted out of a Siberian prison van. 'His eye is forever on bigger, better things; it's the motion pictures next, he says.'

Bellocq was amazed how fast he shook the accident off. At dinner, he felt up to eating fish and oysters, then chicken fricassee and white wine. They were dining together with two brothers the Pinkerton man had met. The talk was of the situation in Honduras. 'The next hot spot's going to be Mexico,' the Pinkerton man was sure. Apropos of nothing, the brother called Otis said he saw no chance for a happy marriage of art and politics. 'Shut your mouth, Otis,' said the other, 'we can't all talk at the same time.'

They went off to buy more drink while the Pinkerton man told Bellocq how he had been down in Honduras helping the army root out the rebels. 'We got the whole shebang up at Willie Piazza's in Basin Street.' He laughed.

'No place better than a whorehouse to hatch a plot! Willie is very discreet. We could have used a good photographer like you; those bastards all look the same. You'd have made good money.' He laughed again. 'The rest of us did our best to get fat dealing in death, fruit and bananas.'

Bellocq was drunk by then, and the others were trying to get a girl to join the table. She had a few drinks, then left with the Pinkerton man.

Bellocq threw up over the side. His nose and sinuses were full of food scraps, gristle and bile. It was not often that he got drunk. He had to piss. He got his fly undone, but it was beyond his power to do it up again, not a button, and that was how he lay until the deck-hand woke him next morning.

Other passengers had slept on deck; he stepped over them to stand by the rail. A lone farm came to life under a haze of smoke. He felt a sense of awe as the sun saw the mist off the flowering creepers. He saw the smoke first, and then the *Pride of Vicksburg* came round the bend, making for New Orleans. She swept past in the usual chorus of steam whistles, the captains hailing each other. He had to fight off an urge to leap into the river and swim across.

After the landing-bell had rung three times, they ran inshore to take on wood at Vicksburg. A mulatto caught the bow rope thrown by the deck-hand; an odour of old cotton bales came off the wharf. The roustabouts took off their shirts to load cords: some had rat's nests of lash scars on their backs.

Arriving at Memphis in the rain, Bellocq was met by Mr Ishihatsu, the Company's agent. He gave a swift bow, arms stiff at his sides, hair oiled flat to his scalp, his metal-framed glasses glinting. He said his stomach was cold, and he felt unwell. He was in need of hot food. Mr Bellocq was welcome to dine with him and his wife.

He had a long thin object wrapped in canvas tied to the frame of his bicycle. Edging it open, he let Bellocq see the hilt of a sword. 'I ride around Beale Street at night I might have to defend myself. You, too – be sure you take care out on the streets.'

He put on bicycle clips and pulled his goggles down, yet did not mount the cycle. He offered Bellocq the shelter of his umbrella as they walked. Naming a chemist with a darkroom who had the requisite chemicals for sale, he gave Bellocq his telephone number and said he had drawn a map of the location of his hotel.

Mr Ishihatsu had sailed from Yokohama and disembarked at San Pedro with sixteen cents in his pocket. Since then, he had never looked back.

A woman in a kimono with a red parasol drew back inside a narrow doorway as they came down to the wooden waterfront building. They were in time to see the bright hem of her robe vanish in the darkness at the top of the narrow stairs.

Ishihatsu called up to her and her feet came back into the light. Her steps were short; her walk was swift – almost a glide. She held her head level, or slightly bowed.

That had been the hardest thing to teach her – that hobbled way of walking. Later, drinking sake, Ishihatsu gave a grunted laugh and said it kept her cunt dainty.

Mrs Ishihatsu said she was a born American. The farm she was raised on was over the other side of the river. She was a country girl in bondage, but where to find an easier life? She had to learn a lot, but the Captain was a past master. Brought up on scripture, she had had a lot to undo. Her father used to give her a biff for this, a boff for that. One time, she was deaf for a week. Only thing worse was her mother saying she imagined it; so what was the blood on the floor? No, the Captain never raised his hand to her. Life did her no favours until she met him, she said.

She was happy in what she called their floating world. 'Look what he taught me. I can put food on a plate so neat the President could eat it.'

She said the dish was *tempura* — prawns, squid, fish, carrots, mushrooms and slices of green pepper dipped in batter to quick fry. She spooned them out onto a napkin, then into square dishes.

Ishihatsu returned with photographs of his family in Japan.

'Whatever a man believes has to be the truth for him,' he said as he drank more sake.

Trying to sit cross-legged, Bellocq found his suit was too tight; the jacket cut under his arms and his pants hurt his groin. His left hand was on his right knee, his right across his lap holding his left arm. He said he had to shun painterly ideas. Men bent nature to their will, extracting its forces and materials to bring an engine into existence. He had to think of that when photographing each piece of machinery. He aimed for an exact image. The photographers he respected worked in this way. Did Ishihatsu know Mathew Brady's pictures of the war dead, or his fine portrait of Sheridan mourning Lincoln? Jacob Riis was admirable, too, for his portrayal of immigrant life in the cribs and rat holes of New York. And there was Robert Howlett's picture of Isambard Brunel — that giant launch chain of the *Great Eastern* hung behind him.

Howlett had him to the life: muddy boots – the stogie – his face stern as any riverboat captain's under the rusty stove-pipe hat.

Making an excuse to go to the lavatory, Bellocq slid a screen aside and found a naval officer's dress uniform. The hairs on his nape bristled. He could not say why – except that he did not care for the way Ishihatsu spoke of the world, now that the Panama Canal was open. The Captain had said he had much to learn from the Foundation Company. One day, Japan would be a great naval power.

Bellocq was dizzy, unable to hear anything apart from the murmur of their voices and Ishihatsu's coarse laugh. Was he laughing at him? He had blabbed too much about Miriam. Was that what the Captain found so risible?

He came out to find Ishihatsu in tears, trying to assemble his camera. Those family photographs were spread out on the table. He wanted Bellocq to take pictures of his wife to send home to his two brothers. He was willing to pay. 'If you feel under the weather, maybe, you bring your camera another time, but it would be better done now,' he said.

'No.' Bellocq stood undaunted. 'Now is as good a time as any.'

He did not like to admit to being afraid of Ishihatsu.

Mrs Ishihatsu came into the room wearing a red kimono. Nothing had been left to chance; it had all been decided. She filled their cups again while Bellocq set the camera in place, then went over and slid a dark screen to one side. Grey afternoon light lit the room, below was the riverside.

Ishihatsu gave a guttural sigh of animal pleasure as his wife let her robe fall. Her body was hairless, shaven;

a fine white powder hung over the blue stubble in her groin.

Seen from the back, hands on her hips, the curve of her breasts showed either side of her ribcage. Left with nothing to do except insert and expose each plate, Bellocq stared at Mrs Ishihatsu, afraid for her and what the Captain would take it into his head to order her to do next. His grunts seemed challenges flung at him also, although he obeyed them as readily as Mrs Ishihatsu.

At his command – '*Rin-no-tama*' – she blushed and took two silver balls the size of quail's eggs from the kimono. Then, head lowered, held them in the palm of her hand as Bellocq exposed the plate. What were they for? Ishihatsu laughed, able to read Bellocq's mind. At his command, she slid them one by one inside her open hairless peach, sinking into a squat.

Behind her, a paper screen showed a geisha with a white parasol, her belly out-thrust to echo the curve of a blue moon. A faint sweat broke from Mrs Ishihatsu's skin. Its sheen spread across her breasts as she worked her muscles. The Captain laughed as her mouth fell open and her head fell back.

Ishihatsu yawned; he rose clumsily and went off at a tangent across the room. Bellocq heard his fingers whisper over the geisha as he slid the screen open and left.

Mrs Ishihatsu put her robe on and tied the sash.

'He'll sleep now,' she said, staring blankly. 'You're not like the other one.'

'Other one?'

Bellocq could see nothing except the moist metal balls she turned in her hand.

'Never mind.' She smiled. 'Mr Ishihatsu is strict. Life's easier if I obey rather than thwart him.' She put the balls in Bellocq's palm. 'I'd be in hot water if he knew.' He felt the *Rin-no-tama* balls vibrate in his palm – copper in one, mercury in the other, she said. 'They belonged to his mother.'

She got up to leave, went to the door and came back. 'He may wake up and want to tell you ghost stories. Don't listen. The other did. The Captain enjoys making your skin crawl.'

Unable to sleep for what had happened, Bellocq could still smell her body as the moths pattered against the paper screens. Then there came another smell; it was dust burning off the mantle of the oil lamp Mrs Ishihatsu carried.

She was naked.

'This is not right,' Bellocq whispered, thinking of Miriam and speaking her name.

'That's why I came,' Mrs Ishihatsu smiled. 'The Captain wants you to have a clear head tomorrow. I'm here to ease your pain.'

Bellocq felt the tears run down his cheeks.

'Lie back and enjoy it, it's so easy to take,' she said.

'Miriam –' he began again. His voice seemed further away, fainter now.

'You said that.' She kissed him, her tongue darting into his mouth. 'Give in – then you won't lie wide-eyed until first light thinking things. I'll have bounced them out of your head easy as a pea off a plate.'

He could smell her face powder as she crouched on him, legs open, arching back as she seized his prick.

The acrid odour of burning dust was gone, the light in the glass shone clear. She knelt; her hand came up between her legs as she ran it down to bring fluid out of her body. She tapped the mauve wrinkles of her anus until they shone, then crooked an invitation with her finger with the same delicacy she put food on the table.

Bellocq lay numb and let her do what she wanted.

As she turned her head her plump cheek stood out like the edge of the moon with a flutter of false eyelashes. Then she sat back on her heels with a low laugh. He must not think of her as anything other than a woman with a good heart, she said, running her hand along his thigh and giving it a pat before going.

Bellocq lay staring at the life-size geisha in her yellow kimono. He strained to hear what he thought was the murmur of their voices. Had she told Ishihatsu she was quenching her thirst, or had she knelt, willingly compliant, again? Bellocq listened. Silence. No hint of that low moan she gave as she sank down on him.

He felt now that he ought to get up and go to the hotel. No, better stay – he would have to face Ishihatsu some time in the morning.

When he awoke, it took Bellocq a moment to realize where he was, and that the sound of the outer door closing had woken him. He went over to the window; Mrs Ishihatsu was a ghost in the mist on the riverfront. The Captain rose high on the pedal of his bicycle as he rode off.

All the next week Bellocq had to fight off the vision of Mrs Ishihatsu crooking her finger. He could not bear to recall the look on her face as she worked those balls, yet he did. He told himself it was a joke they had played, hearing that soft tuning-fork hum as he held the balls in his palm, while Miriam swam in and out of his mind. To fight off those images he took pictures all day, but had no way to blot them out at night.

Memphis! There, joy and anguish were for sale on Hernando and Beale Street! It was by far the worst city for him to be in. None of its many women could hold a candle to Miriam; yet they sold rapture.

No matter how many prints he made he knew that only five or so would meet the Company's criteria.

If only Miriam was there he knew he could do better; but he had to live with that.

Each morning he woke in the hope that it had been Miriam's knock that broke his dream; each morning it was the same listless girl clattering his tin breakfast tray down to open the curtains.

The hotel was a warren of tiny rooms and narrow passageways with tilted floors and crooked corners. The room felt safe; he was in and out of cupboards that had an odour of old dresses and beeswax. His face shone in the shiny boots that stood on the landing every morning, as if the salesmen who left them had died in the night. His own boots were like those of a dead man, too.

Portraits of generals from the War hung on the stairs and, above the bed, an engraving of Audubon – a Homeric figure whose long hair flowed down to his shoulders. By night, the dining room had something of the same comfort as the Hechts' parlour, except it was larger. Some nights, he felt as if he had not left. There he was, talking with Silas Weir, husband to Miriam's elder sister Arabella, with half an ear to the salesman's spiel as he tried to sell her mother a pair of shoes. He saw her tap his arm with her fan, saying, '*Gott in Himmel*!', before bustling off to find her needlework box. Then Mr Bold came in, his hands blistered after a day poling around the bayou, shotgun and leather bag on his shoulder. He shook a brace of ducks and quail to the roomers' applause, standing his ground as Mrs Hecht cussed him for his muddy boots. He twisted her around his finger; Mr Bold was glib, and just had to be smart. Miss Faulkner – *la, la* – waved her straw plait fan, cupping her deaf ear to shout, 'A cottonmouth will get you one of these days; your lights'll be out before you can cry good golly.'

Then he was back, in the dining room, in front of the brass plate that said a catfish in a glass case was four feet long and weighed one hundred and eighty pounds. A musket hung above the chimney under the charred legend: 'Never Say Die'.

A clock strike would jar, numbing with horror. Time was passing; he was alone with another hour gone by. Miriam's time was of another order, waxing and waning in carefree *bonheur*. His shadow falling in the sunlight warned of his frailty, and night was worse. He walked the streets to tire himself. There were fistfights, curses and murderous threats. The pimps fought over whores like dogs over bones. He saw a man slash a woman down to her collarbone. Bellocq could not translate the abuse; there were words he did not want to understand. Most of those saloon girls were lawless, too – a knife would flash in their hand as fast as a man's, if crossed.

Any photographer had to live with the threat from nosy or irate citizens. Bellocq was an object of suspicion each time he set up his camera, and the kids would always want to look through the lens. There were so many, he had to refuse; then they danced around, a band of orang-utans itching at their armpits. Better that than they should try to get under the cloth at a crucial moment.

Nothing else except dreary purgatory. Hammers rang on anvils while a yellow flood slid by with a fresh set of clouds each day. In some deep part of his mind he fought any feeling of being at one with nature. He held on to detail. He would dab at the paper with the clip he used to hang it on the line. He sank it in the tray; the image sharpened. Then he picked it out to hang with the rest. As the prints dried, he pored over them with a magnifying glass. Detail. He would tap the barometer in the hall. The glass was falling. Detail. He would order himself to take an umbrella. Detail.

The closer the deadline, the less he wanted to do. He had to force himself to go to the blacksmith's forge, turning his back to a chill wind all day. The man had a grimy bandage on his hand, and beat iron with the other amid flying sootflakes. He set up his camera over the engines, silently lamenting how men ruined nature's beauty with coal dust and oil derricks. Sluggish black rattlesnakes writhed across slicks of machine oil, dead birds rotted in lagoons of filth. Each time he looked up there was the threat of the blacksmith's sign – a muscular arm raising a hammer. He could not say why he felt so afraid of it.

A Negro and his wife came by. What with the wind, Bellocq lost a great deal of what the man said, but understood that they were off to the depot hoping to hitch a boxcar north. He'd got his name from the white farmer who owned him. He said he felt happier already than he had been in many a year. Laughing at the chain gang labouring on the levee, he said, 'Why, master, I'm free now, going off a ways, not singing to keep body and soul together in that hell they're living out there.' All the time he talked, gusts of wind swung the black door until it shut with an awful finality.

The wind never let up, and the nights were chill.

When he walked the streets he found it was a southerly direction he had chosen, from which he hated to turn back. Twice a week he wrote to Miriam. He got one cool reply beginning *Sir*, and closing with *yours truly*, and with *best respects from her and family*.

Tormented, he wrote to Chenault again. At home he saw him every other night, it seemed. His letters now were more and more frequent. He relied on Chenault's advice above all others'.

If only she were there to guide his steps as Beatrice did for Dante.

The note Miriam sent gave him a lift, even so. He was joyful to be almost done in Memphis. The fear that he might let the company down began to abate. He wrote to Miriam again, urging her to recall the day he took her and her mother out to the amusement park at Spanish Fort. The humidity had sucked any life out of her. She had not felt up to seeing Napoleon House. He had remarked on a little girl – could she imagine having such a one? She said she would never have children. He had given her the violets, but she was cool about taking his arm until her mother did so. The world was his as they strolled along Chartres. He told them of Napoleon's wars, which were more real for him than the war with the Union. He knew the names of all his generals and their regiments. He had fired matchsticks from his cannons, and fought the battle at Eylau with squadrons of lead soldiers. He told them how the French built Napoleon House for the Emperor. How he had died on St Helena before they could rescue him.

★   ★   ★

The night before his departure, Ishihatsu knocked at his hotel door to insist that they have a last drink together. Bellocq could not argue: the man had been drinking already and he was holding the hilt of his sword, which was stuck in his belt.

Boldly, Ishihatsu strode up to the counter of Pecora's vaudeville house. Only an Indian seemed amused, and it was his table at which the Captain chose to sit. Unwillingly, Bellocq had to do the same.

On the table was a tray with jars of ink and dyes. A piece of cardboard with a beautifully drawn sign said 'Tattooing – No Pain, No Scar – 5 Colors & 5,000 Designs'.

The Indian's name was Longhair Tuttle and he was his own walking advertisement for his art. His face and hands were covered in tattoos, as was the rest of his body, he told Ishihatsu. Ishihatsu bared his arm to show a green dragon with talons and fearsome jaws which coiled up his arm.

'Ah,' said Longhair, nodding, 'a good man, a great man.'

'*Hori*,' grunted Ishihatsu, as Longhair revealed his wolf howling at the moon. He said that most of his tattoos had been done when he was a scout for the Union in the War Between the States.

His needles were bound in wooden sticks – the two or three that were ivory were pretty old, he claimed. In Japan they used bamboo, said Ishihatsu.

The last thing Bellocq remembered clearly was writing Miriam's name on a piece of paper, so that there should be no mistake.

Longhair drew the shape of a rose, then spread his fingers wide to tighten the skin of Bellocq's arm, beginning to prick ink into the outline. The wash of blue dye came next and the pricking quickened. Each stroke was bright and seemed to bring Miriam closer, indelible in his flesh. His mother was there in the smoky saloon, too, sure that the whole thing was profane.

By then, Bellocq's vision was blurring fast. Longhair's tattoos had lost their shape; his face kept only the bright hues of a lizard.

The rain fell; Bellocq had no idea where he was going and did not care. Lightning seared the sky with blue flashes; a bolting horse ran out of the dark and was gone as swiftly as an apparition. Lights he saw ahead turned out to be hobo campfires. They hung a blanket on his shoulders as he sat in the doorway of their lean-to. A woman held out a brandy bottle, another came with a plate of stew. After eating, he dozed off in the warmth into a deep sleep that had eluded him for weeks. When he woke, daylight was breaking. He gave the two dollars he found in his pocket to the children. His arms ached.

Looking out the window of the hotel as he shaved, Bellocq saw Ishihatsu ride up and lean his bicycle against an old hitching-post. He had come to order Bellocq on to Cairo. He could understand how that was against Bellocq's every inclination, and how it must burden his heart. Over his shoulder, Bellocq saw Mrs Ishihatsu appear suddenly across the street. Her wave, and her smile, seemed to taunt as Bellocq took Ishihatsu's hand and agreed to go upriver. 'You ran off last night. I promised Mr Tuttle to warn you not to tamper with the scabs that will soon form. Keep the tattoo covered and bathed in oil; they will go.'

The vessel Ishihatsu led Bellocq aboard had seen action in the War. There were holes and splinters everywhere. Left alone, at last, Bellocq lay sleepless above the steam engine, fearful each thud might shake loose every last rivet in the plates. The passengers seemed to share his plight. They were out of a nightmare, fated never to go ashore. They were silent when he passed them in the fogs. He longed to get the trip over, or to hide his ugliness in that fog. Every passenger hid some secret agony, he told himself; they knew the reason for his silence. What could he do? No one could take her place.

A hellish, spirituous fire seemed to dance and burn around the captain. He spat vile juice on the boots of anyone brave enough to complain of the delay or the food. Half drunk all day, he screamed and kicked the Negro roustabouts. He vented his wrath on the pilot, too. Bellocq feared some rift would bring the steamboat to grief on a sandbar. To allay his fears, Bellocq took refuge in another letter to Miriam. He mailed it in the wharf-boat box at Cairo, where a cyclone had torn the roofs off some houses a few nights before. The crew made a great noise and stir offloading a traction engine. The boat would go no further. None of them knew when the ship's engine could be got to work again.

The whole trip, it turned out, was a wild goose chase. The engine of the vessel he had to photograph had been fixed and she had sailed on upriver.

Bellocq boarded the *Tennessee Queen*, grateful at last to be going home.

5

Towards sunset Bellocq met two girls on the Texas deck. They said the band was too loud; they were so hot they had to come up for air. Their names were Adele and Bliss. Bliss's hat had thick black plumes dancing every which way. Maybe both their bonnets were a tad flashy, but their charms were natural enough. They had been to Cairo for a wedding. He could see them any time at Alicia Kite's house in the District, where they worked. If he came by they'd make sure he had a good time. He was a kid again in the circus big top, getting into the ring to pick up red spangles that fell off the bareback rider's costume. He could hear the hoofbeats, the slap of her thighs against the saddle, yet he had to get those spangles! Or had it been a dream?

Later, the girls came sporting and giggling out of a berth astern, arm in arm with two men. They had no time then to look right or left as they swept by. Bellocq guessed the ambience was wrong.

The river became more familiar as the mile markers came and went, and each one brought Miriam closer.

Coming alongside the landing at Canal Street, the calm flood shone darkly treacherous. The air darkened; the moon lit the channel, slick and placid. The Mississippi was not a river to take lightly. Its many twists could alter from one day to the next, creating false shores, sumps, lagoons and deadly currents.

Bellocq felt a foreboding. He sat for an hour in Jackson Square before he could bring himself to go to the Hecht house. He could not rid his mind of that line to Othello: *She has deceiv'd her father, and may thee.* Nothing could calm his anxiety.

He arrived late with the camera in his arms, listening to the hooves of the horse ring in the narrow streets of the quarter.

Alighting, he felt giddy and had to grab the wheel of the carriage. He fell down – no, not a faint: he could not bear the dark weight of the sky. He said her name, sure that her hand was touching his face. 'Are you okay?' the driver asked. Bellocq got up and took out his purse. 'It's nothing at all, nothing to worry about.'

The man drove off, leaving Bellocq too weak to carry the camera to the house. High up, a full moon shone in Miriam's window, twisted out of shape.

As soon as Violet opened the door, Bellocq could hear Miriam and Flis laughing. Coming in, he had a glimpse of them in the parlour, fighting together as they sank shrieking on the sofa. Miriam had her hand over Flis's mouth to stop her blabbing some secret they had shared. The door closed.

Next day, Bellocq met Miriam on the stairs, but she did not want to come to his room. When she did agree, she would only stand by the door. He had to beg her to take his hand, which she did after a while.

Proud of his blue rose tattoo with her name across it, he bared his arm to show her. She gave nothing away as he tried for her lips. What had he done to cause that coolness? Why had she not written? All he got were sullen asides. She had things on her mind she did not want to talk about. He tried to laugh, saying he was all at sea, the floor rose and fell underfoot as if he were aboard the steamboat. Had something in his letters upset her? She could see that he was hurting. He asked her, had she changed in his absence?

'How do you mean that?'

'Did you lose your heart to some other man?'

'Who would that be, pray?'

'Why are you this way, then?'

She shook her head. That was enough of that nonsense. She had not thought he wanted a reply to his last letter or she'd have written one. Her manner was tart, evasive — sullen too. He could get nothing out of her, and had to let her go.

He sat still, knees together, cold in his stomach and chest. Later, however, Miriam told him that Mr Bold had left, as well as other salesmen of whom he had been jealous. Would she bring his breakfast in the morning, as usual? Maybe so, but she could not promise.

Waking, he felt uneasy when she did not knock. He caught glimpses of her around the house, but they did not speak until the Sunday. He found her in the parlour when he went for a newspaper. She smiled and handed him one cordially. Unable to make head or tail of that, he left to find his friend Chenault. Perhaps he would be able to advise him.

Out of his senses, he did not know where he was until he heard and smelt the stockyards. He turned back, knowing he had to go to Miriam. Her manner had been so absurd he did not know how to deal with it. He said the truth was he had never seen her like that, and did not care to see it again.

She had nothing to reply to that, yet her look was warmer as she left the room. It lulled him into a false calm. He saw her again after sunset, but she would not come to his room. She could hear him quite well by the door; besides, she had too much to do.

'*Bien,*' he said. She smoothed her apron. If he came close, would she shy away again? She sat by the door; she gave her hand, and they talked for half an hour.

He told her of his misery in Memphis – how her silence had hurt him, the more so because he had not understood it. If no one had come between them – why was she so cold?

He had to get rid of the notion that things would go on in the old way, she said, those days were over. He remarked that she looked peaky; well, she said, she had no time for looks. She did not feel ill, and no, there was no one else.

Then, later, he saw her come out of a lodger's room onto the landing. She wore a loose-fitting dress and stood to comb her hair up from her nape to show a clear profile. She kept her eyes downcast as he went by. He asked, 'Are you my queen?'

She lost her temper at that. He took her hand but she pulled away. He felt a pang, sure now that something or someone had come between them. She did not care enough even to tell the truth. He ran halfway down the flight after her, then rushed back. He slammed the door, choked on his fury and jealousy. Tearing the locket from his neck, he broke it underfoot.

He couldn't stay there; yet he could not quit the room. He heard himself scream her name. They all ran up to see what the ruckus was – father, mother and the roomers. He locked the door to hide then flung it open in a rage. Hot with shame, he faced the crowd. Miss Faulkner, sure beyond doubt she'd heard Miriam scream, cried, 'She's murdered!' He would never put Miriam in any jeopardy, he shouted as he tried to get out of the room. Mrs Hecht seized his arm, weeping. 'For Heaven's sake, Mr Bellocq, you can't go anywhere in that state!' she said.

Mr Hecht was at a loss – as if he had no idea what was going on. Bellocq could see in his eyes the certainty that his lodger had gone mad. 'If he wants to go, let him!' Hecht said furiously. Bellocq tore himself away and onto the stairs as they asked, 'What has Miriam done?'

'Killed me,' he shouted. 'Put me in my grave!'

He ran out of the house, sure that he would never go back. The night only made his plight worse: dogs snarled in the yards, a wind howled. Unable to get Miriam out of the tempest in his mind, he went back.

Mr Hecht opened the door. Bellocq said he had lost control; it would not happen again. Seizing Mr Hecht's arm, he drew him upstairs saying he must speak to him. Hecht came behind glumly, not eager to hear an explanation.

Bellocq urged him to sit. 'You see, I am quite calm now,' he said. 'I need your advice.' He had no way to go at things other than in a forthright fashion.

'You know your daughter best, Mr Hecht, but do you know how she beguiles and charms?'

Hecht said he had taken quite a blow. He'd had no idea how serious things were between them.

'No man should be as alone as I have been all my life,' said Bellocq. 'All I want is to marry Miriam. Judge then how I feel, coming home from Memphis to find this change in her.'

'She was always flighty, an odd girl,' said Hecht.

'Fast with strangers yet cold to anyone who cares for her, you mean. All I want is a final yes or no – all or nothing.'

131

Hecht said he could not answer for Miriam; he could not push her to act one way or the other.

Bellocq nodded. He said his friend Mr Chenault had always given him the best advice, urging coolness whenever she came near, no matter whether she was loving or cold.

Hecht agreed that this was good advice, urging him to sleep on it.

The next morning Bellocq's body ached as if he had taken a fall. It was early; a factory whistle sounded over the city. He was calm, and lay watching until the sunlight reached the mirror. His breakfast did not come. At nine, he shaved and went down to the dining room. He was alone there. Violet came in to serve; Miriam was unwell, and had not slept last night. Bellocq went back to bed, and lay adrift in bad dreams. He woke in a sweat after being on a high ledge, so narrow he had to squeeze his body tight against the rock or fall.

Violet was knocking. She said that Abe, the boy from the Foundation Company, had come with a message for him. The *Dauphine* had gone aground across the river east of Natchez. Mr Bellocq had to go by train to take pictures and send them as quickly as possible. One of the brothers would meet him at the railway station first thing in the morning.

Feeling sicker after lunch, Bellocq went around the room and picked up the pieces of the locket to put them in a paper bag. He asked Flis if she would come up to help to pack his things, and to tell her mother that he must go to Natchez in the morning. He gave her a parcel and a note for Miriam, asking her to return the photographs. Enclosed in the parcel were Poe's *Tales of the Grotesque and Arabesque* and the *Poems* of Keats. He hated her to have the pictures now; they were proof of his idiocy. Flis brought the books back with the message that Miriam had no use for them. Her grandmother had the photographs, but she would have them for him by late afternoon. 'Well, if she doesn't want the books, you can have them,' Bellocq said to Flis.

Just after three o'clock he was in Jackson Square to meet Chenault, who was not there. On his return, Flis had a parcel for him. He did not see how it could contain photographs until he felt it. They had been framed. Untying the string binding the package, he found them wrapped in blue velvet. There was also the copy of *Lucrezia Floriani*, George Sand's novel based on her life with Chopin, which he had given her. She had cut her name and his dedication off the flyleaf. Had she done this before or after he asked her to return the photographs?

He told Flis to go to her. 'Beg her to keep the Keats; say I send it with my love.'

'Miriam loved the Keats best,' the little hussy piped up, her shrill laugh cutting as a whip.

He heard that catch in his breath, which he could never prevent, as he asked, 'Are you sure?'

'She always said so,' Flis said.

Bellocq could not help feeling fresh hope surge in him. Flis's throwaway remark swept a real Miriam back to fill the shadows of his loss. A child will say he sees something simply because he wants it to be so. Bellocq gave her two dollars.

What was it for?

'It's for you,' he said. 'Try to grow up less cruel than your sister is.'

Left alone, he sat at the window staring at the traffic; an hour went by without a knock. Had Miriam thought twice about a meeting? After three hours Bellocq could wait no longer and sent a message.

When Miriam did come at last, she said, 'I'm here; what is it you want, sir?'

He said he would like to talk to her as a friend. Offering the rocking chair he begged her to make herself at home. 'If you think I'll sit there, I'll leave now,' she said, going to the door. He begged her to stay.

Only if he did not try on anything of that sort again.

She was not always so cold.

That was yesterday! Why did he shame her now in her own house with his tantrums?

Bellocq shook his head. She ought to have known that there would be a scene.

The fault lay with him. All he had to do was give up with those words: for ever! 'You are not back from Memphis five minutes and you start harping on again,' she said. 'I intend to heed my family, now, especially my aunt who is my best friend. No lodger will get within spitting distance.'

Bellocq went down to see Mrs Hecht to make sure his room would be there when he got back.

'She was such a good child, kind and dutiful, yet with a lively sense of fun,' said Mrs Hecht reassuringly. 'You've no cause to fear a rival, Mr Bellocq.'

All the family could vouch for Miriam; ask any of them. Even Violet would tell him she had no time for other lodgers, only him. She had loitered hours in his room, despite Mr Hecht's concern. 'I told him that you were of old New Orleans stock, and would never treat Miriam badly.'

The door opened then and Miriam ran into the room laughing, as if nothing ill had passed.

Feeling that he was going mad, Bellocq kissed Mrs Hecht's scrawny hand, moist to his lips. He could not rub away the taste of her skin hours after!

It was out of the question that Bellocq should tell a hero of the charge at San Juan that he did not want to go to Natchez. Besides, the brother had the railroad ticket ready in his hand! He hoped Bellocq had had experience of being out on the river in an open boat; that was the only way to get there. He said the *Dauphine* had been under tow when a storm drove it aground on a sandbar. Shaking hands as the train began to move, he wished Bellocq a safe journey.

At Natchez the hotel was near the station, so that wailing trains kept Bellocq awake and homesick. A dry oak leaf fell out of a magazine a guest had left. It had marked an article about Chester Gillette awaiting execution. Gillette's parents were poor; he used to go with them into red-light districts as an evangelist for the Salvation Army. It was his craving to be rich that had led him to murder eighteen-year-old Grace 'Billie' Brown. Both had worked at his uncle's skirt factory, Billie as a secretary and Gillette as foreman, until he got her pregnant. She threatened to tell his uncle if he didn't marry her. He took her on vacation to Big Moose Lake, where he hired a rowboat.

Later, after people saw him drying his clothes by a fire at Eagle Bay, he booked a room at the Arrowhead Inn. Billie's corpse surfaced the next day. When Gillette asked at the hotel if anyone had been drowned, the police arrested him. His trial lasted twenty-two days. At first, he said that Billie killed herself – then, that the boat capsized, but he had tried to save her from drowning. The truth was he had hit her with a tennis racket to make sure she fell out of the boat.

In an inset picture Gillette sold signed copies of his portrait. It showed him, wing-collared, in his ball and party-going outfit of happier days. Appeals kept him alive for a year before they buckled him down and sent two thousand volts through his body. There was also a photograph of the chair, which had been first used at Auburn in 1890.

Bellocq could feel for Gillette in his despair and desperation. Deschamps had probably felt the same passion for Juliette as his father had for Josune Baulaz. All for love! If a plague bubo broke out on Miriam's flesh, he would caress it. At the first dry whisper of parching fever, his lips would drink in his death as deeply as he longed to taste the life in her.

Early next morning Bellocq stood by the wharf under a yellow storm light. He wore a Yankee officer's cape; it was a souvenir of the War that gave off a whiff of stale perfume. It was heavy and would be too hot if the weather changed, but it served to keep any light out of the camera, and as a darkroom when necessary.

The boat that came alongside seemed too frail to navigate such a powerful flood. Would the engine hold up long enough? A lamp hanging from the mast was still alight. Oil drums nudged and rang in a smell of tar and kerosene. Bellocq could smell the brandy on the man's breath long before he offered him a swig. The black dog that sat in the bow was sure where they were going; it had been there before and survived.

The boatman slung an anchor out into the mud. Said

he would wait until dark, then, if Bellocq were not there, head back to Natchez. He tossed him a pair of gumboots saying he would need those, advising him to watch out if the mud began to suck too much. He got Bellocq ashore on his back, telling him to look out for sand.

Bellocq set off, and was soon deep in more yellow mud; ahead, there were slate-blue lagoons and sumps with red veins. Fearful of sinking, he had a job to haul his cart and keep his footing.

The going firmed-up when he came onto the sand but was not much easier. He found a stick to scrape the mud off his boots; it broke, but he got them clean with the stub. He halted, looking back along his straggly trail to the boat, now a dark shape in the greyness. The only light in the monotony was a white flight of pelicans coming and going along the river. Of a sudden he was back, fishing with Jomy that day they met with the Chinaman in his black cotton pyjama suit and coolie hat. The sail of his pirogue was made out of battens and strips of canvas. He worked it like a fan and could fold it away just as neat and quick. He could play any tune they asked for on his twelve-string banjo. They refused the catfish he offered, having nowhere to cook it. A fog came down that sent them inshore, where they chanced on the submarine. So far as the old man knew, it had never seen action in the War. Sure, for a dollar Bellocq could photograph it.

Bellocq set up his camera between two rusty artillery pieces to wait for the fog to lift. Later, they went to the opera, where an old woman took umbrage that Jomy stood on the exact spot Ulysses S. Grant used to smoke his cheroot.

A sudden wind drove a rainsquall across the mud. Already weary, Bellocq sank down with the cart between his knees and drew the cloak over his head. It was the same as waiting for that fog to lift – except that he could not make out the shape his life would take. He had no solace save his trophies, those items of clothing that held the aroma of her body, which he had been at pains to get hold of. He took a satin brassière out of the pocket of the cloak and held it to his cheek. Deep down in the bottom of the cart were the blue silk knickers he held onto last thing at night, drugging himself with their musky smell. They gave relief when he was apart from her. The rain stopped. Bellocq stood, feeling tears run down his cheek. What sort of creature was he, sniffing her undergarments out in a muddy river? Setting off again, he came round the edge of the trees, saw the *Dauphine*, and heard a sound of humming voices. Beyond the vessel, a chain gang of niggers were singing as they dug a channel ready for the next high water. Bellocq walked the length of the vessel lost in a dank odour that came off the side, a stink of crusted river slime. A patch of new planking shone white through fresh tar. A pile of dead ash lay on a sheet of iron on the mud – they must have used that to heat the tar, Bellocq supposed.

The captain was still in his dressing gown and pyjamas. His handclasp was abrupt and firm. He was too old to be in charge of a riverboat. Dark bags hung under his heavy-lidded eyes, and there was a grey wart in the corner of his nose. Instantly he began to justify himself. 'I knew such a night would come,' he said. 'Had she been under her own steam it would never have happened, you tell the brothers. Never mind, they know me; they'll see it already. Damn the pilot's eyes on that tother scow! He's soaking up whiskey in some bar in Natchez now where he belongs! Soon as I get off this bank, the little fucker will answer to me! Go on, say different –' He glared now at the mate. 'I knew it the minute I saw him. Didn't I say, now there's a man whose underwear is too tight to circulate his blood?'

'Take a load off, Captain,' the mate said, urging him to sit.

'Quit looking over my shoulder, I say!'

His voice was dry, reedy; it did not carry far. How did he get his orders over? Probably relied on the mate.

'Gloria will give me hell – you know how long we been high and dry?'

He led the way, agile and quick on stairs, up ladders; testy as he took Bellocq to those parts he had to photograph. Bellocq spent the best of the morning doing that. Then, with a crewman to haul the camera, he went off to take a picture of the stranded vessel, which the brothers wanted as a record. The crewman spat as he stared at the hulk. The captain had the wheel that night was all he was saying.

None of the pictures he took aboard the *Dauphine* had turned out well. There had been something wrong with the chemicals. He had to go over the river and do them again. So, held up in Natchez, Bellocq wrote to Chenault to urge him to see Mr Weir. He must beg him to mediate with Miriam – his sister-in-law, after all – on Bellocq's behalf.

He said he had been so confident, so sure of her, when he bought that cigarette holder and the flashy necktie to go with it. Why had Chenault not had the heart to tell him that he was as vulgar as a third-rate conjuror? He was lovesick. Had he ever been anything but gentle with her? His crime had been to prowl around the house hoping to catch her out. He had done that only after hearing below-stairs chatter and laughter that he could not explain. He ought to have shut his eyes to it! Stupidly, he had taken her word. He had only himself to blame. Things would have been fine if he could have seen her as easy. He had refused to play her game. He had threatened her freedom dreaming of marriage. He recalled every syllable of their carping fights over her fine sense of propriety. It was awful; there was nothing he could change, and he would do it again in the same way. She had lost none of her power to charm.

Chenault's reply came swiftly. He had met Silas Weir, who had been open and friendly. Chenault was sure that he felt for Bellocq in his present fix. Weir wanted to do his best by the two of them. Although he saw obstacles to a marriage, he did not say that it could never happen. He did not want to take sides; all the family felt the same way – that Miriam ought to decide. Weir had no idea what she felt deep down, although he had told her the gist of Bellocq's letter. She had given him to understand that matrimony was the last thing on her mind. Yet he could not say that she would never agree to it. He was forthright, with no side at all. None of them would go to bat for the marriage, but none of them would stand in the way.

Chenault had asked Weir how they might view Bellocq living in the house. If he were to do that, Miriam should treat him as she had before. Weir could not be firm on that, but said he would take Bellocq's part. He did not want to put Miriam in a jam. The upshot was that he could see no bar to Bellocq's return, or to Miriam greeting him in amity. They had shaken hands on it, and he had left Weir to talk it over with all of them.

Bellocq read the last paragraphs several times over: 'You upset things, E. J.; you let good sense fly out the window in the heat of your passion. Only you can judge whether chasing after her is wise, but she has been ripe for the picking all along. You gave the whole house a fright when you took off that way; they all see you as some wild man now, and they worry on Miriam's behalf.

'Weir said his sister-in-law was *a good girl* who would make any man *a good wife.*'

Chenault felt that he would not say such a thing if Miriam were what Bellocq seemed to think she was. He knew her well. After all, he'd married her sister. Weir could not see why Bellocq should not try his luck with her again.

Chenault could imagine Bellocq's face on reading the letter, but he was simply relaying what had been said. Anyone less like a marriage broker Chenault could not envisage; Weir was an auctioneer with probity hiding his lust to be a senator. He would talk his way to Washington, if anybody could. The truth was that Bellocq had never felt worthy to be loved.

After praise from the brothers for his persistence in doing such a good job, Bellocq left for the Hecht house with the highest hopes. He was happy that first night to be sleeping under the same roof as Miriam. When they met, she took his hand; but she had changed. She was pale, and played deaf and dumb. He put it down to her reluctance to speak about marriage.

The third day, however, they had a long talk after which he felt that everything was fine. She was at work in the parlour and said, no she could see no reason

141

why he could not sit. They were close together in the window seat.

He could find nothing to say except that he loved her, body and soul. In time, and too late, she would see that. Could he hold her hand?

She saw no harm in taking his hand, but did so as obediently as a zombie.

He felt easy again. She seemed candid, they were talking calmly as of old. He wanted her to be as loving as before. She began to cry, which was not a thing she did, and he hated to see her tears. He thought he saw regret and pity in her eyes, but he was more afraid of the resolve lurking there. He could get no reason out of her for her tears. She said she had to go.

He sent Flis down to ask Miriam to come to his room. He waited an hour – nothing. The next day, he spoke to her mother, saying that Miriam had seemed fine until the night before, and he could not plumb the change. Mrs Hecht said he read too much into it. Then Flis came in with the message that Miriam had gone out.

Bellocq went down to speak with Mrs Hecht again. She fetched port from the pantry to drink his health. He tossed his back and strode out along St Charles to eat at Fabacher's, where he had set his mind on taking Miriam.

It was a Monday. Unable to bear being out of the house for long, Bellocq did not linger over his food. Going home, he urged the cabman to drive faster, only to find that Miriam had gone to bed.

All Tuesday morning he had to steel himself from begging her to be his wife. In the evening he could endure it no longer. He went to knock on the parlour door. Flis told him that Miriam had gone out to see

her aunt who lived over on La Salle. Bellocq sat on the
window seat awhile, Miriam's favourite place, his heart
heavy in his side. He felt full of misgivings that she sat
there looking out for someone else. Mrs Hecht, who was
dozing, woke abruptly and ordered Flis to put her book
away. It was way past her bedtime.

Darkness fell, bringing a thick fog. It was no night for
a woman to be out; those that were had to be whores.
The streets were unsafe even for a man.

Bellocq told Mrs Hecht that he would walk out and
look for Miriam. She said that Miriam could be staying
over at her aunt's, what with the fog.

It was hard to see anything, the slimy mud was treacherous underfoot and he could hear the foghorns on
the river.

He saw Miriam by the light of a shop window on the
corner of Cromwell. She was heading on to where he
stood. His first urge was to run to offer his arm, thinking
that she was alone. A band of people moved aside to let
her pass. It was then that he saw the man. *The murder
was out.* At first, Bellocq did not know him; he was tall,
handsome, young. Bellocq passed by without a word, sick
with disbelief, hoping to seem just another shadow in the
fog. Stricken, he came to a halt and turned. They had
stopped, too, to look back. Coming towards each other,
they passed in silence again.

Bellocq fled back into the house and climbed to his
room swiftly. It took him some time to realize that the
moans he could hear were his own. When he did, he
had to stifle them with a pillow, striking at it with his
fist. Then, thinking he had not heard the door, he went
out again to catch them coming.

He ran across the road into the shadows. On reaching

the door, the fog came down to hide the kiss, if there was one. The man called 'Good night'. The door opened and closed. Bellocq waited, counting to fifty before going up into the house. He rang for Violet. 'Say to Miriam that I feel calm, and I must see her now,' he said.

Miriam came quickly, tapping on the door and entering with a smile.

'I must know who he is, and how things are between you,' Bellocq said.

'Mr Bold, you mean?'

Mr Bold! It was Bold, of course – it had been him all along! 'Why did you deny it? If you do want him, I hope that you will be happy, never mind that you used to say you did not care about a man's looks!'

She had never seen Mr Bold as handsome, and she had not changed her mind. Only a man's heart and soul could move her. She had no time for skin-deep beauty.

'You said you hated him! You said he was vulgar the first day he became a lodger. You hated that sad catfish moustache of his!'

She had put that to one side when she got to know him better. She said he lived around the corner, where he had moved six months ago – just after Bellocq left for Memphis, she had told him the last time – and they had met by chance in the street. 'Surely there's no harm in him seeing me home a night like this?'

'You were coming from his lodgings?'

He listened to her lies; what else could he do? He said he hoped she had not stooped to a liaison with Mr Bold. Such a man could never have a fraction of the love he had for her. Miriam had nothing to reply. Thanking him for his concern she stood up to go. Even then, he could not hate her.

No longer able to stay in the house, for fear of another outburst of anger, he ran out again, anywhere. The streets were emptier now; he heard music and saw the lights of a saloon in the fog. Who but Mr Bold was about to go in? Bellocq seized his arm just as the door swung shut and said they had to talk.

Bold's calm wink was man to man, warm and tolerant. They sat at a table near a small stage. A few white couples were dancing to a Victrola; a black girl leant at the counter, smoking as she talked to a Negro barkeep whose white beard was cut close. Bold asked what he would drink.

Whiskey, Bellocq said.

They talked an hour or so. It all came out. Those three months before Bellocq left for Memphis, Miriam had played the game with him. She'd bring his breakfast up first, flirting with long kissing, then say she had to go up with Bellocq's ration. She used to deny any affection for Bellocq. She said he was just a roomer who meant nothing to her.

Bellocq told Bold how he had believed that Miriam could not forget her old lover. He had felt that was why she had scarcely written and why, on his return, she was cold. Bellocq closed his eyes, overcome by sudden fatigue. When he opened them again, a huge Negro with a guitar had got up on the stage. He sat down on a chair, legs apart; his pants, halfway up his calves, clung to his knees and crotch above red ankle socks and shackle scars. He was majestic. Nothing had come easy to the man, not even his music. It was difficult to make out all the words he sang. Some notes barely left the gravel depth of his throat or came forth over his humming; they were clear only when his voice rose to a shout. The song was his own, yet he seemed to be making public Bellocq's life. He was a man in trouble, whose woman no longer loved him. 'Not much to smile about, but when he does I can't say I care for it,' said Bold. 'Niggers in these dives have such nasty know-it-all grins; they just cut a man down to size and shrivel his balls. I don't think I can take any more of that sound.'

Bold tapped a good-natured punch at Bellocq's shoulder. 'Don't feel so bad. You fish one out; there always another you can play. That's what they're for, and that's all – every last one of them.' With that, he said good night.

Left alone, Bellocq dozed off. When he woke, the blues singer sat with the black girl who had been at the counter. The corner by the stage was dark, but Bellocq could see that one leg was round his waist, and the other round his neck. The soles of her feet shone yellow in the light; her toes clenched each time she thrust her body against his. The bartender was polishing glasses, nodding his head with a grin as she moaned.

At home again, Bellocq locked the door of his room and would not come out, said nothing when any of them knocked. Miriam was artful, a past mistress of cheats! One of her glib sayings, idly buttoning and unbuttoning her gloves, had been that she defied any man to read her mind. She admitted to envy of her sister, Arabella, who had always gone one better; she had married herself an auctioneer who would be elected senator one day.

'What deep mystery lies in those eyes?' Bellocq had been stupid enough once to ask, dreaming on her serenity.

No, she was not one to crow over her victims. She was a perfect actress and could flounce across any stage

– cute, heroic even. She astounded him still with that dainty sense of how far to let a man go!

If Miriam had made a clown of them both, what sort of fool did she make of her Boston lover?

She was shameless if caught out in a fib. 'So what if I tell lies,' her toss of the head seemed to say. Rare blushes were her only signs of grace. No wonder it came easy for her to say that she had no great affections.

Hungry, Bellocq had to leave his room to see what he could find in the kitchen. He thought all the house was asleep.

The air was chill on the stairs; the front door was ajar. Miriam leant close to Bold on the doorstep. Bellocq could not hear what they said. Then she led him in, whispering in the gloom of the stairwell. There was light from an open door. Bold's hand came out of the dark to take Miriam's from the banister and bring it to his fly. She knelt and took his prick in her mouth, holding onto her hat to keep it from falling off as she sucked.

Crazy now, Bellocq could not sleep. Did she glide into the room, naked, cold and dead? Half in a dream, he rose on his elbow to touch a phantom bride he had longed to bed. It was the grey of first light that flooded the room and his mind. She was lost for ever, and every tender feeling he had had for her was gone. He had fallen in with a whore. Miriam was of the same sort as those women with whom Chenault found comfort. They took his wages with a smile, ran off and spent it, then squirmed back onto his lap to wheedle more. He could see Miriam bilking her marks and scuttling off with her earnings to a pimp. She would go on that way until some heartless drifter laid her low. She was a jade her mother let loose among the lodgers; no doubt she was proud of her share in her daughter's cheap triumphs. Yet, even now that he saw Miriam in her true colours, at her basest, what could he do? Murder her and thrust her bloody corpse up the chimney? He stared at his face in the mirror, those flecks of white mucus in the corners of his mouth. Thirsty, he drank half a jug of water.

Putting the Emperor Concerto on the phonograph, he opened a score on his knee. The only image he had in mind was Miriam holding onto her blue hat in the stairwell. That low white moon shone again, and he could feel the heat of Pearl's thigh.

He tried to lose himself in the music until Violet's pail clanged below. He opened the window. She was another child of calamity, fated never to lie in the same bed or grave as a white. Her voice had the depth of feeling of the Negro blues singer, the moan of a slave. His lot did not compare with theirs but, yes, he knew something of their grief.

He had his things packed before breakfast. He left a note with a week's rent for Mr Hecht, saying that he would send for his things in a day or so. After shaving he put on his best suit. As he got to the foot of the stairs, he heard the genuine Black Forest quail-and-cuckoo clock whistle a quarter past eight in the parlour. Mrs Hecht heard his step and called, 'You slept well, I hope, Mr Bellocq?' He did not reply, but left the house swiftly, without a glance back to see whether Miriam was at the window.

6

The yard was between Rampart and Basin Street. Chinese women hauled on slender poles then let them go to drive long strings of steaming noodles through a sieve. They hung them up to dry. An old man in black robes and a round, black silk cap fell but did not cry out. Bellocq knew that he had broken his ankle. The man lay against the wall with a faint smile, as if chiding himself for being so foolish. He was as small as a child, and weighed only as much when Bellocq went to pick him up.

One woman spoke English. She said the old man's name was Jun-li. She led Bellocq, still carrying the Chinaman, to a warehouse which an acting troupe had turned into a theatre. No amount of incense could kill off the underlying greasy smell of cotton. The actors had made a stage hung with scarlet and gold banners. Later, Bellocq saw dancers mime a sword fight to clashing gongs and the clack of wood blocks. They could teeter on a non-existent gangplank in such a way as to make it visible. Jun-li told him later that the Chinese name for it was opera.

The doctor was a Taoist priest, Jun-li said. Bellocq watched him twist and turn the old man's ankle, then stick needles along his leg and back. The Chinese called it Plum Flower acupuncture, Jun-li said. China had such cures two thousand years before Christ was born. The good man could have used shiatsu, finger pressure, which was also useful against pain. An old woman gave the priest a bowl of duck soup when he had finished.

Bellocq had seen lone coolies loitering out of place in various parts of the city, usually by the river. He had not given much thought to the separate society here — its stores, markets, a bank, a theatre even.

Jun-li's shop was filled with carved chests and boxes, the scent of spices, the click of abacuses all day. Next door, metalworkers beat gold and carved ivory. Some merchants were rich enough to own rickshaws, said Jun-li, which they rode in down to the river to see their cargoes offload. They knew to an ounce what was in each hold.

Silent women went in and out of rooms with ceremonial calm, lighting red joss sticks on the altars. Ever ready to serve a husband, they put his coat on his shoulder if it slipped, or lit his cigarette. Always busy doing something — yet, if they did sit still, they were wreathed in calm.

There were family photographs: the dead shared pride of place with the living.

Some weeks later, Jun-li showed Bellocq a field by the river where they were hoping to grow rice. The women's shrill singsong voices rang as they swung along in line, planting shoots. The old man delighted in the kites the children were flying, vivid birds that rose higher with every breath of wind. Their shadows sped from side to side of him, as elusive as the shapes above.

The rickshaw man padded behind as Jun-li limped along.

The Quan Kai's two entrance columns had staid black Chinese characters. Opium smokers felt nothing for each other's misery. If they spoke, they could all tell dire tales of false paradise. Some of those men lying in the bunks drove Bellocq off only to fall back feebly; others smiled, deep in dreams, unaware of the camera – simply not there. The dregs queued in the alley behind to buy *yen shee*: the dottle the boys scraped out the bowl of the *gong* and mixed with water to sell as pellets. Most chewing those had sores break out on their bodies.

'Yes, the pipe is known as the *gong*, but in Chinese it was *yen siang*,' said Jun-li. 'We call the bowl *ow*, and the dipping needle *yen hock*. As you see, they are kept in *yen hop*, the box which also holds the lamp, *yen dong*. Here are *kiao sien* – the scissors I use to cut two pieces off the opium brick. What we have now is *yen pock*, the pill.'

Jun-li shaped the opium to fit the bowl of the pipe, and handed it to Bellocq who, after a few puffs, laid his head on the *chum tow* rest and went back in dream to the Hechts' parlour. As of old, he knew that any roomers there had just done mocking his plight. The opium would deepen their howl of laughter, making it universal. He would brave the stuffed beaver again, now a vile beast threatening to drag him under the river of time.

Bellocq spoke fluently with those strangers in the photographs of Hecht's Alsace kinfolk that filled the sideboard. Then he was an ape, baring his teeth to spit fighting abuse at a tribe of chimpanzee salesmen, yelping in rage about evolving into Charles Darwin. His animal eyes wary, he went from side to side of his cage, the stench of his rutting flesh in his nostrils. He could see Miriam, a vision of light, going round the table with Violet to serve supper. 'You would never know, safe here at this table, that fallen women were fornicating two blocks away!' Miss Faulkner's laugh was a little bell. As a poor relation of an old plantation family, she defied anyone to prove that a lie.

A swift wipe with her napkin, then another full spoon went into her open mouth and left empty again. Another dig, and the same – without let-up until her plate was clean. Soon, though, those very women were there too, sure enough, giggling as they went flitting to and fro, spectral, tempting with those fleshly delights Miriam withheld.

Floating in dreams, real or unreal, Bellocq did not know whether he was aboard the *Tennessee Queen* or not as he looked up to see Adele. She smiled down at him then she lowered her veil and moved on into the shadows.

Of one thing he was sure: his nightmares took shape out of those real events that made up his life. His fall had to end somewhere. If the familiar was strange now, or had gone, the hardest to bear was the piercing sense of loss which haunted his life.

Leaving Chinatown, Bellocq went to Mr Ahada's pawnshop to redeem his father's watch. 'Go see my daughter, Sharon,' said Ahada. 'She is looking to rent an apartment.'

Bellocq had a strange feeling long before Mrs Ahada said a word about Mischa, the rooms' previous tenant. Then, shaving one morning, Bellocq tilted the mirror; two photographs slid out and fell into the bowl.

In one, a peasant woman stood in a field with a rake; in the other, she drove a bony team of bullocks. Mrs Ahada chose that moment to knock and enter. Seeing the photographs, she said she had looked for those but never found them. Mischa had said they were of his mother. Mrs Ahada was soon wiping tears away. She held her body stiffly against the memory of the event, the loss, touching her lips with her fingertips. A long sigh was a sure sign Mischa had been in her bed whenever she could get him there.

He had done it before, raping girls. She knew that. He told her he was too weak to fight off those devils that got into him, but the girls had been been ashamed and kept quiet about it.

The last time he did it he was with another boy. You get the idea, one to hold the girl down to make it easy for the other? She'd never yet met that *goyim*, but he was in trouble from birth, but lately for poisoning horses at the track. 'One horse, he broke its legs with a baseball bat for three dollars. So yes, him – he'll fry for some crime, that boy. I hope so, too: he was no good for Mischa, who would still be here if it were not for him. One day, he will murder some person, as I foretell, just for the hell of it. I know the kind.'

So, truly, it was not only rape – it was attempted murder. It was the *goyim* trying to do the murder – no, not Mischa. He was bad – but killing? Never. Yet he was the one took out on the lam to wander this cruel world. Some said he had stowed away on a riverboat and gone up north.

Mrs Ahada's house was near Rampart, and Bellocq had spent a morning buying a bed, sheets, linen and cooking utensils. After arranging to get his father's desk out of storage, he had gone back to see if he could find any of his mother's furniture he had sold. The chest of drawers leant against a tree, wet after rain. Dead leaves had blown there to fetch up in a sodden mass, so that the furniture seemed to float on a sea of yellow. The dealer was asking twice what he paid for some pieces. 'We're all a tail on a kite,' said the man. Bellocq bought a daguerreotype of Billy the Kid, a victim of his likeness, who reminded him of Rimbaud.

The Life Drama of Napoleon and Empress Josephine of France was showing at the Vitascope. Bellocq had decided to see it in the evening. He had made a vow not to see Chenault until he stopped feeling sorry for himself. Otherwise he would rehash the whole affair, and he could not face that. He felt he was doing well enough: never again would he waste time flicking playing cards one by one into his hat, waiting for Miriam in the fading light.

He ran into Chenault by chance a fortnight later in a barbershop. Chenault had been drinking and was on his way to The Arlington. He had been to the Hechts' house, but nobody there knew where Bellocq had gone. The sudden flit had upset him. Chenault said he was relieved to see him in one piece. 'Never set your face against your friends,' he said. 'You are going to get over this. In any man's life one woman, at least, will make a sap out of him. Come along to The Arlington. I'll find you a girl for the night. There's a peach there; she'll soon straighten you out. You'll forget your troubles in no time.'

Bellocq went to see Leo feeling he had to confess to killing his mother. But, seeing Guersaint up near the altar, he left again. He had rehearsed what he would say. He knew now how his mother could slide so easily in and out of past and present tenses, slick as a snake – it was a trick he had never fathomed as a child. He could not let Leo see how near he was to throwing in his hand. His guilt was not worth sharing. As Louella said once, 'God has been in this family too long, and whenever God's around there's never any peace.' Besides, he told himself, Leo had his hands full now, hearing the confessions of the waterfront dregs of New Orleans, men dying of knife wounds.

With Miriam gone, nothing made sense any more; the only thing he could do was to take photographs to forget. He went to the slaughterhouse to see Chenault.

It was raining. Sheltered under an umbrella, he ferried his camera and apparatus into the place. He felt alien among the men, cracking wise, clumping around in rubber boots and aprons between the cattle pens. There were axes to avoid, and hooks and tubs full of coiled yellow and purple entrails. Slimy hides swung by, dripping blood and shit; some gave off a bluish light.

Amid a clang of pails, men hosed the tiled floor awash with blood, flushing scraps of fat into the sinks. He did his level best to work, but the stench soon got to him.

They brought the beasts down with a blow from a sledgehammer, then hauled each carcass up on a pulley, slitting the throat and belly so that the guts fell in steamy coils. He could not bear the sound of cattle moaning, nor to see so much meat hung up – a cow, a pig, got a number before he could blink. The light was so poor that he told Chenault to quit before he went blind. When he asked how a man of his taste and sensibility could work in such a place, Chenault said maybe he had to blunt that sensibility.

Bellocq watched his friend scrub the blood off his boots, saying how he could never get it out of the laces. They killed and butchered four or five sheep or pigs every hour, which was not as fast as Chicago cutters did it – they butchered a hundred cattle every hour. 'It's not the blood I mind, it's the shit, E. J.,' he said. When he was younger, he'd wanted to be Bob Fitzsimmons. He was eager to make easy money knocking men down. He had gone to work for Sol, a sports promoter, who had a tent and some heavies he took to fairs to knock the shit out of hayseeds. 'I'm too old for body-blows now,' said Chenault. The truth, as Bellocq knew, was that his friend drank too much. He had hit the canvas too many times. They were making potato-mash of his brain. Once he'd known every Shakespeare sonnet by heart; now all were gone.

'Why stay here? You could hire out as a strong-arm man.' Bellocq was sure he could find a union job with the waterfront locals. 'You can see me helping to fill ballot boxes for those people?' Chenault laughed. 'Jesus wept! Did you ever read Karl Marx, James? We get out of the freezer of a night to warm ourselves at the braziers. I hear men argue about wages, their hopes for their families. There's no looking up at the stars any more. Come morning, the pigeons quit the ledges, gulls drift in from the Gulf to scavenge. Nothing can stay the same. Everything has to change.'

7

Lulu White's name shone in a white arch across the stained-glass fanlight. Bellocq did not expect to deal with her — if, indeed, she was around that time of the morning. The girl scrubbing the step got up and stood aside to let him pass.

A maid in a white starched apron came, pinning on her cap. She was pigeon-toed, and had one strap of her button shoes undone. Bellocq did not know the man who followed to catch her arm. He was not George Killshaw, Lulu's lover, whom Bellocq had been expecting to see.

'Step this way, Mr Bellocq,' he said, giving the maid's backside a pat.

His beard was close-cut. He waved fine manicured hands to give Bellocq an idea of what Lulu had in mind — see, this view through into the parlour, to get the parquet flooring and the fireplace and the white pillars there. And the chandelier, of course. 'Lulu insists you feature that,' he said. 'The way the guy got those lights up like open flowers cost plenty.' Bellocq nodded, happy to settle on a view that left out the worst of the overblown furnishings, the rich hangings and the sculptures of 'artistic' nudes.

'Anything you need, you sing out now. I'm your man,' Bellocq's guide said, leaving him to it.

Bellocq set up the camera and took photographs.

There was a hubbub outside. Two men ran in through the open door carrying another by his arms and legs.

Blood ran from a wound in his forehead. One of them said he had been run down; the other said, no, he had been set upon and robbed – they'd better phone an ambulance. Two girls had come out of the kitchen in their négligées. One, still eating her toast, asked, 'Is he drunk, or what?'

'Can't you see he's bleeding?' The other girl knelt to have a closer look. 'That leg looks funny to me; I think it's broken.'

One of the Samaritans reached to loosen the wounded man's tie. They'd brought in a minister, he said in surprise.

'He must be from out of town,' said the other man.

'Who'd want to hit a clergyman?' the girl with the toast wondered.

Just then, another man came in the doorway, hat in hand, holding a book.

'Is that his Bible?'

'It was out lying in the street,' he said. 'I chased the guy as far as the cemetery, but lost him.'

'Send for an ambulance,' one of the men was calling.

'This here's no Bible.' The other girl had opened the book. 'It's a rent-collector's tally.' The others snorted a laugh. 'Somebody got away with the crib rents.'

Her friend put the toast down and picked up the telephone. 'This is Main 1102, Lulu White's. There's a preacher here needs an ambulance. Quit laughing, you asshole, and get yourself over here!'

'What's all this ruckus?' The voice was strident; Lulu White – the Diamond Queen herself – stood at the top of the stairs. She wore a bright, unreal, red wig. There were diamond rings on every finger, even her thumbs. It was too early yet for corsets, so her belly swung from side to side as she came down the stairs.

She denied any Negro blood. She was born in the West Indies, she said, and put it about that her father was a Wall Street broker who took her to New York as a child. After his death, she'd been left with a property in Customhouse Street. The truth was that she had been born on an Alabama farm. She'd finagled the money to open Mahogany Hall from an oilman, a railroad tycoon and the owner of a department store.

'Who is that lying in my hallway?'

'Some preacher was robbed, just now.'

'Well get him out of here, that's all.'

'He's hurt,' said the bearded man who had greeted Bellocq earlier, as he came downstairs. 'Best avoid any shit with the Church, Lulu.'

'Fuck the Church! What did a parson ever do for me? Who brought him in here to bleed all over my rug?' She rounded on the men who had carried him in. 'You, who are you? You got business here? No? Then piss off! Get his head off there! Don't you know how much that cost?' She came face to face with Bellocq. 'Who are you?'

The bearded man said he was doing those photographs of the parlour. Lulu went towards the kitchen, heading for the lift. 'If I find that sonofabitch still lying here when I get back, I'll have George kick his ass and throw him back into the street.'

The lift gate slammed shut. As Lulu began to ascend, the preacher came round, moaning with pain.

'Some days that's one lady I come near strangling,' said the bearded man softly to Bellocq. 'You got the job done, right?'

'Fine.'

'You can see that things are a little haywire here. When can you show Lulu the pictures?'

159

'Would tomorrow be all right?'

'Sure. That would be good. Do a few copies: Billy Struve will have to okay them, too.'

'I'll find a cab, pick up my camera later, if that's all right with you?'

'Sure. Sure. Nobody here is going to mess with it.'

Bellocq put on his hat and went out. Two ambulance men were coming up the steps, sniggering as they drank a beer. One had a rolled green canvas stretcher on his shoulder.

Bellocq was unsure now where he was going. The cemetery lay ahead. A woman shrieked at him from a gallery. It was Adele, the girl from the riverboat. She was sitting on the rail, swinging her leg. She got up to sidle along under the fans, staying abreast of him and twirling her parasol. 'Sure, you remember,' she said. 'You were out of your head the last time, at the Quan Kai.'

'Did I see you there?'

'We all need our little trespasses,' she said. 'Your eyes were open, but you were not at home. Step on up; I told Bliss I knew you'd come and see us.'

She leant down at an open window and said, 'Our Mr Bellocq is here, Bliss.'

It did not take long for them to worm Lulu White out of him; then they were all set to hear about Miriam. 'Those hard-luck stories are a dime a dozen, Mr Bellocq,' said Adele. 'Take a leaf out of your friend Chenault's book. He treats a woman same as the meat he works all day. You best learn to see a body in the same light. We got the same natural needs as any other flesh on the hoof.'

What he needed was a pinch of Goofer Dust from Julia Jackson, the conjure woman, said Bliss.

Bellocq shook his head. '"Goofer Dust"?'

'You dry earth off an infant's grave, and you got Goofer Dust.' Adele lit a cigarette. 'Julia dusts the guy's pillow, and he'll never bother you again. She's some powerful lady. I cross the street when I see her – any broad puts one over on her finds her cunt closed tight in the night so she can't turn tricks no more.'

Behind the house, Bellocq heard a girl laughing as she helped the maid hang out washing. He was happy in that atmosphere; he liked the easy way the women talked about men. He could appreciate now why Chenault spent all his nights there.

Sure, they worked for Mrs Kite, but they all stuck a tongue out when her back was turned. Mrs K. saw all men as pigs; they were two-faced, and you had to watch them like a hawk, or they'd run off with your teeth. Her girls better make sure they got the money in their stocking first. Mrs Kite was not going to pay some bully to beat it out of the john.

'Why stay here, if she is so hard?'

'She's not all bad,' said Bliss. Mrs K. had been the 'other woman' too many years; that was not something to set you up for life. Of course, she was young then, and didn't know any better.

'Any woman can run things as good as a man,' said Adele. 'Men won't rest until they get you under their thumbs. They beat you into shape, and that makes you cruel and artful. No woman is born that way; with men it's natural.'

'That first nip you give them to skin them makes my flesh creep,' said Bliss. 'You do it, but it's plain filthy, and how many of them ever wash their foreskin out? What the hell it can tell you about how bad their condition is, I'll never know!'

Adele heard it from Phoebe, who left the house two years ago. She said a nurse at the Charity told her how Alicia Kite's pimp threw her down the stairs.

'Having to use that cane now, no wonder she's so mean. No woman is harder than a red-light landlady,' said Bliss. 'Mrs Kite's no exception.'

Neither of them knew how Mrs Kite came by the money to set the place up. She kept things to herself, never had a pimp, never went out anywhere, but was partial to orchids. A fresh one every morning – you could see her coming.

One of the girls had epileptic fits. She would lie naked in bed after an attack, perspiration soaking the sheet. 'I don't know how much longer I can put up with this,' said old Mrs Kite. 'It'll happen with a client one night, I know; he'll keel over with a heart attack and give the house a bad name.'

'She has one of her turns, and a john thinks he's giving her one hell of a time,' said Sippie Brooks, with a laugh. 'You let her bite on a stick, it soon passes.'

Adele put a feather, a *lagniappe*, in Bellocq's hatband before he left. Force of habit, she said. All the johns got one of those; it was a sign to other houses that there was no point in trying to fleece that particular mark.

No sooner had Bellocq left the house than he wanted back in, and could not wait to go again.

Life there was not as grand as it was at The Arlington or Mahogany Hall, they told him. But any novelty on offer was as good as it was at Josie Arlington's or Emma Johnson's, and the johns paid less. Mrs Kite said her fillies had the same form as any whore Josie or Emma could field.

Bellocq was in the house one day when an old woman

arrived in a carriage. The tall Negro who drove the rig lifted a shrouded figure out and carried her swiftly up the steps. She held a sheaf of gladioli and spent an hour or more locked tight with Mrs Kite. Later, Adele told him she had to be Mrs Kite's mother. She got a whiff of her once — camphor, Bourbon and old piss. She was an immortal, and you don't ask about those. Nobody knew where she lived. Some said out Carrollton way, others in squalor on a plantation outside the parish limit, a Miss Haversham. One day Adele had seen her come out the Hibernia Bank and Trust Ltd, so she must have something salted away.

It had not been a good day for her to show up. Mrs Kite was having her courses and felt nervy and sick.

The door of Mrs Kite's room had red baize fixed with brass studs. The first time Bellocq saw her, the curtains were half drawn. She was going about with a copper kettle watering her plants. She asked about the pictures he had taken for Lulu White. Then told him which of her girls she wanted to see in the *Blue Book*. 'If that sow Lulu White is selling her wares in there, I'm having a page, too. That nigger gets her pitcher to the well ahead of mine all the time!'

'You have to ask the women about that,' said Bellocq.

'I'll do no such thing!' said Mrs Kite. 'Any bitch under my roof has anything to say can pack her bags right now.'

Mrs Kite saw people only for what they were worth, cash on the nail. Bellocq was beneath her notice, but he had his uses.

Was it an illusion, or were the women not up-to-the-minute? Why did their perfumes and hairdos linger on from his mother's time? He found them easy-going – rarely devious. They would talk and play cards, sit in their white fur stoles and muffs as if waiting for a carriage to take them to the opera – Bliss showing off fancy-striped six-dollar stockings as she drank. None of them did much – it was always too hot to stir, they said. They would ride as far as the shops or sit reading magazines and novelettes or play the Victrola and drink too much. They were waiting; that's what they had to do a great deal of the time.

Bellocq put his vision at their service. He knew exactly what he wanted. He could tell how each of them would turn out before he made a print, although he used more than one plate. Even then, he got a thrill seeing what would emerge in the darkroom, late at night, anxious to discover whether he had caught the right light. Things changed so fast.

He took none of their portraits cold; they were not ship's engines. He had to sit and talk about everything under the sun except photographs. He drank tea and coffee, often a little wine. They had all the time in the world; there was no rush. Everything stopped on the day that Bliss's sister came to visit. She was caring for Adele's baby boy.

Amaryllis and Adele were bedmaking – whooping, tossing fresh sheets and shaking them out in cool billows that wafted the smell of peaches from the fruit stand as Bellocq sat brooding. If he had never been much of a man, it was his mother's fault. She failed to make him a priest, but she had formed his body, with its natural desires. She had shaped him in a form to preclude any relief. He saw his head, trapped halfway out of her uterus. He had lost her; they had torn him out of her body. He used to pore over

164

a book on obstetrics – Jean Poullet's foetal extractor. A doctor worked the tongs by tightening a strap around the head, to nip the spine where it met the skull. Was that the tool they had used on him? In the museum, his brother foetuses were afloat in glass jars, the same curiosities as Seminole flint arrowheads or the coins and pistols in nearby rooms.

It all came out of a naked body from the start. Having found Mrs Kite's by accident, he needed those women now. The more exposures he made the more pictures he had to take. He was making up for lost time.

One that did go wrong was the group portrait that Mrs Kite had wanted. He felt nothing with the women standing on the porch out back. They were talking too much, even when he hissed at them to be quiet so that he could focus. They left off chattering, and stood smiling at their reflections in the mirror he stood beside the camera.

The grouping was similar to the one Leo set up for him: girls in white confirmation dresses holding their lilies. Their eagerness to change their lives shone through their devotion. What did they think change was? Most would marry and have children; but some were bound to end up in the District, by this or that route. Some of the girls on the porch had come from good families – not that he pried. Women had to have their little secrets. They paid no mind to what he thought or how he looked, and if they made fun of him, they were never cruel.

'If you are a hoot, it's because all men are,' said Sippie. 'We get a laugh out of them all day long – all night, too, I guess. Surely that's the only natural thing a girl can do?'

★　　★　　★

165

It was Bliss's birthday; they had all kept quiet about that. Bellocq knew she was feeling low when he took the group. 'For Heaven's sake, it's her day. She can look any way she pleases, even down in the mouth,' said Sippie. 'Let it go.'

Alicia Kite rented a house with a garden to stage the event. After dark, a hired jazz band came drumming and blowing along the alley. Bliss's eyes lit up. 'I'll say one thing for her, Mrs K. sure knows how to lay on a swell do,' said Sippie. There were crates of French champagne on the grass; couples waltzed under the magnolia in flower. Bellocq found Bliss and Adele on the swing; the plank hung from iron stays could sit three girls at a time.

'So, you were born here, when?'

Bellocq told Adele the date.

'Why, that's next week!' Bliss cried. 'Are you going to have us to your party?'

'Party? I never celebrate,' said Bellocq.

Adele could not believe that. 'Never?'

Bellocq shook his head.

'Why, Mr B., if that's not the be-all I've ever heard! Say, what are you? One of Jehovah's people? Your birthday – and you don't ever jig around, get drunk or blow a candle out!'

That was why, three days later, they wore the masks as a special treat. They would always make a fuss of somebody having a birthday, a cake and all. Sippie put on make-up to hide her black eye.

Adele laughed. 'I know you'll really feel it's your birthday if we get our glad rags off!'

'Whatever you want,' he said, feeling heady. 'Money's no object!'

'Money? That's the last thing on your mind when you're deep in that box,' said Adele.

Bellocq smiled. 'I'm too fond of you to short-change you ladies.'

'What I mean is you could make plenty, Mr B.,' said Adele. 'You drink in that South Rampart saloon ever? It has the room upstairs full of dirty photographs!'

No, Bellocq had not.

'Well, aren't you the good boy!' said Sippie. 'We'll have to think up something tasty for you, later.' Her sly smile held a fairground promise. 'I've got what it takes to satisfy you to death.'

A Negro page-boy stood guard on the doorstep. He wore eighteenth-century knee breeches, buckled shoes and a white wig. Mrs Beukes owned the house. The girl, Elzadie, worked there as a maid. Mrs Beukes said she was going elsewhere; there was no way that she could raise a baby there. What had the little slut been thinking of? Having a kid wouldn't change her life. She had gone part the way with a couple of bucks towards the abortion – the sooner the better from the look of things. She was only being helpful because the stupid chit had got herself knocked up on her premises, and that was against the law. The player-piano in the parlour was beating out 'Meet Me Tonight in Dreamland'. 'Tell Elzadie we'll be back around eight to pick her up,' said Bliss.

Chenault had hired the car. He offered to drive if Bellocq did not feel up to it; but Bellocq had promised Bliss. 'Are you sure? It'll piss down before morning.'

'Crank the engine, and I'll get going,' said Bellocq.

Adele, Ruby, Bliss and Elzadie were waiting around

the corner from Mrs Beukes's house in the doorway of an Iberville crib.

'I don't know what we're doing!' Adele said. 'Why can't her own kind look out for her?'

Bliss took her to one side. 'If you're about to start, Adele, you better get on home now. I am doing the best I can for Elzadie. Elzadie did her best for me one time. So shut your mouth and keep it shut!'

After making sure that she and Ruby had settled Elzadie safely in the car, Bliss said to Bellocq, 'Get along now to the racetrack.'

The greasy medical chart on the wall did little to allay Bellocq's sense of foreboding. The shabby room had nothing to do with surgery. Priaulx's breath stank of whiskey. He wore steel-rimmed glasses that dangled on a black silk cord, and he needed a clean shirt and a shave. 'She left it late,' he said, touching both sides of Elzadie's neck, with a nod. 'Could turn out to be a tricky business. I need five dollars more.'

Bliss took a purse out of her handbag.

Priaulx put on a white coat, reading Bellocq's mind. 'You want to see my medical diploma?' he laughed. 'I must have one of those around someplace. I forget just where.' He came under the light to stare at Bellocq. 'You still live on Conti? Your mother died – now, how many years ago? You'll know exactly.'

'What are you trying to say?'

'Never mind. Your guilty secrets are no concern of mine, just as mine are none of yours.'

Bliss helped Elzadie take off her cotton drawers, saying, 'Come on, Elzadie, come on, girl, nothing is going to get done else.'

168

Bellocq stood by the window. Half the light-bulbs on the hotel sign next door were dead. Ragged bursts of cheering rose every now and then from the livery stable across the street. A bare-knuckle fight was going on — by rights, that was where he should be, Priaulx said, not poking in some black bitch's insides. It was then that Bellocq placed the smell: a blend of liniment, iodine and the acid sweat of fighters.

Elzadie had given herself up for dead. Let it happen, if that was how it was going to be. It was there in the corner of Bellocq's eye, and he could not turn away from the dark cleft under her swollen belly, hair a nappy frizz thickening round plump bluish lips that gaped pink as Priaulx forced her legs apart. 'A shot of morphine will cost you extra yet again and is probably not worth it,' said Priaulx. 'There's no feeling up here in these girls.'

A smell of disinfectant spread as Priaulx washed his hands. Ruby and Bliss held Elzadie's legs, trying to soothe her while Priaulx edged an enamel pail with his foot to catch the blood. He took up a speculum, ordering Bliss to hold the lamp still so that he could see what he was doing. 'Why is he pressing her throat?' Bellocq whispered. He was with Adele now in the open doorway.

'Maybe to stop her screaming,' Adele said. 'I don't want to hear that. He has to know what he's about; he's done it often enough.'

'Shut up, or get out of here!' Priaulx called.

Elzadie sobbed, legs open, hands holding her knees. When she took them away she put them up into the light each side of her grimacing face, palms upward, her fingers clawing against the pain.

Bellocq felt sick, too. Priaulx probed an instrument in her uterus, and was tossing bloody cloths aside in disgust, one after the other. He would wash them later as matter-of-factly as a knife or fork. Bliss stuffed a handkerchief into Elzadie's mouth before she had time to shriek. Bellocq did not know what it was slipped out of Priaulx's hand and slid across the salver. If it was not a minute, skinned baby rabbit his fevered imagination said it had to be the foetus.

'There's still a lot of bleeding,' said Bliss, alarmed.

'I've done the best I can.'

'Suppose it won't stop?'

'I want her out of here, right now,' said Priaulx, filling a bowl with hot water from the ewer.

The storm broke suddenly. Lightning flashes lit the sky. Bliss and Bellocq had to fight the wind to get the hood up ahead of the rain. Elzadie seemed more scared of the thunder than the blood leaking out of her. Ruby leant close to Bliss. 'What are we going to do with her? Mrs Beukes won't want her in the house in this state.'

'I don't believe I'm doing this,' said Adele.

'That fucking butcher!' cried Bliss; then, to Bellocq, 'It's over! Get us back as fast as you can.'

When the car drew up outside the house, the page-boy ran out with an umbrella to open the door. Bellocq knew what was going to happen next.

'She looks just awful,' said Mrs Beukes. 'I'm not having her die here. I got my troubles, too.'

'Then she better come with us, you bitch!'

Bellocq did his best to stay out of the way as Bliss and Ruby got Elzadie back in the car.

'Mrs Kite is going to have a fit.' Adele puffed at a cigarette nervously.

'She'll be asleep now. We'll worry about that when we get to it.'

The flow of blood had soaked the towel under Elzadie.

'She's not going to last till morning if we don't do something,' Adele breathed into Bellocq's ear.

'Drive!' Bliss ordered.

Bellocq helped to get Elzadie upstairs at Mrs Kite's. The coloured girls brought pails of hot water. Bliss and the others got Elzadie into the bath. Ruby came out saying it had done nothing to ease the bleeding.

Bliss followed, and took hold of Bellocq's lapel. 'She has to go to the Charity,' she said.

Josie knew that no poor nigger girl bleeding from an abortion would get in there so late at night.

'She has to, or she'll die.'

When they brought Elzadie out of the bathroom Bellocq knew she was going fast. He and Bliss drove the maid to the Charity Hospital, where he sat waiting in the corridor. He could hear voices raised; Bliss was doing the shouting.

When Bliss shook him awake he did not know what time it was. It was still raining, and Elzadie was dead. 'I put you to a lot of trouble for nothing,' said Bliss. 'The little fool kept herself going too long on promises. If I'd known sooner, a dose of calisaya might have done the trick and she'd be okay.'

'You look worn out,' said Bellocq. 'Let's get you home.'

'I don't want to talk about her now,' she said. 'I feel sick. Ask me tomorrow.'

Elzadie had known as soon as the priest went through the ward ringing his bell. By then, everything was inflamed – lymph glands, pleura and peritoneum. They had a lot of Latin words to cover it, a lot of questions.

Bliss took off her wet stockings and walked barefoot to the car.

★   ★   ★

The rain fell heavier at first light. Bliss insisted that Bellocq take her couch. The house was too hot for sleep; he ducked under the sash and stepped out onto the gallery. The women wore only chemises, sighing as they walked back and forth with fans whirring overhead. Josie had cagebirds she would hang in the gallery, and they were singing. Adele sat on the railing, one foot on the tub, with the orange tree brushing her long hair. Every so often one of them squealed at a bolt of lightning. Below, the maid ran with a basket of fruit from the market: lemons, apples and a pale green watermelon.

A car braked under the overhanging chinaberry tree. Two men got out with umbrellas, picking a way over the streams that ran down the street.

Sergeant Sprague and Lieutenant Judge had a list of women on a clipboard. It was a routine instigated by some doctor at the Charity who'd had a bellyful of such cases. The men didn't want to waste time running around in that weather. They called down those who were in their rooms to question each separately. Finally, Judge got around to Bellocq.

'No use asking if I know the man,' Bellocq said. 'I wasn't there. All I did was drive the car.' Bliss had told him to say that.

'So it was a man, huh?' Judge nodded.

'Well, none of the girls will say a word,' said Sprague. 'They figure they might need him again. Never mind he kills a one of them now and then.'

'I don't know anything else.'

Sprague cornered Bellocq in the hallway, and backed him into the kitchen. 'I'll tell you his name: Priaulx. And you know it,' he said.

'If you know – why ask?'

'What I got up here' — he tapped his forehead — 'is of no use in a court of law. I arrest him, I'll be a laughing-stock.'

Nothing was going to happen, anyway. After the funeral, Bliss took the girl's parents to Mrs Beukes to collect her few things. Nobody had much to say to them, and they were not expecting anything. The father was drunk, and the mother said that's what he did when he could not cope. He swept the streets of the District, and it was some miracle how he kept his job.

Alicia Kite brought Sylvie in as a novelty, fresh blood. She was a ten-year-old. Some of the women were not happy about it. Bliss said that Mrs Kite ought to 'take that child to the House of the Good Shepherd rather than sell her ass'. Mrs Kite laughed when she heard. 'Bliss is jealous. Either she was drunk or jossing with you, Mr Bellocq. Emma Johnson auctions a virgin every Saturday night, sweet as a peach, with the bloom of down just on her. She has circus ponies and horses that her man, Wash, grooms in the stables out back. Now, why does she keep those, do you think? If she had Sylvie under her roof, she'd soon have one of them fucking her while men watched. You're too soft, Mr Bellocq. Ask her, and she'll tell you she has it easy here; all she has to do is suck them off.'

None of them could budge Mrs Kite when she was set on something. She wagged a finger at him in reproof. 'I let you hang around to amuse the girls, not give advice on brothel-keeping. Sure, Mr Bellocq, in case you've forgotten, that's what this place is.'

Sprague came in barefoot, smoking a cheroot, his shirt-tail hanging out of grimy white pants.

Bellocq knew about Sprague's visits from the driver. He

would wait outside while Mrs Kite gave Sprague a glass of whiskey sour and a taste of her switch, which she kept for special clients. Bellocq had heard the sound first then Mrs Kite came in sight, swinging the cane as she crossed the doorway to where Sprague knelt over a low table.

Sprague had got his start in life as a member of the Red Light Social Club. He helped to haul a U.S. Mail sack around the District, collecting the weekly pay-off the maids left out on the doorstep of each mansion.

It was Sylvie peeking round the edge of the door. She wore an orange kimono with Japanese characters and blue dahlias. 'I thought you had left,' she said to Sprague. 'I came to find you.'

Sprague did not look at her. He fixed his eyes on Bellocq as E. J. went to the door. 'You don't get rid of Bix Sprague as easy as that, honey.' It was a threat.

Passing Sylvie gave Bellocq the whiff of a singed cat hiding among wild flowers. Turning his head as he left, Bellocq saw Sprague hug her, a hairy hand squeezing her buttocks.

The sun was going down. Sylvie crouched over the bidet, her back towards the door, an impish, brazen smile over her shoulder making Bellocq an accessory. Her client came into view, laughing as he buttoned his flies. Bellocq had expected Sprague, but had not wanted his suspicions confirmed. He longed to be the man, whoever he was, and Sylvie knew that.

It was what they paid her to do. She would wash Bellocq, too, if he paid. Bliss said he did not know the half of it: how Mrs Kite had city fathers – French mostly, of course – who came to see Sylvie act out unnatural dumb shows with Josie.

'Sylvie is a French name,' said Bellocq later, when they talked.

'Papa came from Antibes,' she told him. 'He died soon after I was born. Then *maman* put me with the nuns to run off with her new flame. Mrs Jobas paid the convent cash on the nail. I could never understand much of what some of those nuns were on about, but I know my catechism. Would you like to hear it?'

She had hated that convent. Everything was locked, and all you heard morning, noon and night was the sound of keys. 'Even the floor polish smelt of God. *Mon Dieu*, what was the word for all that holy stuff?'

'Ecclesiastical?'

'You could be right.'

With the sun below the horizon, the lurid dusty pink of the afterglow set Bellocq afire with as much joy as grief. A group of men standing on the corner were listening to the whine of a steel-string guitar, long time gone, drawn out and mournful. Sometimes they cupped their hands around a match to puff at a cigarette.

'Prison has to be the same as a convent,' said Sylvie, 'doors forever slamming and bolts being shot, that whispering. I hate to shut a door. I don't mind who sees me on the bidet. What I liked best about that place was the garden, milking the cows, the corn for the chickens. I used to take my shoes off and walk about in the shit. That was good. All those nuns had lost their minds, though – no, I mean it. I learnt a lot more than my catechism.'

She was another Florrie. He had already taken one picture of her without her knowing, staring up at the two plates she had spinning on wands. She wore a black ribbon around her throat, a younger Olympia, and sucked a lollipop. She had the appetite of a bird. She lived on air.

'Do you speak French?'

'*Comment allez-vous? Combien?*' That was about all she could remember of her past, she said, that and her mother's name was Eve.

'Well now, that's something we might have guessed about you,' said Adele with a laugh, as she came into the room.

Adele did not say much when Sylvie was around. 'You can't say whose ear she whispers in. I come here to the District to work every night. Same as punching a clock, only I don't want to think of it as that, nor do the johns. I give a tub of lard a massage, some slap and tickle, and he'll blubber, groan and fart with gratitude. Sex? It's mostly about mothering, pampering no end. They breeze in here all steamed up, huffing and puffing; my job is to find a way around them going out crestfallen. I don't mind that sort, but now and then you'll get a john wants to cut every stitch off you. He'll read poems while I play with myself. Says he writes them, too, but he'll never read those.'

Sylvie heard Mrs Kite and left. Bellocq watched Adele deal the deck again for solitaire. 'Sprague is up to fuck her after Mrs Kite's licking whips some life into him,' Adele went on. 'You got any other ideas about fidelity? Forget it. No gal here but has her price. Any emotion costs that us fallen women weave around a fuck, Mr Bellocq.'

They were dolling up for the funeral of a girl whose pimp had cut her throat, 'so bad her head near came off'. A doctor had 'stitched her up real good'. Bellocq lacked the nerve to take his camera, much as he wanted to. She lay in full warpaint in the big brass bed: strings of cheap pearls, black silk gloves so fine the blood-red nails shone through, eyes closed as if sleeping. When the undertaker came, Sippie pulled back the bedclothes. The dead girl was wearing a silver shimmy dress, black stockings and high heels. It was the girls had paid for her coffin, the hearse, the cemetery plot and the band. The musicians were drinking on the veranda while they sang.

Every month, the changing of the moon,
Every month, the changing of the moon,
I say every month, the changing of the moon,
The blood comes rushing from the bitch's womb.

'I thought they were going to play a funeral march,' said Bellocq to Chenault, whom he had invited.

'Oh, they'll get around to it shortly.'

'That's a pretty awful song,' said Bellocq.

'You know how these things go,' Chenault croaked, touching the bandage around his neck. He had been cut intervening in a fight at the slaughterhouse. His visits to the mansions were even more frequent, now that he was supplying Alicia Kite with meat.

Sylvie's face lit up in a smile as she painted Sippie's fingernails one afternoon. 'Why, I do declare, Mr Bellocq,' she drawled, 'there is no sweeter pastime than sucking Mrs Kite's cunt until she squeals.'

'You never do that, Sylvie!' cried Sippie, slapping her arm.

'Jethro will tell you – he knows,' Sylvie answered. Jethro played banjo at parties and ran errands for the girls. 'He came in one time when I was at it; he got hold of my arm on the stairs, and shook so hard I thought it would come off. He said I better wash my mouth out with permanganate.'

The women were always touching – they would tickle each other into hysterics. Then, catching themselves in the act, they would slow the tickling into a caress. Bellocq had seen Bliss let her legs fall open so that Adele could cram her fingers into her. 'No camera, Mr Bellocq? Will you look at him sitting there, the cat that's got the cream? The one game he'll never play is forfeits. Any minute now he's going to say he's in love with all of us.'

Amaryllis had not drawn the curtains but the smell from the chamber pot had nowhere to go except out onto the landing. Louis Danzig, a retired riverboat man, said the Germans downstairs smelt worse than Amaryllis's juice. 'They all stink! Dolts!' He lit a cigar as they listened to the drunken officers' blundering horseplay below. Bellocq would not believe why they were there! Why was the German high command so curious to know how fast American roustabouts could strike a three-ring circus marquee?

Bellocq shook his head. 'Are you sure about that?'

'What else are they? Military spies,' said Danzig. 'They are not here to fuck girls brainless. They are shits, and I can see us having to shoot some of them dead in the near future.'

'You are drunk, Louis,' said Bellocq.

Danzig was sober enough to use the camera one of the officers lent him. He snapped Bellocq taking photographs. Bellocq tried to teach him: 'For a picture to be any good, the person who took it must leave all his obsessions on show; that, or he is working for someone who can pay to have his pictures sharp enough to please.'

Danzig said that Bellocq ought to stop feeling sorry over spilt milk. Any woman in the house was ready to lie down and perform any trick he asked.

'All I would have to do is admit that none of it has anything to do with true feeling,' said Bellocq. 'Then she'll wash my penis, open her legs and give the empty counterfeit.'

'Don't you like that?' Danzig shook his head. 'No, you don't, I can tell.'

They lay on the bed drinking, staring at the print some sailor had left.

Danzig said the artist was Hokusai. An octopus was sucking a pearl-diver's cunt. 'You can *smell* the whole thing,' said Louis, fondling the red garter Bliss had left around his neck. 'Will you *look* at its eyes, those arms palping on her – that itchy tentacle is so canny – and Jesus, what about the baby with its beak in her mouth? My God, those slimy things *know* what they are doing writhing around like that. They are driving her out of her mind. She can't let on, in case they stop. She'll say how one thing led to another; she's as drunk as I am, and clearly in her element.'

Too tired to reply, Bellocq dozed off. When he woke, Danzig had gone and Bliss was into the room. There had been a nasty scene in the parlour, and Sylvie had run off out of the house. Mrs Kite had sent Jethro to look for her. He had come back empty-handed. He was downstairs drinking coffee but he would be off again in a minute.

Bellocq got up and put on his jacket. 'What happened? What's it about?'

'How do I know?' Bliss said she had been out when it happened. 'Mrs Kite won't say a thing. Whatever it was, the bastards paraded Sylvie afterwards and gave her a medal. I do know one of those motherfuckers shat in her mouth.'

When Bellocq got home he found Sylvie asleep on his

bed. She had told Mrs Ahada that she was his sister's child, and had been let in. She had tied a cloth around her head, inking in a red cross. She was nursing a rag doll with black ringlets, the only thing she had brought with her.

Bellocq moved as quietly as he could, but she awoke and sat up, rubbing her eyes as a child does. 'I've come to look after you,' she said.

'What did they do to you?'

She did not want to talk about that, but she was never going back there. She broke into tears when he said she had to. She was leaning against the wall – a waif hurt yet again. She held a hand over her mouth, her head jerking each time she fought back a sob. 'You took all the women's but never my picture,' she whined. 'Do it now.'

Bellocq felt he had to humour her. He spread a red cloth over a box and told her to stand on it. She could hold on to the chair-back. At that height she was level with the camera; he did not have to adjust the tripod. After he took the picture, she said he had done the other girls with no clothes on. Before he could say no, her dress was off and she took up a lewd pose on the divan, linking her hands above her head.

Her breasts were small; she had only a lick or two of hair on her vulva. He was torn between a need to shave it off and an urge to hold the tuft and never let go. Not content with that she got on the box again, slouching, a hand on her hip.

When he had finished she came over to the bed and put her head in his lap. He lay back, overcome by a sudden stabbing headache. She shook him. 'Do you want to fuck, or not? Mrs Kite said you're a dumb nebbish with no idea what your cock is for!'

She tore his flies open. He heard the buttons pop. One

pinged off the horn of the phonograph. She rode him – there was no other word. That slip of a girl was a contortionist; her body struck his hips with each thrust.

Feeling along her delicate ribs, he moved up to her breasts as she came down on him with the vigour of a succubus. He lay awash between her thin thighs, drowning in those fluids. She probed her fingertip inside herself, her buttocks clenching. She threw her head back, her chin tilting into the light, panting, her lips open.

'Never do that again,' said Bellocq. He felt hollow, beaten, used, yet he knew he wanted her again already. She smiled, taking hold of his nose and twisting it. 'I mean it,' he said, as sternly as he could.

'I don't want to go away. I want to take care of you,' she begged.

Bellocq got off the bed. 'You can't stay here,' he said. 'You're a child; the police will soon come knocking on my door.'

Bellocq could fix the cops, she was sure. Mrs Kite always did. 'Tell them I'm your daughter,' she said. 'I'll never make any trouble, and you know how nice I can be.'

He could not put her out in the street at that hour. He turned away, only to feel her curl up at his back.

An awful idea struck him. Had she some intimate disease? He thought of his father, and saw the man in his coffin.

What could he do about it, if she had? He thought about the morning. He could not take her back to Mrs Kite. Before he fell asleep, he decided he would ask Danzig's advice.

Sylvie had gone when he woke. She had been in his tiny darkroom, broken some plates and scratched away

181

the faces of Adele, Bliss and others. How could he blame her? He tried to place the broken shards of a plate together. The finished jigsaw showed Sippie naked in black stockings. Her face was missing.

Sylvie had left a parcel. In it were two dresses – on one was pinned the 'Iron Cross' she had earned.

Two nights later, a grocer heard screams on Canal Street Wharf. He thought he saw a man run off. Whether Sylvie had jumped or the man had thrown her in the river, no one knew. Anna Kjeld, a new girl, said it was nothing Sylvie did at Mrs Kite's had drove her to it; no, no bullying officer was to blame. 'Some girls just want to die, and that's about all.'

The next day, Sprague left a message for Bellocq to meet him at the Franklin Street death house.

The nuns had left the religious card, the doctor told Bellocq. He folded Sylvie's hands, and remarked how she bit her nails.

Sprague came soon after. The two-tone shoes he wore were what a lowdown pimp sported. He took the sheet off Sylvie's body to find that the doctor had dressed her in a green alpaca chemise. 'Take that off,' Sprague ordered.

'No. They'll bury her decent,' said the doctor. 'Why do you want pictures of her naked? She drowned. Where's any foul play here?'

'Oh, you're sure about that, are you, Doctor?' Sprague said, with weary scorn. 'Just do as I say, or you'll be out of a job tomorrow.'

Bellocq always hated everything about the death house; the room's pale yellow bulb did nothing to brighten the gloom. There were dirty white tiles, a stench of corpses and disinfectant. An infant lay in the next alcove. The sickly aroma of the dying flowers begged from Poydras market followed Bellocq wherever he went. He could not look at Sprague, who was putting on a pair of cotton gloves.

Aware all along of what Bellocq had felt for Sylvie, Sprague relished his reaction as the doctor stripped off the chemise. Bellocq knew how the river treated bodies. He had not expected to recognize Sylvie. He was glad that she had been cleaned up. He was relieved, too, that they had brought her ashore before she had swollen. But what was left of her face was a puffy blue, cut up by her voyage, eaten by catfish. Bellocq had to swallow his vomit when he saw the deep clefts in her rotting feet.

'This has nothing to do with any investigation,' said Bellocq.

Sprague laughed; then, looking at his watch, said he didn't have all day. 'You do it, or I can cuff you and take you down the station to explain why you threw her in the river – but you didn't do that, did you?' He laughed again. 'No, not you, Mr Bellocq.' He spread Sylvie's legs to show the kind of photographs he wanted. Bellocq had used his own pictures of the dead girl in the same way, his gaze fixed, mouth open so that he heard his own breath, in a ritual to resurrect Sylvie, wanting her alive and eager to do those things it was too late now for her to do.

Sprague left, telling him to bring the prints to his office first thing next morning. As Bellocq packed his camera and plates away, he talked to Sylvie – not a corpse on a slab, but the girl frisking around his room. He did not know why, but he asked, did she recall the night Chenault came drunk to Mrs Kite's with a package the women helped him untie? How he had torn the muslin off, and it was a side of pork? How he took it up in his arms and waltzed it around the room, amid the giggling women? Why recall that? The vault whispered Bellocq's questions back as he saw the sow's tender nipples.

A man came hosing down the tiles along the passage. 'We had rain last night; the raft-men walked in a lot of mud.' He stared at a tin bath where Sylvie's ragged dress had been left to soak. 'The night they brought her in, two of them were swilling a bottle down, and they gave the third guy trouble to get them to do anything right − not that the poor girl was much to carry.'

Afterwards, Bellocq went down to the waterfront. A Victrola was playing aboard a charcoal schooner. He could smell banana boats unloading. There was nothing he had to account for, now that Sylvie had gone. He did not have to. Nothing could stop Sprague giving Mrs Kite the news, but Bellocq had his mind set on burying Sylvie. Anything else did not bear thinking about. 'You'll be sorry. You'll beg me to come back, you'll see − and I won't,' he heard Sylvie say.

The doctor turned a blind eye when Bellocq came with a handcart that night. He took her body down to the cemetery and hauled it up over the wall. He brought her to the vault where his mother lay. He closed his eyes, but there was no God to pray to. All he could cling to was the tuft of hair between Sylvie's legs.

8

Sippie Brooks and Josie came upstairs together, their arms loaded with Christmas presents.

Bellocq followed the girls into the parlour. 'Now look what you made me do,' wailed Josie. She raised a corner of the cardboard box she was carrying. 'I can't eat this gateau now; it's a mess!'

'Forget it, forget Christmas, too,' said Sippie. 'I need a drink. I've run myself ragged before it's even started.'

There were cards on strings across the walls. The air was laced with the scent of the tree, on which they began to hang more baubles.

'My God, he was not somebody you could buy off,' said Sippie.

'Are we trimming this tree or not?' Josie wailed.

It took Bellocq a while to realize that Sippie was talking about the Ripper. The girls could not help themselves, swapping stories each more horrible than the last. Bellocq, drawn in by their hysteria, could not stop listening however much he tried.

'They never caught him,' said Sippie. 'I hark back to that time when all of us thought the swine was right here, in this house.'

'Judas priest, don't talk about that!' Josie cried.

'He knew what those women had in their pockets: a broken comb, a bag of sweets, a stub of pencil, a spoon, a knife with a bone handle,' said Sippie.

He had those gruesome postcards he kept in his wallet – pictures of the rooms and alleys where he made out those women had been found. He used to tell about the kick he got among the crowds at railway stations every time the police brought in a suspect. Sippie could not say for sure he had been the Ripper, but it was possible, wasn't it? For all any of them knew, the Ripper could have been standing in any alley in any city.

'For Christ's sake, Sippie, you do go on! I don't want to hear any more.'

No, maybe he wasn't the Ripper, Sippie said, but he knew an awful lot about those killings. Besides, he had that leather bag and that dog-tooth hat with the earflaps – a deerstalker, he said. 'Mind you, I lose count of the freaks,' Sippie sighed. 'He was here three nights, and had a different girl each time. He half strangled one. She quit the next day.'

Ruby came in with a bunch of mistletoe to tie on the lightshade. Did she remember the john, Sippie asked?

'Never said his name.' Ruby got up on a chair. 'Did you know it?'

'None of us did, not as I recall,' Sippie answered. 'He made out he was a doctor. What the fuck did he know about medicine? He just got a kick out of scaring women.'

Sippie thought now that he had been a sideshow geek, the man who bites the heads off chickens. He stank worse than a polecat. 'There was a carnival in town that time. That's why he talked about the Ripper, and why he left the letter where we'd find it.'

Josie didn't know about the letter.

Written in red ink – that ink was the worst part for

186

Sippie – the letter was to a Mr Lusk. It had some stomach-turning horror about frying and eating a woman's kidney, and how the police were spoiling his game.

'Life is a mess of red herrings,' said Ruby. 'A guy you got a taste for and felt might have hung around awhile didn't and, anyway, those things always turn out bad – but this one, soon as he's gone, you tell yourself he might have cut you open as neat and fast as Jack ever did.'

Bellocq thought of Platt. Those wild horses came round again as he asked, 'Where is this letter now?'

Sippie shrugged. 'Mrs Kite'll have it somewhere. She hangs onto those things. She took it seriously for a while. I heard she was at the public library looking for books and newspapers. Ask her.'

'Men always take it out on women,' said Ruby. 'It gives them a hard-on to do that.'

'It's Christmas, for Christ's sake!' Josie did not want to hear any more about it.

Mrs Kite denied any knowledge of the letter. 'Those girls got nothing better to do than sit around all day making things up?'

Bellocq said that the books must still be open on those murders. 'They could charge you with withholding evidence.'

'You think so, huh? The man's dick was the size of a peanut, so he needed a gimmick.'

In her book, men were the natural enemy; they danced in front of women – jab, jab – the way boxers stood up to mirrors. Then they took them like dogs, anywhere, up against the side of a barn, on a kitchen table, in some muddy field. Men! She knew one built a cage for his wife in the corner of their parlour. He'd lock her up weeks, and not let her change her clothes. In the end, the bastard

187

stitched her vagina. He came to her house after the poor woman killed herself. He was in a bad way, saying he hadn't been the same since he got back from the war. 'He was sure one of my girls could save him from his worst impulses. Shit, he expected a lot.'

'Are we talking about Sprague?'

Mrs Kite's laugh was derisive. 'Sprague!' Her voice found a new level of spiteful contempt. 'Sprague has other problems. Was there a boy born who didn't want to fuck his mother?'

'I never did.'

'Well, bully for you! So, what are you trying to prove with your pictures? Do you like women, or what?' All men were in need of some time in a mental institution.

'You can't believe that.'

'I do. I never had a husband, and I take pride in that. Marriage has to be the final insult in a life of insult and injury.' She lay back on the sofa, closing her eyes. 'Why drag it all up? I'm tired, I don't want to go on with this.' After a flick or two with a black feather fan, she laid her hand on her brow and began to toy with the tassels on the light switch.

Two fat winged cupids, painted gold, seemed to fly out of the green wallpaper.

'What will you do?'

'About what?'

'If they close Storyville.'

'Retire, I guess. I couldn't put myself through it all again.' She sighed. 'A war starts, that's when men reveal their true faces. They get a sudden rush of blood to the head; they see the big profits, never mind the battlefield dead. You get a sudden spate of morality, too – and that's the excuse they use to shut us down, even though they need us most, then. There is worse to come, I feel sure. You can bet your life on that.'

All of them knew that nothing would come of Bascum Johnson's chinwag with Tom Anderson. Josephus Daniels would get his way in spite of that. Sure enough, the upshot was that the New Orleans City Council had to comply forthwith. 'Say what you like about Mayor Behrman, he has been a good friend to Storyville since 1904. He did get up to Washington to protest what the Navy Department was doing. It wasn't his fault they shut the door slam in his face, same as Daniels and President Wilson.'

In September, an order came from the military for the Council to close the District down, or the army would do it for them.

Bliss said, 'Somebody put on "Everybody's doing it", will you?'

That wasn't the piece they chose. They were soon laughing over a singer's wheedling complaint that her daddy wouldn't buy her a bow-wow. What was so funny about that, Ruby asked?

Josie was laughing. 'She's going to give up sex. She's a whore and she's going to give it up. Out of sight, out of mind? She'll drag her scut along until she's old and grey, glad of a dollar. Who does she think she's fooling?' she said.

Bellocq was with Ruby. 'Where will you go now?'

'Up north,' she said. 'There's plenty of johns with dough in Chicago.'

'Open a bar,' said Josie, 'get some help behind it, and sit around drinking Raleigh Rye all day.'

'I'm going to find out how much is in my pimp's bank account,' said Ruby. 'He saved fifty-five cents out of every dollar I made. I'll put my feet up awhile, turn a trick only if I feel like it.'

'Get out of this racket,' said Adele. 'Find some guy, have a family, raise some kids.'

Bliss got up, heading for the phonograph. She chose 'Oh, You Beautiful Doll'. 'I'm off someplace I can cut a fine figure – Saratoga, maybe,' she said. 'I'll run with the best of them, for a change.'

'From now on it's going to be aggravation all the way,' said Mrs Kite. 'Willie Piazza is off to France; says she'll live out her days on the Riviera. She'll never want for anything – she has enough dirt on the honest johns of this city for that.'

In October, the *Picayune* gave the insurance companies a helping hand. The paper knew for a fact that Basin Street was set on burning the brothels. An investigation turned up no evidence, but the companies reneged on their policies all the same.

There were yet more of those farewell parties, part business but chiefly pleasure. They would last three or four days now. Men came and went until the small hours; by then, the jazz was over and any leftover Negro was singing lowdown dirty blues. Bellocq would go home, but when he came again the same faces were still there.

'Chin-chin, Mr Bellocq,' Mrs Kite had said to him at some point. Then he heard her say, 'Get him off that couch. He can't stay on the landing all night!' When someone tried to take his glass he held on tight; they had to give up for fear it would break.

He saw a man in long johns wearing a cap with the earflaps down – hardly right for Crescent City. Some river rat whose face was old putty yellow. The man groaned as he bent over; his hand went to the small of his back. He said he'd overdone it.

'Overdone it! He had me on my knees all night, a goat ramming away! Pleurisy, he says, can you believe that?'

The man capered around, blaring '*Haw Haw*!' He slapped Anna Kjeld's buttocks as she went by in her gumboots and underwear.

Bellocq was still fully clothed when he awoke; sweat bathed his throat soon as he wiped it away. He got one arm out of his jacket sleeve, but fell back in a half swoon. The moon shone at the rear of the house now; a dwarf stood in its light. Bellocq felt for his father's watch. The dwarf gave a grinning nod as he found it, then turned away and was lost in the darkness at the head of the stairs.

The ringing of the hallway telephone woke him again. He listened, waiting for someone to reply, but no one did. When it stopped, he heard the kitchen door open and close.

He got up and went downstairs.

'What can I do for you, sweet thing?' Aphra asked. She hoped the johns up there with no home to go to weren't peckish, for she felt low and might keel over any second. Did he want some tea? It was herbal and was the best for fixing any blinding headache.

She had a frowsty look, having just got out of bed.

'Some know it, some do not, but we live in these whorehouses when we sleep,' she said. 'Our dreams are about them, even if they're gone the next morning. We've come to the end now, all of us. Our shoes are gonna pinch. Got to up and go — but where? A many men'll miss this crib — and their wives, for sure.'

The gooseberry tart sure was tart, but he was welcome to a slice. He better spoon on some sugar, or his tongue would cleave to the roof of his mouth and he'd lose skin to get it loose.

She squeezed a dish rag out and hung it beside the sink. He heard her fill the kettle, then the rub of her straw slippers across the tiles to the stove, where she set it down. A rank odour of wet rusty iron came from her underarms. The solid, scrubbed white drawers had brass handles set in metal recesses. He winced at the rattle as she opened one.

She said she was put in the St Louis orphanage to stay on the straight and narrow. Life was but a row of mean stitches, and she must never drop one! Sweet Jesus, her thighs ached she had to keep her knees so tight together, and was there ever enough light to see by?

The leaves still clung to the trees there, yet snow fell already.

Aphra lay down across the slab of marble, wide as the table. Said it was to cool her down.

'Any time you want, up until I let the stove go cold, you come again. I'll cook you something tasty,' she said. 'You need filling out.'

Some madams had already set up shop in other wards. Gertrude Dix brought an injunction to stop the City Council enforcing the writ. The State of Louisiana Supreme Court turned her down. Many of the brothels had already closed, and the police turned out in force to see off any protest. There was none.

Then the vultures came down to pick the bones; the something-for-nothing pikers got their hooks in.

Bliss was angry. 'They tell me Willie's white piano, the one Jelly Roll used to play, went for a dollar and a quarter!'

'You'd think we are a plague of rats they're driving out,' said Mrs Kite. 'They are all smiles now, but they'll learn – a whole lot of people are going to find out where the shoe pinches.' The cement that held Storyville together was old, and very hard. There were two thousand women busy there; most girls earned seventy or so dollars a week. That came to one hundred and forty thousand bucks a week. Every house – and there were around forty-five – bought in over a thousand dollars' worth of alcohol a month to sell at a big profit. Never mind the gambling money – she didn't know about that, but even a piano player had a thousand dollars a week in tips. Add the figures up any way you liked, her total came to something around a quarter of a million dollars a week – ten to fifteen million a year.

9

Smithline had a studio in the Quarter; elegant was the word. It had a wine-coloured velvet half-curtain on a brass rail. He would ask Bellocq to help out, mostly during Mardi Gras. 'We can make real money, then,' he said.

He had left a message at Beaubien's and, when Bellocq rang, asked whether he was free to earn five dollars photographing Charlie Einhorn's Red Hot Rolling Jazz Band? 'They need them for publicity.' He would provide the plates and paper.

It was coming up to two o'clock when Bellocq found Pete's barbershop, which Smithline said to look for – haircut twenty-five cents, and a shave fifteen. Five dusty Negroes were smoking on a bench out front; the one in overalls sat patching an inner tube over a pail. Next door a storefront chapel had a flight of rotting stairs built against the wall in the alley. Bellocq held tight to his camera, climbing until he stood on the landing near a humming telegraph pole.

There was a flaking sign – *Proprietor Gordon Tamblin, Jnr.* – but the name on the rusty mailbox in the alley said Bub Strother. Smithline opened the door to his knock. Below, a burst of idle applause came from the Negroes. Smithline waved, grinning over the handrail, before ushering Bellocq into a long attic where the walls and ceiling were draped with black cloth. Bellocq made out a skylight. It had been painted out. Apart from one bulb, any light there was filtered in from where slates were missing. A metal microphone and long strips of cloth hung from the rafters. Under the microphone were platforms, high and low. Mattresses against the wall made the air – stifling hot already – even closer.

Bellocq shook hands with Charlie Einhorn, piano player and leader, then met Sonny Briscoe on clarinet. The others were Negroes: a horn player called Pigfoot; Matt Severin, soprano saxophone player; Billy Tutt, trombonist and singer, Jody Clampert who played cornet; and a guitarist name of Broonzy. Philo White, on drums, fed a tame white rat with breadcrumbs. Bellocq had seen Billy Tutt and Clampert go by playing in funeral parades.

'Where's Mauvetu got to?' Einhorn took out his fob watch.

Muffled thuds and laughter came from the stairs. Smithline hauled a mattress aside and the door banged open. A black girl came strutting into the room, sniggering as she poked the palliasse with the toe of her shoe. 'You laid this in for us, sugar?'

194

Behind stood Bud Mauvetu, a huge Negro with a double-bass, darkening the doorway.

'What the fuck's she doing here?' Einhorn took the girl by the arm to show her the door. 'You know the rules about twists when we play.'

'Onie goes, you don't have a bass. You want that, Charlie?'

'She keeps her trap shut or I'll toss her down those stairs. Understand, Mauvetu?'

'You hear that, Onie?' Mauvetu said. Unless the girl behaved, he'd bust her in the mouth himself.

The Negroes' laughter was cordial. Onie went and sat down in a corner.

Some of the players sat three feet above Einhorn's piano and Philo White's drums, walled by mattresses. Broonzy, by the piano, had his guitar upright on his knee, turning to one side to let Mauvetu get his bass under the microphone. Billy Tutt, Severin and Clampert sat in front of them. Bellocq lost a great deal of what was said; they were using the *gumbo* patois.

Einhorn went over to Bellocq. 'Now we all got our asses on chairs, we better start,' he said. 'You take the pictures after the set.'

'Nothing will show up in this light,' said Bellocq. 'I need the skylight and the door open; if not, I can line you up outside the barbershop.'

Smithline crouched beside Bellocq. Billy Tutt's trombone was in use in an army band before he found it in a pawnshop, he said. 'Sounds as good as the day it was made.' Einhorn had been lucky to get Broonzy – the guy you could call the regular guitarist had gone to Tampa to see his sick sister. Another absentee was the cornet player Tommy Ladnier.

When the band hit their stride, Bellocq found it hard to keep up with the hectic massing of notes, the snatches of other numbers woven into the fabric. Suddenly, it all faded without trace; there was only the hum of the power cables and telephone lines outside. An engineer appeared from behind a screen to shift Briscoe next to Severin, so that he was under the microphone. 'You got us right, now?' Broonzy's tone was edgy as the engineer asked him to turn his body, his guitar, so that he could pick it out. Broonzy said he didn't feel at all happy sitting that way.

Einhorn set a pattern around which the players felt and found their way into solos. He was quite sure about what he wanted to hear, Smithline said. With the warm-up number over, the players had their breath. They were at ease – in touch with one another. Einhorn riffled a quick solo on the keyboard, leaning forward as if reading sheet music. The others exchanged grins. The recordist came out again to say what his buzzes were going to mean. One buzz would ready the band; on two they would start. 'Give it two beats in the head, first. You hear?' He was a harried white man with spectacles, sweating sourly in his shirtsleeves. 'We're in your hands here. You get it right,' said Einhorn coldly. All that the engineer left in his wake was unease on the platform.

Einhorn need not have worried about Onie. She was soon deep in a magazine she took out of her bag. The test needed cutting down – from five minutes to three minutes, six. The engineer was not happy at all; he was using his wax up too fast. Billy Tutt could not, would not, sing the same lyric for each master. 'Let's get it right, boys,' Einhorn said. 'Let's get the thing done this time round. There's nothing you need do except the same thing again. I can feel it moving fine.'

To anyone schooled in classical music, jazz could not but seem too free; it broke the rules. It was an exciting sound, though Bellocq found it hard to follow. Yet, at times, Clampert's cornet had the shrill, brazen tone of any in Bach.

The number ended with Billy Tutt singing wild and high, and, as the last bars of the number died away, Philo White let loose on his drums. Pigfoot tooted his horn, and the band rolled into a march, playing way off the beat, calling out the names of dead New Orleans musicians. Gradually the great machine seemed to slew round and fade into silence.

Charlie Einhorn took a handkerchief from his breast pocket, shook it out, held it by the corners and waved it back and forth. Then, leaning back, he let it drop over his face with a laugh. 'What the fuck, who's going to pay to hear a noise like that? That was for burying rascals, and I think we did it pretty good.'

Bellocq and Smithline undraped the skylight. Bellocq told the players where he wanted them to stand. The sound Einhorn and the others had scored into wax would be there for a listener to extract at any time. Bellocq wanted his photographs to match; he wanted to capture the event with chemistry, lock the light, the day's heat and stillness into the emulsion.

All done, he opened the door for a breath of air. A youth perched on an Andrews Coal Company cart looked up from the alley. Seeing Bellocq, he sang out to his mule, 'Come up, Lady, we got places to go.'

Smithline's suits were three-piece now, with box-back jackets and two-tone shoes. The barber slicked his hair down with scented oil. Someone was taking an interest in his looks. Back at the studio he told Bellocq he was getting married.

'Isn't that bigamy?'

'Who do you plan to tell?' Smithline laughed, preening in the mirror, as he smoothed his hair. 'You're not going to grudge me a little happiness so late in life?'

'Who is the lady?'

'All I can play is the hand that fate dealt – who can do more?' The lady had a sugar-daddy, an outfit boss – *capo*, she called him. He would kill them both if he found out. Smithline was worried by strange telephone calls that came in the night; nobody said a word – just heavy breathing. Sometimes he woke with a feeling there was a prowler in the studio. 'What those guys do, they shoot you in the leg, in the belly, then put one in your head. I have to take care of this Paolo Lippi or get myself killed.'

'Take care of him?'

Smithline opened his coat. There was a pistol under his arm, in a bright yellow holster. He had to carry it to protect himself, but was not sure he could use it if the time came.

'So, how do you plan to do it?'

'Look for some guy outside the rackets and pay him for the job,' said Smithline. He leant down to peer through the window. 'Here she comes now!'

It was Bliss pulling up to the kerb – older, perhaps, but clearly Bliss. Her dress was powder blue and her cloche hat had a turquoise buckle on the sash brim. She began to take hatboxes and parcels off the rear seat. 'One thing I know,' said Smithline admiringly, 'that is one hell of an extravagant twist!'

Bliss turned to head for the studio, and saw Bellocq. Never at a loss for what to do, she smiled and waved for him to come out.

Smithline shook his head. 'It's you she wants out there!'

Before Smithline had time to think, Bellocq left. Bliss kissed his cheek and heaped parcels into his arms. 'Say nothing,' she hissed.

Bellocq shook his head. 'I had no idea you knew him.'

'Some guys hate to find out that a girl has been through the Storyville mill. Say we met on the river; that's no lie.'

Bellocq turned, hearing Smithline open the door.

'I didn't know you knew Mr Bellocq, Ethan,' Bliss said. 'We ran into each other on the *Tennessee Queen* long ago. Ask him up for a drink, baby. I brought you tequila. I know you like that. Just give me a moment to tidy the room.'

'On a riverboat?' Smithline frowned.

'You remember,' said Bellocq, 'I worked for the Foundation Company – I was on business for them; Bliss had been to a wedding in Cairo.'

Bliss called to Smithline to hang a closed sign on the door.

She had not tidied much – underwear, corsets, silk stockings hung out of half-closed drawers. Nothing changed. Her room had been the same at Mrs Kite's.

Bliss drank off a quick one to steady her nerves. She was sure some gorilla had been tailing her, one of Paolo's men. She had run like billy-o until she got to the car. Smithline was at the window looking out. She shook her head. 'I wouldn't have come if I hadn't given him the slip!'

'Bliss says to leave – and go where? I'm not running,' said Smithline. He had too much at stake in New Orleans, and he couldn't give the jazz up.

'Ethan thinks he's proof against anything,' said Bliss. 'He doesn't know Lippi.'

'I have to take a leak,' said Smithline, humming his way along the landing.

'You gave me a start, but it was good to see you, Mr B.,' said Bliss. She turned to him, now distant, asking, 'Who were we, then, do you know? I don't any more.'

'Are you in touch with the others?'

'I hear nothing of Mrs Kite. Josie died last autumn. Ruby is in a hole in Poughkeepsie – I send her a few dollars now and then. Adele stopped using opium, but she sniffs bernice now, cocaine. She's in a hurry, but God knows where she's going. I see Anna Kjeld from time to time. The door closed. Some of them think they can hear music in the ice cubes still; they drink to keep it going.'

'Who is this Paolo Lippi?'

'I met him at Mrs Kite's. I saw him on and off, until he went back to New York. I was at the racetrack a couple of years ago, not long after the District closed down, and there he was. A bigshot! Ethan thinks I've been living with him all along.'

Lippi disappeared a week later. The news gave Smithline a fit. 'I'll have to hide out until he turns up. There was a cop came round yesterday to talk to Bliss.'

After he left Smithline's studio, Bellocq's nose started to bleed. He bought some ice in Poydras Market. When he got home, Mrs Ahada told him she had come in to find the door open. Somebody had been upstairs making noises in his rooms. Bellocq told her he could not think why, or what they were looking for. Vulnerable and afraid, he went for a drink in the bar over the road.

'Somebody bust your nose, Mr Bellocq,' the barkeep said, aiming his finger.

'No.' Bellocq looked at himself in the mirror.

The barman wrapped ice in a cloth. 'I tried that,' said Bellocq.

'Was it the guy here looking for you?'

'Did you know him?'

'He was here. Asked if I knew you.'

'What did you say?'

'He was the one?'

Bellocq said no, his nose bled at the slightest thing.

The barman said he was glad about that, since he had given the stranger Bellocq's address; he was Italian. 'Said he was looking for a photographer.'

Afraid to stay in the apartment now, Bellocq told Mrs Ahada to telephone the police if the man came back. Packing a suitcase, he left, making sure he was not followed, and booked into a hotel.

The bellboy seemed familiar. 'Don't I know you?' Bellocq asked.

'Sure, Mr Bellocq. It's Abe. I ran errands for the Foundation Company. They fired me after their stuffed pelican got stolen.'

Bellocq felt Miriam's presence at the window again. He realized with a pang how rarely now she came to mind. Abe was no longer the haunted street urchin whose suit was too short in the leg; he had filled out, his old, natural cunning had taken on a fresh knowing smartness. He had white gloves tucked under the shoulder strap of his monkey suit.

Abe came along the corridor with Bellocq and the porter. The tray of drinks he carried was for a guest across the hall. He was a naval lieutenant, and his hand shook as he signed the tab. A woman in the room called out, 'Ask if he has the time.'

'Do you?'

'It had just gone six when I came up,' Abe said.

'Here's a couple of cents; don't spend it all at once.'

Abe tipped a salute. He stood by the door of Bellocq's room as the porter set the suitcase down.

'You come into money you live in a hotel now, Mr Bellocq?'

'My stay here is temporary.'

'Same as mine.'

'Why, what do you plan to do?'

'Right now, the best I can,' said Abe. 'I was lucky I got this berth when I did. You know I could sell it tomorrow for a thousand dollars? Only way I could make more is to be a pimp. I've been run off my feet since the District closed down – so has every other bellboy. You don't see that girl?'

'No.'

'The Hechts left that house.'

'Did they? I don't go down that way. Do you know where they went?'

Abe shook his head. 'Forget all that, Mr Bellocq. I can get you a girl who'll do it standing on her head if you want, just say.'

Bellocq laughed. 'You know what a pimp is, then?'

'I got wise, Mr Bellocq. One day I'll own a swell house.'

'Somehow, I believe you will.'

The room had a brown sunken easy chair, with orange piping hanging loose. The standard lamp was a dusty, fly-flecked flambeau. The small electric fan on the table did little to cool the air. Bellocq opened the desk and took out the Bible. The text said it all: *I know thy works, that thou art neither cold nor hot: I would thou wert cold or hot.*

202

So then because thou art lukewarm, and neither cold nor hot, I will spue thee out of my mouth.

The hotel was behind the Vitascope on the corner of Canal and Exchange Place – where Bellocq had seen *The Life Drama of Napoleon and Empress Josephine of France*. The place had moved with the times and it had a projection room now. With the window half-open he could hear the pianist during the battle scenes, strumming threat and passion.

From his room, he could see the projectionist, a man alone whose life seemed unenviable. He cranked the film reels, steamed the glass up making coffee, then paced between the two windows as he drank it. Sometimes he sat outside in the shadow of the fire-escape. All this until, late in the afternoon, an usherette came into the booth.

She took off her cap and ran her fingers through her hair while the projectionist poured a drink. Then, off came her stockings and uniform, folding them neatly on the table while the man played with his erection. One foot on his thigh, she sat astride him; his hands held her buttocks as she slid down on him.

These encounters went on seven days a week. Bellocq bought a pair of opera glasses. They only made things worse, more tantalizing. He felt he had survived a shipwreck and he was using the glasses to pick out the flotsam and jetsam that would keep him alive. He knew the room better than his own, so intent was his gaze. Above the reels hung a rusty fan made in Milwaukee. As he inched his glasses over the wall, a calendar riffled in the breeze, the cornfields of an open prairie dancing to the movement of the fan. The usherette stood by the window, shaking ticket stubs out of her pocket. Loosening her belt, she took off her skirt and undid the rubber buttons which held her stockings up. Bellocq had the same view as the man's bloodshot eyes, two pairs of lips bluish in the light.

Sometimes she came in before the film started, all hasty fingers and thumbs as she tore off her uniform. She came again after the show. People lived secret lives all over the city, lives he could never share except by their smell, their shadow, their sound.

Close up, through the glasses, the projectionist was ugly. But he was blessed. How could a man so haggard and worn stand ready twice a night?

The man Bellocq found in his room wore a dinner jacket with a diamond-studded horseshoe tie-pin. He was looking at the photographs. He said his name was Tony Laudati, and Bellocq had nothing to fear. The maid had let him in. 'This one of the girl with the butterfly, I like,' he said. 'You posed her there, but why? She was drawing the butterfly on the wall, or was it already there? Why was she doing that?'

Laudati got up, revealing his club-foot as he moved towards Bellocq.

'Those Storyville days were good times. You caught all those backstage goings-on pretty good. Are you as happy now, Mr Bellocq? We were looking for you at Mrs Ahada's.'

'Yes, she said that.'

'So why are you hiding out here?'

'I was afraid you might come back.'

'Afraid?' Laudati laughed. 'Yes, I think so. So, where are Bliss and Smithline?'

'I don't know.'

'I'll ask again, because I have to be sure you understand what that means.'

'I do, Mr Laudati.'

Bellocq said he had never had much to do with Smithline, and how he had met him in El Paso. He saw him rarely now, mostly when the man put work his way.

'That Bliss was always going to be bad news,' said Laudati, 'but Paolo — you could never tell him anything.'

Some people sang opera when they saw Paolo's body. They called for blood. Some were so mad they didn't care whose blood it was. None of them would sleep until they spat on the grave of Paolo's killer. Laudati knew that a lot of that was for display. Sure, they came to press his hands, but he'd had little comfort and, so far, he had none to give.

Never mind that, his feelings ran deep, and he had to see justice done. He and Paolo were born on the same street, the same block, even. Paolo had not died straight off. Someone cut your throat you had a little time to look at the moon. Nothing could be worse than lying there alone, looking at the moon. Dying men had done that since time began, and none of them was any the wiser. He swung round. 'Do you get headaches? I have them so bad some days I go to bed and dose myself with painkillers. I say this because I'm not here to argue. I want things to go smoothly between us. Okay?'

Bellocq said he could understand that.

'No need to be afraid.' Laudati gave Bellocq's arm a pat. 'I'm going to buy you a coffee at a place I know. It's nice there, and you won't be so nervous. It's just around the corner, and we can talk.'

Bellocq's terror grew with each step. He tried not to stare at Laudati's club-foot as he ducked awkwardly under the washlines. There was a fence of bedheads wired together, chicken feathers flying everywhere. A black woman swung a pump handle to fill a pail. Easing up, she pressed her fists into the small of her back and stared. Her husband loomed in the doorway in a vest and pants, a towel around his neck. He told the woman to bring her pail into the house.

Afraid he was about to die, Bellocq was almost sick. He tried to listen to what Laudati was saying. How it was for the Italians in Crescent City – and everywhere in America. Having to learn a new language, yet few of them could stop dreaming in their own. Bellocq would appreciate that: his accent said so. They had their customs, their ways. They were aliens in a strange country – the grit in the oyster. No immigrant, so far as he knew, had a hand in writing the Constitution.

'Take a look around here. You see a lot of people who have nothing better to do than wait to die, Mr Bellocq.'

The café had an Italian name, but the man behind the counter had no accent. 'I didn't ask for this pie,' an old woman was saying. 'I ordered tea and a slice of the raspberry tart. I said it plain.'

The owner waved the waitress's pad to prove his point.

'See that, it says apple. Why is that?'

'She got it wrong, that's why. I don't like apple.'

'*Padrone*,' said Laudati, going over and giving the counter a rap to gain attention. 'Let the lady have what she wants.'

'Well, who are you?'

'Just give her what she asks, okay?' Laudati spoke each word as a threat. The owner scraped what was left of the pie off the plate and put raspberry in its place. Laudati gave it to the woman. 'That's perfect, huh?'

An old woman craning out from the kitchen serving-hatch pursed her lips and shook her head.

Sitting down with Bellocq again, Laudati said, 'These old ladies get confused. Is your mama still alive?'

'I must go,' said Bellocq.

'Go where?'

'I have to be sick.'

'There's no way out through there.'

Laudati was right. Bellocq held the edge of the bowl tightly. He retched, gagging a few times, but could get nothing up out of the acid turmoil of his stomach. Splashing his face under the cold water, he was about to use the roller towel but the stink of it put him off. He took out a handkerchief.

The man at the corner table was familiar. It was only when he took out a fob watch to see the time that Bellocq realized he was the Vitascope projectionist. Waiting for the usherette? Suddenly the man got up to come over. 'Do you know me?'

Bellocq shook his head as he moved in closer.

'Then why stare as if you do!'

'He doesn't,' Laudati put in. 'Go away, unless you should want I break your arm.'

Laudati leant back in his chair as the man turned for his table. 'You owe him money. Is that it?'

Bellocq said no.

'I know you are short. So, there will be dough in it for you, if you find out where they're hiding. Some compassion is in order. Think of it that way. Paolo was more than a good friend, he was family. Nothing will happen to Smithline if he's innocent. We just want to clear him of Paolo's murder.'

'I've told you, I don't know where he is.'

'Maybe yes, maybe no; but there are ways. We think he's still in the city. All his jazz friends are here. Are they

207

hiding him? You've known Bliss a long time, you know both these people better than we do.'

Someone the projectionist had been expecting came into the café. Bellocq turned, anticipating the usherette. It was the man's wife, laden down with shopping. Her thick eyebrows grew together above her nose. She was a woman who put a thing down, then had to pat it to make sure. The projectionist had no interest in what she had bought. His mind was elsewhere – with the usherette? The disturbing thing about his wife was that she used her hand to cover her mouth, in the shy way of Chinese women.

The old woman took a last mouthful of raspberry tart. She raised her fork in salute to Laudati as he lit a cigar at the gas jet on the counter. In the street, a man turned a barrel-organ. A woman threw back her head to sing an aria from *Madame Butterfly*. She was trying to outdo the knife-grinder's cry: 'Step right up, folks; step right up! Sharpen your hatchets here! Your knives! Come on down and get an edge; get keen!'

'Think of me as a friend you are doing a favour – that will help,' said Laudati, handing Bellocq his card. 'This is a number you call as soon as you have something to tell me. If I can do anything, just ask.' He sniffed the air, head nodding to the aria. 'I shall miss this city when I go. *Buona fortuna*, Mr Bellocq.'

Bellocq sent Abe down to buy a newspaper. The front page had a picture of Lippi's coffin at the railway station. Inset was a photograph of his wife, Irma. She looked like a glum diva – certainly she was as stout. She had seen it all, and her eyes were dead. Tony Laudati stood beside the flower-laden casket, which she was taking to New York.

Abe knocked later to say that Smithline was on the

telephone. He was in jail. The police had arrested him and Bliss boarding a train for New York. Could Bellocq hire him a good lawyer? The police were saying that the two of them had killed Paolo Lippi.

Sprague was on the front steps, talking to another man from the police department. 'I got a call,' said Bellocq. 'You have Smithline under arrest as a murder suspect.'

Sprague pushed open the gate that led to the offices and holding cells.

'If Smithline didn't do the job himself, he knows who did,' Sprague's companion said.

'What about that?' Sprague lit a cigar.

'He's not my friend,' complained Bellocq. 'He was an associate.'

Sprague said, 'You mean those pictures you took of Charlie Einhorn? You came close to breaking the law there.'

Bellocq laughed. 'Photographing a jazz band?'

'If Einhorn has two girls grinding for his fancy clothes, he has a dozen,' said Sprague. 'Aside from that, I hate the slick Jew bastard, and I'm going to hurt him, one of these days. Be careful — you run with all the wrong people.'

'I don't understand what you are trying to say. What does all this have to do with anything?'

'He means that you are failing in your civic duty,' said the other detective, coldly. Then, turning to Sprague, 'I thought you said this guy would be a help.'

'I don't have to put up with this,' said Bellocq. 'I have a right to talk to Smithline.'

'Are you his lawyer?' Sprague spun round and struck Bellocq with his fist. He fell on his backside, jammed into a corner, the blood spurting through his fingers. Sprague blew on his knuckles, then pinched Bellocq's cheek and

209

gave it a slap. 'You don't want to piss us about, unless you want more. Who did Smithline pay to do it?'

'You know Paolo Lippi was screwing Bliss Davenport,' said the detective.

Sprague rounded on Bellocq. 'What about Bliss? She has a car.'

Bellocq did not know what to say except to blurt out that Sprague had known her too. 'Can you see Bliss having anything to do with Lippi's death?'

'She was a Storyville whore; she couldn't tell the truth to save her life,' said Sprague, waving to a turnkey. 'Think it over in a cell.'

'What you doing here? Having a bad dream, huh?'

The man sighed, fingers rustling along the wall of the cell; then, as the sound of his stick grew surer, Bellocq heard cockroaches pop under his shoes, and the hiss he gave each time.

'I don't know. I came to bail a friend out.'

'Who would that be?'

'Ethan Smithline.'

'The guy cut Lippi's throat?'

'Ethan couldn't do that.'

'One thing you better not do is piss on the floor, no matter what. It's against regulations. I hear that snuffle. Who bust your nose?'

'It doesn't take much for it to bleed.'

'That no-good piece of crap Sprague, huh?'

The man seemed to detect Bellocq's nod.

'Ask to see Lieutenant Judge. He's the man – except he's out of town right now.'

A prisoner sobbed in the dark.

An Irish felon homesick for the Emerald Isle, said

Bellocq's cellmate, before shouting, 'Stow that!' He turned back to Bellocq. 'We all need a sense of humour in a crib like this.'

'Are you a seaman?'

'Sure, and anything else besides.'

'What did you do for them to put you in here?' Bellocq asked.

'I drink to forget I got no wife, nor a place to live. You don't have a cigarette?'

'No.'

'A cigar?'

'No.'

'Not even chewing tobacco?'

The man sighed again, faced about and went to sit down in the corner of the cell.

The stench said that a lot of prisoners had broken the regulations recently. Bellocq closed his eyes. He did not know how long he had been there when he heard a door unlocked and the footsteps of the turnkey. He took Bellocq back to the office where Sprague had hit him.

Smithline stood at attention in front of Sprague's desk, his face as grey as alkali dust. He needed a shave, had no tie and held his muddy jacket tucked under his arm. Seeing Bellocq, he whined, 'Listen, did you get a lawyer? You can't let them do this. How could I do a thing like that?' Bellocq did not want to reply. He had no idea what Smithline did, or didn't, do.

Quail hunters had found Lippi's body out on the road to Thibodaux. He had only his vest and pants on. A wild boar had eaten his pecker and balls, and torn a piece out of his leg. Lippi had Smithline's card tucked in his vest. 'I keep telling them, I hand cards out all the time. I swear to God, I had nothing to do with it.'

211

Sprague's colleague asked, 'What did it cost you, then?'

'All that was just hot air,' Smithline said, staring at Bellocq.

'I don't believe either of you. You're not worth a damn,' said Sprague.

'I have no jurisdiction here, Sergeant Sprague,' said the detective. 'I can't tell you how to run the show. All I want is to close the book on Lippi. I'd say we're on the wrong track here. I don't believe the woman or either of these two had anything to do with Lippi's death.'

Bliss and Smithline talked to the papers on their release. Asked what their plans were, Bliss said they would marry quickly. She came to Bellocq to help her choose a trousseau. She said she needed his advice, and had always trusted his eye.

Bellocq said she would be beautiful in anything, even a man's suit.

'Don't say that. I know how I look. I used to wear one in a combination I did – don't remind me.'

Ethan was worse than useless at such things and, besides, she could not let him see the dress – her luck was bad enough already.

Bellocq went with her to see her try on several, then shook his head. 'You're right,' said Bliss. 'Better I get Bess Nunley to make one up.'

'If we are going to do it on the bias, we can cut to your shape, bring out your curves,' said Mrs Nunley.

'You know I hate my neck, Bess. It's all wrong – too thick. I'd rather keep it hid. Some see-through stuff to come up under my chin, I think.'

Mrs Nunley led the way into a back room where she

offered them a glass of port. 'Is it okay to do your bust with him here?'

'You are joking?' Bliss laughed. Mrs Nunley slipped a tape measure under her arms, and round her hips and waist; then she began to pin paper patterns.

Bellocq was intent on Bliss's red nails as she began to pick over the bolts of material Mrs Nunley spread. He saw only the hands, deaf to what the women were saying. Rank sweat came in waves off the two black girls working sewing machines; a younger one stitched with needle and thread. Bliss was saying, 'You see, that bastard Paolo had a wife all along. I used to pride myself on being able to spot a married man, but I erred there.'

'Is this Mr Smithline up to the job?'

'Why, Bess Nunley, you surely don't think I'd tattle about that!'

Bliss asked Bess Nunley archly how long they had known each other, then said the only thing she kept from Ethan was her Storyville stint.

'Those were the days, huh?' Mrs Nunley sighed.

'What he doesn't know won't hurt him.'

'You think so?'

One of the girls took her foot off the treadle. The wheel idled to a stop. The other two burst out giggling; Mrs Nunley hit the table with a ruler and told them to get on with it. 'Trade fell right off soon as it closed down,' she said. 'The only blessing is that I keep girls now. I used to lose them in droves to those sporting houses.'

Bliss laughed. 'You should have paid them more.'

Again, Bliss seemed to think that it was part of the best man's duties to go with her for the fitting, to oversee the hairdo, to help choose the chaplet of white flowers.

213

Bellocq learnt he had known nothing about Bliss or her aspirations in the narrow milieu of Mrs Kite's. The only detail that jarred, and he said so, was the red sash round her waist. 'It's too late to change that now!' She was in a fluster as she took up the bouquet.

Bliss left nothing to chance; everything about the ceremony was meant to see off any gossip. The carriages were hung with flowers and ribbons, and the drivers wore eighteenth-century livery. Smithline could have afforded only a fraction of the cost. It was Bellocq's guess that Bliss had been salting away Lippi's money for some time.

Anna Kjeld was the one guest from Bliss's past, and she was sworn to secrecy. Smithline had not wanted her to come; there was that something about her that rang false. Bliss was adamant, and got her way. Anna held the same arcane place in her affections as Elzadie. 'Anna was my friend long before I met you. Unless she comes, I won't be there.'

Bliss could do nothing about the weather. Rain fell all night, and did not let up until after the carriages left Jackson Square. Bellocq could hear the thud of raindrops on the banana trees; a mangy stray, dragging its tail between its legs, stood to watch the parade go by. Without his knowing why, the image of Marta, swaying back and forth in her straitjacket, or reading the Bible Smithline had left her in her rat hole, came into Bellocq's mind. How long did inmates live in those places?

Smithline had hired Cajun fiddlers from Jefferson Parish for the waltzes and the slow numbers, but Charlie Einhorn's band was there, too. Charlie's bowler was tilted raffishly over his right eye, and he sported a diamond in his front tooth. He took out a cigar case, offering Bellocq a smoke before lighting one himself. Two girls were with him: Carmen, tall, thin and black – also a nervy white girl whose name Bellocq missed. She told him she used to be a waitress. 'You know, that was a nice job you made taking our pictures,' said Einhorn. 'It was a pity they spoiled that record; it never saw the light of day. That's the story of my life. Things never turn out the way I want. Maybe we could get together some other time.'

Mauvetu's Onie went around saying that any wedding she was ever at would end in fireworks, people beating each other up with real blood in their eyes. She paused to let the words sink in, then went on to tell some other guest.

'Ruby coughs night and day now,' Anna confided to Bellocq. 'I don't want to say the word, but I think she has tuberculosis.'

'Holy Mother Mary and Joseph!' said Father Faul. 'What in Hades did you put in the punchbowl, Mr Smithline?'

Bellocq was relieved that he had already taken the wedding portraits. Marta's face would not go, nor those of other people in places they could not escape. He felt faint and confused. He had drunk enough to want to confess that he had suffocated his mother. Where to start?

'This is not the time or place to hear confession.' Father Faul shook his head. 'You come and speak to Guersaint in the appropriate place, Mr Bellocq.'

A couple brushed past Bellocq talking in a haze of smoke. The woman was saying, 'I asked him, is that so hard a pill to swallow? Then he got it all, how it was going to weigh heavy against him.'

Chenault was playing billiards in an anteroom. He had kept his head during the catering arrangements, but he was the worse for drink, now, he said. He told Bellocq he knew who killed Paolo Lippi. 'Lippi had the markets in his pocket, the fruit trade too. When he tried to cut himself a slice of our meat, two butchers took him for a ride. They had to do it, or his boys would do it to them. When the Lippis of this world get their teeth into you, you pay for ever. He took it well, I hear. Those outfit *capos* have to live with the prospect every day. You know what they made him do?'

Bellocq shook his head.

'On his knees, he had to kiss their feet. Not very nice – they had their work boots on. Right then, just as he did it, they cut his throat.'

'Who were they?'

'One was not quite right in the head. Probably why he got the job.'

'Who chose him?'

'Somebody takes these decisions.'

'Who?'

'I don't think you'd want to know, E. J. Ask why they didn't drop him in the river, though. Surely it would have been an easier way to get rid of the body?'

'Well?'

'He was lucky we didn't feed him to a couple of rats.'

'Rats?'

'You starve them, then strap the cage between his legs. They eat their way in. The idea was left open – if a hog did take a bite out of him, it would warn the rest off.'

Bellocq realized suddenly that Chenault had been privy to the killing; but he did not want to hear him confirm he had been present at the death. Chenault said it was all much the same thing. 'You put it all together, you could even write it down; it doesn't give it a smidgen more of a meaning.'

Carmen looked up from the mirror, then pinched her nose. She had been sniffing a line of white powder with a straw. 'I can't pretend any more. I've wasted my life doing that, with one man or another. You got a wide-eyed look. What's your mind? Spit it out.'

'Nothing; nothing at all.'

She laughed. 'If you don't want my peaches, better not shake my tree.'

She glanced over to Einhorn at the piano. 'Charlie tries so hard. He wants to be Tony Jackson,' she said. 'That glass of whiskey on the lid, well, that's all for show, too. Booze doesn't mean a lot to him – or anything else, get right down to it – but Tony drinks, see. Dressing like him is part of it; one thing he isn't is a black fruit. It's all a dream, and those never come true for Charlie. Tony is a natural, and good-natured with it. As to the piano, well, we all know Tony can drive it hot with anything, from opera to blues. Charlie earns a living, is the best you can say.'

Carmen went to the ladies' room when Charlie took a break. He came over, glanced at the table, and shook his head. 'That woman costs more than she's worth, or I can afford,' he said. If he'd known she was kicking the gong when she was fourteen, he would never have brought her to New Orleans.

'Well, what about all these flowers?' Anna Kjeld's voice was too brittle. 'Is it their perfume that's making me feel giddy?'

'You're talking champagne,' Smithline said coldly.

'Do I know you, darling?' Charlie stroked Anna's cheek.

Anna drew back as if a hornet had stung her, a hot pink spot where he had touched.

Charlie shook his head as she stalked off.

'What was that about?' Smithline asked.

'Beats me. I've seen her somewhere, though.'

It was never long before Smithline got to jazz. 'Some good people are hanging on, but the bands are lost without the houses and the honky-tonks.'

'Easy there, Ethan, it's old Charlie here you're talking to.'

'Well, you know as well as I do about those flashy solos up in Kansas and Chicago. They'll ride the rails on to New York, where the record companies have all the big sticks now. The further jazz goes, the worse it seems to sound. I can't tell you what happened. Did it lose its roots? It lost the tribes in Africa, and what was left of them in Congo Square.'

'Sure, the *joie de vivre* has leached out of some things,' said Einhorn. 'So, what else is new? What I mean is that jazz was *low* and dirty, and some of the fellas who played it had to go up against every rule their daddies made. They were working stiffs who did it for the hell of it, the joy of the thing. A lot paid the price. Buddy Bolden gone loco, throwing fits and walking in his own shit up in the asylum. Now, everybody the world over is wild for it, and the phonograph is going to make some people rich, but not us musicians.'

'Is there a full moon?' Bliss strode up and down. 'Is that why I have this feeling crawling round my neck? You seen Anna anywhere?'

Bellocq said how he had been looking to find something in the cupboard the other day and come off a ladder.

Grabbing at the first thing to hand, it was a cardboard box full of his old prints. Everything came down, and he lay there under faces from Mexico to Chinatown – 'You, Bliss, and Adele, and the other women. The last time I had control over my life was when I took *photographs*. I could leave things out I didn't want to see.'

'None of us can hide from change by buying new chair covers,' said Bliss. 'Other than that, I don't know what you do.' Then, suddenly: 'Where's Chenault?'

Bellocq went with her towards the billiard room.

'Well, for Christ's sake, can you believe this? Not at my wedding, Anna – how could you?' Bliss crouched under the table shrieking. Anna Kjeld had her thighs locked up around Chenault's ears. 'I'm going to turn my back and count to five. If you're not out of there by then, I'll beat you out with a broom.'

Bellocq had a glimpse of it in the mirror: Anna, naked to the waist, coming up from under the table with pink breasts and cheeks. Bliss smacked her face.

'Whoa, Bliss, no need for that, now!' Chenault ordered.

'Jesus, you hit me, Bliss?' Anna had tears on her cheek. 'Nobody could see under there. It was nothing strenuous. You know yourself these things take but a minute.'

'That damned Carmen sniffing it right in front of where I stood! What do you all think this is? Well, it's my one and only wedding day! Christ, what happens next – rats run out to eat my cake? No, Anna, I don't want to hear any more. Just go.'

Chenault had Anna on his arm, going out as stately as she could.

Bliss closed her eyes and leant back against the table with a tight smile. 'You think you'll get a kiss on the ass. You didn't know, but I was going to hire an actress to play my long-lost mother for the day. I got cold feet when I realized that Ethan would expect her to keep it up.'

Bellocq felt sour when he woke. A breeze shook the palm fronds, and the net curtains shimmered as they rose and fell, the sunlight coming and going. Two white doves billed and cooed under the tree that overhung the yard, where a dog lay panting in the shade. It raised its head, then let it fall with a shuddering sigh. Bellocq was back in those evenings, the last days of the District – that last night he had seen Albert Jomy.

Bellocq had told Albert he would go with him to the railway station, he remembered. He'd been in time to see his friend jump down off an army truck, with rifle and kitbag. Albert had held up a bundle. 'I haven't looked but I guess there's food in here. My sister won't hear of me eating army rations.'

'I had no idea about this until Beaubien told me you'd enlisted,' said Bellocq. 'I was sure it was a joke. I never believed you would.'

'I thought I was over the hill, but they said I was A1.'

'If I had known, I would have brought a camera.' Jomy made a joke of putting on his army gas-mask there and then, plucking nervously at his chinstrap.

Bellocq said that a uniform made him look younger, yet mature. 'You joined the army to get girls, Albert,' he said.

The one-legged soldier in a tattered uniform, a medal on his coat, sat beside a large pastel outside the church. It was a copy of Watteau's *Voyage to Cythera*; it had taken him the best part of a month. Later, he said, he would cover it with a tarpaulin and sleep there. He had a sign asking for two bits. His pallid chest was bare; every rib stood out. He had no teeth, and had hacked his hair short. 'If you get away with being shot, that's the fate awaiting you, Albert,' said Bellocq.

'Maybe so, but I'd rather not hear you say it.'

Bellocq embraced him. 'Take care of yourself.'

With Albert off to fight the Kaiser, influenza had broken out in the city. The epidemic had not abated until the end of 1918.

All Smithline knew was that it had been some party at an out-of-work musician's crib in the Garden. Einhorn had stopped in before he went off to play aboard one of the Streckfus Brothers' boats. There was a ruckus over money. Some guy was trying to shake Charlie down, and then a fight broke out, razors flashing. Charlie had always tried to make out he was a hard man, but he was gentle, really. Fisticuffs, or any sign of trouble, he faded. So, it was Carmen pulled the .22. She put the fear of God into the guy with the razor, and he tried to jump her. The gun went off. The bullet blew Charlie's diamond tooth clean out and struck up through the roof of his mouth into his brain. He lingered in the Charity awhile, not knowing where he was until he died. 'Carmen's out on bail,' said Smithline. 'I haven't seen her, and I don't know where she is. She may have skipped town already. She's scared sick she'll drag a cotton sack on some farm the rest of her life.'

Smithline could not lift his head. The funeral was due to leave from the corner of Liberty and Perdido, where they stood. There was a bass drum sounding already to start things off. Only half the musicians Bellocq had photographed were there. Mauvetu and Onie were holding on to each other, in tears.

When the parade was over, Bellocq went home to find a letter waiting. It was from an Austrian war widow who had sat at Jomy's bedside in the American Hospital in Paris, where he had lain for two years since the armistice. She had hoped to take him to Karlsbad to convalesce, the spa town where she was born. She had wanted him to be happy. Now, grief-stricken, she had to tell Bellocq that Jomy was dead of his wounds. Life was a bed of nails. It struck Bellocq as odd that Albert should go halfway round the world, only to end up with a widow.

10

Tony Laudati sent Bellocq an invitation to a farewell party – to make amends, he said. He and his family were leaving for Chicago. The party was aboard the *Tennessee Queen*, which set Bellocq thinking of Bliss and Adele. He was too afraid to refuse. A jazz band played on the wharf; another in the stateroom. The vessel was ablaze with lights from stem to stern. The same captain smoked his cigar by the gangway, sweeping off his planter's hat to kiss each woman's hand. Bellocq had tried to envisage the event but failed. He was left feeling that he ought to be wearing something more in tune with the occasion.

'I don't see a camera,' said Laudati.

'Was that what you expected?'

Laudati shrugged. 'We have a guy around somewhere. Not many people aboard are crazy about having their picture taken.'

The man with him was over six feet tall, and big. He weighed some two hundred pounds or so, which he carried with a shambling walk.

Bellocq felt a sudden panic as the vessel shuddered. The paddle wheel rumbled as it began to turn. He had thought that the party would be there, moored at the Canal Street Wharf. 'Where are we going?'

'St Louis,' said Laudati. 'I have business there. I'll go on by train to Chicago.'

'I have to get ashore,' said Bellocq. 'That's a thousand miles. I have no money. I did not plan to go anywhere, certainly not to St Louis.'

'Enjoy yourself as far as Baton Rouge. I'll pay your passage home. You want anything, just ask. On this river you can never know what you're liable to feel. All the girls are free.'

The bodyguard got quiet in the stateroom using a megaphone. Laudati stood in front of a lifesize ice swan. Behind him, the buffet had a silver salver heaped with caviare. There were lobsters, crayfish, oysters and prawns, also vast Mozzarella and Gorgonzola cheeses the size of cartwheels, and bowls brimming with black and green olives. 'How many of you know why you're here?' Laudati glanced around at the crowd. 'You must have said to yourselves, Tony is throwing a wild party, and never gave it another thought – except you ladies, maybe, what with all that fuss about what to wear. Paolo Lippi is the reason we are here, of course, God rest his soul. It was Paolo's idea to have a party aboard a riverboat, and he used to talk all the time of making this trip. Sadly, he had to go before he could make that dream come true. One thing I do know, he would want all of us to have a good time. So, that's what I ask you to do, too. Anyone wanting to sleep can; then wake up and start all over again. Right?'

There was applause, cheering. Men cried, 'Laudati! Laudati! Laudati!'

A master of ceremonies came on stage; the Storyville dwarf in tails, cracking a ringmaster's whip. He took off his top hat with a flourish as two girls in black stockings and coats burst through a paper moon lit by a spotlight, dancing around with walking canes. They wore red cravats, and waved derbies. The one who fell down got a big laugh and applause.

A man who took hold of Bellocq's arm said with a laugh, 'What do you think, you can eat avocado with chopsticks? What you do here? You're not Italian, yet you got that accent. What is that?'

Lorenzo Tovoli had a razor scar on his right cheek. It was stitched so badly it gave his face a lopsided leer. He was balding, going to and fro, hands waving, ready to prove a point. Five years ago he knew nothing: he was a raggedy-ass kid in Sicily beating a shitty mule up a slab rock path. If his father could see him now his mouth would hang near his knees. 'I don't ever look back after I come to America,' he said. 'I make *gelato* in New Orleans. All the ice-cream they eat here! I had a real artist carve that swan. You like? You see those flowers I froze in there? A nice touch, I think. The hell of it is, it will be water again before you can blink.'

'Are you moving to Chicago?'

Tovoli smiled. 'These guys – they look forward to being in the hotspots, smoking fat cigars and listening to Jelly Roll all night. I'll tell you, some of them won't be laughing. They had it easy in New Orleans, but things will be tough in Windy City. Not all of them will pick up where they left off. Nobody is about to leave a warm place by the fire and say, come on in and make yourself to home. Question of numbers, and what there is to go around.' Tovoli combed his hair, glancing sideways in

224

the mirror. 'You see those old *padrones* at the table in the corner? They can't get it up any more. Some of them could need a doctor before we dock at St Louis. Too much too soon, if you get what I mean. They are sweeties now; they kiss each other, where's the venom in it?'

Tovoli asked who pulled his strings, and Bellocq thought first of his mother, then of Miriam, before shaking his head.

'Somebody always pulls those.' Tovoli was sure. 'What the fuck you do here, anyway? I guess Tony has his reasons.'

There was no holding Tovoli once he was in his stride. Life was not all they cracked it up to be. Nothing you could do about that, except learn to take the rough with the smooth. Some things he knew, he would rather not know. Other things they didn't mention because you *caca* your drawers. Could Bellocq see Carmine Togliatti there, solid as a brick shithouse? 'Don't ever step on his toes, or you'll wish you hadn't. He can lift a horse up – I seen him do that trick.'

Togliatti stood guard as petitioners came to Laudati to seek royal justice.

'The outfit is what it is, and always has been,' said Tovoli. 'Forget you heard a word I said. Anything gets back to me, I'll come round to find you. You'll regret it. Nobody knows anything about us, except us. Understand?'

'What did Tovoli have on his mind?' Priaulx came round from behind Bellocq's shoulder. The handle of the walking-stick hung in the crook of his arm was silver, shaped like the head of an elephant. Its trunk was uplifted. His hair, greyer and longer, fell to his shoulders. His greasy bow-tie hung loose. 'You sitting this one out?' He tried a goatish caper, saying that Tony Parenti and Irving Fazola were in the band. 'Parenti is the clarinet player – the one wolfing candied fruit.' They were playing 'In the Good Old Summertime'.

Bellocq wanted to ask about Josune Baulaz, but saw Priaulx as part of that audience gloating over Sylvie's antics. Instead, he said, 'What would Amateau know, if anything, about my father?'

'Amateau is a fine lawyer. He was of great service when I had to get shot of a bad tenant. He has more facts at his fingertips than anyone I know; he would certainly be the man to ask. We all speak French, are born into our class – we all eat and sleep each other's business – one big happy family, heh? You know how families are, though – soon as their faces turn away you have to learn to live with your loneliness and fear.' His laugh was taunting. 'I don't see how any son could know the far end of his father in this city. Every family here was sprung from tainted stock. You can smell it on the midwife's hands.

'You don't really want to know about your papa, that he was useless at most things he tried – same as that Étienne Deschamps. You recall the case? No. You must have been deep in your studies to worry about such things.' Priaulx laughed again. 'No whiff of any scandal with his patients – but heh, what did they know when they were under? Jean Lafitte's gold?' Priaulx could not stop laughing now. 'He had himself a time with that girl – what was her name? Many's the time I heard him boast how eager that child was for a poke. Can *you* believe that?'

Priaulx slid his thumbs up under his suspenders to stretch them.

'You still got stuff rattling round in your head – spit it out.' He puffed his cheroot.

'Did my father steal Señor Mezcua's money?'

'Put it this way – if they didn't catch him with his hand in the till, he knew whose it was, and nobody knew better how to spend it.'

Never mind about that. Guilt was in the air Bellocq had breathed since he was a child; it had come with his mother's milk. 'We wake up and it's there on our doorstep, a stray cat mewling to come in,' said Priaulx. 'You've felt all along that you carry the burden, too. You're an easy book to read – always down on your knees at some keyhole, telling yourself lies all the time. The truth would be too hard to face – others have the truth. They own the substance of that shadow you chase with your camera.'

Smiling, Priaulx went off, leaving Bellocq alone with the rattle of roulette wheels and chuck-a-luck layouts, the thud of dice against baize.

Laudati had his wife on his arm when Bellocq saw him again. He introduced her as Orla. Bellocq had drunk enough to feel bold. He wanted to ask Laudati if he had killed anyone, but could only demand why Priaulx was there. 'You know what he does?'

'He checks the boxers out. There is a fight tomorrow.'

'I hope he has more care with them than the women he aborts.'

'Abortions? You sure about that?' Laudati looked at Orla.

'I saw him kill a girl one night.'

Orla Laudati fluttered her fan as her husband went over to Priaulx.

Bellocq rocked on his heels. 'Something to do with the fight?'

'You have a poor opinion of Tony.'

She leant back against a green tabletop; it rested on an Arab boy's turban.

'What does my opinion matter? Everybody needs a bootlegger, these days.'

'Yes, that's what they call them now.'

'I don't know, Mrs Laudati —'

'Orla. Call me Orla,' she said. 'Tony has always felt he had to achieve more than other men. Since I've known him he's owned a restaurant, and many other businesses. That's what he is — a businessman.'

'With interests in the waterfront, the meat market —'

'No. Not those, so far as I know.'

'Why does he need a bodyguard?'

'You mean Carmine?' Orla laughed. 'Carmine is Tony's cousin, though I admit he does look like a bodyguard. I must go. No doubt I'll see you later.'

Laudati had waved her to join him. Bellocq watched Priaulx bow low to kiss her hand.

Turning, Bellocq flinched at seeing Lieutenant Judge, afraid that Sprague was not far away. Now Laudati was close behind him, saying that Priaulx may have done a few abortions, but he gave up that line of work years ago.

'Sprague, that two-bit chiseller?' Laudati was scornful. 'There was no chance of him getting aboard.'

Judge was showing the New Year photograph of the officers and men of the New Orleans Police Department to Henry Maranga. Maranga had run a honky-tonk in the District until it was closed down. Maranga held the picture to the light with a fond smile.

★   ★   ★

228

The queue of men fell silent as Bellocq passed with Orla. She was cooling her cheek with a fan. 'It must be hot in that cabin. They say the girl was in a convent. How can she do that?'

'She's in great demand,' said Bellocq.

'Animals!'

'Ask your husband; he knows more than I do,' said Bellocq.

Orla was amused. Tony went to mass Sundays and they had a happy family life. They had two children: a boy, and a girl who was a prima donna – what she would, what she wouldn't eat! They had gone ahead with Tony's mama on the train. She could not hope to find a better husband. He was attentive, kind; he doted on them. He never ran around, and there were few times in the day when she did not know his whereabouts.

'You, though, you must know all about what life was like in those houses.'

'You've seen my photographs?'

'Tony has a couple, framed and all,' Orla said. 'One of a girl with a butterfly.'

'Where did he get them?'

'He said you had a friend, Ethan Smithline, who sells prints in the Quarter?'

What she admired was that he had treated all the women the same way. They all seemed to live in an Inner Light – none was any more beautiful or ugly than another.

As they moved, the air became inert, almost a substance, and so laced with her gardenia perfume that Bellocq felt like a fly drowning in cosmetic cream. Those women had been objects of desire; neither he nor any other man could possess them. The men paid to live other

229

lives for a while, to have women defer to them. Those women were open in front of the lens, in a sunlight that had seemed timeless. His exposure fixed them. He asked for nothing, and they gave any- and everything they felt would make him happy. 'I tried to stop the clock for a while, mine and theirs,' he said.

No. He was not trying to avoid her question.

Sex was not the same for Catholics, Orla said, as he must know. All they had was Jesus holding a lamb in His arms. Quite the worst thing about the convent had been that the girls had men on the brain. They taught her every Latin word for what you did in bed. She had them all pat: *vagina, fellatio.* 'Half the time I didn't know what Tony meant,' she laughed. 'You think I'm not a virtuous girl, I talk this way? America is the land of the free; not like the old country, thank God. There, women kneel on pillows to be blessed, and the rice falls like hail. A girl can get herself stoned to death.'

Later, when Bellocq passed the room again, the girl over the bowl, rubbing her throat with a piece of the ice swan's foot, was Sippie Brooks. She raised her skirt with a grin to show stocking-tops bulging with dollar tips. 'You get around, Mr Bellocq,' she said. 'You're a live one, and a sly old fox.'

By now, a few of the guests were drunk enough to imagine that they could sing. The band played 'Tiger Rag' again.

'They carried him upstairs on a bloody stretcher,' the woman said. 'The maid was scrubbing for a month to get the stains out of the carpet and sheets. He was dead, of course; he had gone. Nothing could be done that wasn't done. I wiped the dust of the street off his face. I took his teeth out and put them in the glass by the bed; he would never permit that when he was alive. Now I live hand to mouth.'

Laudati tried to pacify her. 'I don't care to hear you say that, Mrs Ruscio, because it isn't true, and you know it. We take care of you; you can hold your head up until you join Angelo.'

'Nobody blames you, Tony, but what should I do?'

'It's well past your time to go to bed,' Laudati told her firmly.

Tovoli hovered at Bellocq's elbow again. 'That old lady is a holy pain in the ass. Never mind she's not right in the head. I know now about your pictures. Tony says you're good.'

'I take them to please myself. Sometimes, I have to pretend that I have clients,' said Bellocq.

'Come on, I've got a little something you might like to see,' Tovoli urged, leading him into a room. 'I had a hand in it myself before they closed the District.'

He said they shot the film to sell in Chicago and New York. The room was dense with cigarette smoke that made Bellocq's eyes sting. A nude girl was kneeling on the floor, in the usual posture, the man's cock in her mouth; her feet beat a frenzied tattoo as she choked on him. Tovoli grinned. 'On my mother's eyes, if I do say it, you'd go a long mile to see a better performance, heh?'

Bellocq was upset that many of the women were masked. None of their bodies had the same nakedness he had recorded. One girl made him recall Florrie, another Sylvie. When two men tied her to the bed, he looked away, not wanting to verify his suspicion.

'Tony never came to you?'

'What do you mean?'

'You'd be a natural in this line of work. He said

231

you knew how girls could tell just where a camera was.'

'Is that what he said?'

Tovoli heard the bitter note in Bellocq's voice. 'We all piss in the same pot, those of us who can,' he said. 'We make it up as we go along. We do what we want, when we want, and we're no better or worse than any other business outfit. I don't write the rules, and I had no hand at all in making this world.'

Bellocq heard the twang of the Jew's harp first, then a baby's cry. The raft came swiftly out of the dark and went past fast under the lights, with the family staring up. The woman's wedding dress was off one shoulder as she gave suck to a babe. A girl held her father's hand; in his other, two tied geese were struggling. It was a dream, or someone had put something in Bellocq's drink.

He turned to find Sippie Brooks at the rail. 'You saw that?'

'Saw what?'

She was being sick. 'This is not such a good trip after all, Mr Bellocq.'

At daybreak it was raining at Baton Rouge. As Bellocq left the boat he passed partygoers waiting to board. There was an old man with a girl he said was his granddaughter. She wore a purple hat with a dark-blue silk band. A boy by the gangway held a large umbrella so as to shelter them; he was no more than twelve. Laudati followed Bellocq down to embrace the old man, whose name was Fiorino Ortolini. 'Now, Fiorino,' he said, 'this is not the weather or time for a kid his age to be out. Take him up; get him into some dry clothes. Feed him, and find him a bed.'

'You've come a long way since I last saw you, Tony,' said Ortolini.

'I did not choose the way it came about. But, yes, things changed after Paolo died.'

'That was bad.'

'Sure. What could I do? Shoot just anybody?'

'It might have looked better. You sure you'll be happy in Chicago? There is going to be big trouble in Cicero; opportunities, I agree, now that Prohibition's here to stay but opportunities – what are they? I can see a lot of people fighting tooth and nail to get their snouts in the trough.'

'Don't they bill this as the land of opportunity?'

'You mean George Washington was Italian?'

'Torrio has it all sewn up, now that Colosimo is dead,' said Laudati. 'His motto has always been that there is room for everyone. John I knew in Brooklyn, and he wants me up there.'

'Come Christmas, I'll make the trip to see how things turned out. Your lovely Orla is aboard, of course?' Ortolini crouched down, grunting for breath, and took off the girl's satin shoe. 'At least you have a future; I have only a past. You do me great honour, Tony. I kiss your hand. See. I'm going to drink long life for you out of my granddaughter's slipper. All this,' he laughed, with a wave of his hand, 'there's only one word for it: it's a fairy-tale.'

Laudati shook hands with Bellocq, who was left holding the boy's umbrella. '*Arrivederci*, Mr Bellocq. I'm sorry you're leaving us here. Everything has been taken care of.'

All Bellocq could find to say was to watch his step in Cicero.

'You can make a book on that.'

Laudati's party left Bellocq with the same feeling as when the District closed. After the auctions, gangs of workmen tore the fittings out – the doors, the mirrors, the floral toilets, sink bowls and taps; the panelling, wallpaper, and shelving. Bellocq felt for the dazed dwarf outside the sporting house. He had hustled johns and run errands for the girls, anything from hairpins to opium. 'Maybe if I sit here long enough,' he had said, 'somebody will tell me where to go. They told everybody else.' Bellocq had lost the women too. They were fading, the light was not the same – yet he could see them dancing for ever round that phonograph.

The lights died out one by one as the riverboat went round the bend. A thin streak of yellow widened slowly on the horizon to etch the trees with acid light. The air had a dead smell of geraniums, but none were growing there. A heron launched up from the tree line.

Three years later, Bellocq read in the paper that Laudati had been shot. After a game at Wrigley Field, he had stopped off to get a shave in a barbershop on Wabash Avenue. The two men came in separately but fired seven shots together to make sure. Mrs Orla Laudati, who had just arrived by car to pick up her husband, saw it all. The killers were 'persons unknown'; there were a lot of 'persons unknown' in Chicago then.

11

The headlines were about Lindbergh landing in Paris, but the big news across the South was that the Mississippi was forty feet above its usual level. Louisiana was flooded, and New Orleans was under threat.

Bellocq stood in the rain behind two women waiting for the streetcar. He listened to their talk. One said how much money she owed and could never repay – the worry would kill her. 'I swear to God, I'll stab him next time he comes round to get his piece of my flesh. I stand there, knife in hand, and think about it every week . . . What *is* that smell?'

'I don't care for it, either, it's the fish I bought,' said her friend.

'I was looking at the hatchet he uses to cut off those heads, wham-bam, wham-bam, all day long. I got murder in my head, and I can't stop my mind running on it.'

If old women were not able to tell you something about life, who could? They were boring in the end. Bellocq hesitated on boarding the streetcar, not knowing why, suddenly afraid, thinking of his mother's last days, of his petty rages when things went wrong, a chemical failure, or a light-bulb broke. 'You get on right now, or you can stay there,' the conductor said.

Bellocq got aboard, disliking the motorman's smile. He wore black pants and a white leather belt.

A hand touched his shoulder; a voice said, 'Is that you,

Mr Bellocq?' Bellocq turned to see Joyboy in the front seat of the Coloured section. He was wearing a sou'wester.

'Why, Joyboy, what a surprise!'

Bellocq could remember the day he'd first met him, at some picnic Louella took him to. 'How is Louella?'

'She's fine. Rough waters, Mr Bellocq, but we're still shipmates together. The meat rolls soft on her old bones and it can still move me. She'd be glad to see you, you know, if you would come around.'

'I'll try, if I can find the time. Give her my best regards for now.'

Bellocq had always seen Joyboy as alone, a jailbird and a hobo. Louella had taken some of the distance out of his eyes, but the blood pulsed in the twisted knots of veins on his brow.

'Are you well? Your health okay?'

'Oh, better now,' said Joyboy. 'I ate a crab that was bad, and was in the Charity with food poisoning.'

'It smells tasty whatever you got in there.'

Joyboy laid a big hand on the parcel in his lap.

'A ham, and some pig's feet.'

They rode on in silence for a while. Then Joyboy came out with Nature being like that old Pandora's box. There was everything in there, but it was hard to say what was going to jump out next, even a flood to threaten his life. 'That old river can sure be mean. Maybe it'll take us all this time.'

'No, they'll dig that ditch,' said Bellocq.

'I hope so.' Joyboy laughed. 'I'll die smiling if I can. I told Louella to scatter my ashes on the racetrack, and she said why not – I'd blown more dough away there than I ever won. The ponies always had a mind of their own when I put a dollar on their nose. You sad the District went? You were around there, I heard. Wasn't that one hell of a place? Nothing's the same since it shut down. Well, this here's my stop, you know.' Joyboy got up and shook Bellocq by the hand.

The streetcar moved on. Joyboy was left standing in the rain, in serious thought.

A knee-high statue of a grinning black jockey in racing colours and a yellow bow-tie stood on the lawn in front of the house. Bellocq knocked at the front door then stood clear of the raindrops falling off the wisteria above. A black servant showed him into a large parlour, and Elroy W. Braidwood came through the adjoining doors. 'Afternoon, Mr Bellocq,' he said, knotting his tie, blue with red spots, and slipping suspenders onto his shoulders. Bellocq noted the man's gold signet ring set with an amethyst as he stood at the mirror slicking the hair back over his big ears. He turned, ready for business.

The fan above set the chandelier tinkling so that light spots chased around the ceiling. Over the mantelpiece hung a painting of an eighteenth-century sea fight somewhere off the coast of Europe.

Braidwood had come out of the Irish channel, like those saloon owners Tom Anderson and Frank Early. The slums were the same, but they had left them far behind. Braidwood was respectable now. His boots creaked as he went to the drinks cabinet. He was having bourbon and branch water; would Bellocq take the same, or something else? Bellocq nodded, and said, 'Then the figure we talked about is acceptable?'

'Why, of course. Isn't that why you're here? As I said, I've seen some of those pictures you took at Mrs Kite's. They catch the very bloom on things – ah, those sweet memories! Now there was a woman who made a man feel at home. It got so bad my wife had a private detective on my tail. I don't think there's a missing collar stud she doesn't know about me. If she has a fault, it's that she sleeps half the day now,' he mused. 'I don't know where I am with her.' He paused. 'You don't mind my being frank.'

Bellocq shook his head. 'It will help you feel at ease with the camera.'

'Is that what happens? I feel at ease?'

'I hope so.'

'I have a lot on my mind right now, Mr Bellocq.'

'I see that.'

'Let's keep this short, eh?'

Bellocq got up to unpack the camera.

'I'm dealing night and day with a state of emergency across Louisiana,' said Braidwood, his arm spread wide. 'The cards when they fall are awful black at times. I sent for a digger, but the damned steamboat ran foul of a floating tree and shed the thing over the side, so the dog-tired men I got out there are slaving to save this city by hand. They can't rest up, night or day, or we'll all swim like rats. I'm housing thousands of refugees who have lost everything. There are hundreds of them here who didn't make it to the high ground at Vicksburg.'

'Are you going to do it, hold back the flood?'

'Oh yes, I think I can say that. What I'm less sure about is the cholera threat getting to us; there could be any amount of dysentery and pestilence.'

Bellocq said he had a friend – Chenault – helping with the ditch.

'Along with a lot of good men.'

'Get off your soapbox, dear,' his wife said, coming into

238

the room. 'Mr Bellocq is here to take your picture, not vote for you.'

As Bellocq framed Braidwood, he recalled where he had last seen him: a shadowy figure in the cigar smoke watching the pornographic film at Tony Laudati's party. He was older – fatter, too, after civic dinners and late nights at Fabacher's.

If Bellocq would like, he could hitch a lift out there with him; see how his friend was getting along.

The storm had blown over but the pavement was wet. Tannehill, a journalist Bellocq knew by sight, was waiting by the car. Braidwood followed his gaze up at the sky. 'Sure, it's let up for now, but for how long? You're on the dot, Tannehill. You know E. J. Bellocq? You'll have seen him around the District, I guess.' Bellocq shook hands.

'Your chauffeur won't credit that Babe Ruth earns more than Coolidge,' said Tannehill, shedding his oilskin. 'Money talks, eh? How much would you say you're worth, these days, Mr Braidwood?'

'Now what sort of fool question is that, for Christ's sake? I hope you're not out to ruffle my feathers, Tannehill!'

Tannehill had worked in the District; he had seen Bellocq's nudes in the *Blue Book*, and would like to see more, sometime, even if those girls were not what you could call odalisques. He had cut his teeth at the *Mascot* as a cub reporter, with pieces on social evil and police vice in Storyville.

A maid came out of the front door and waved the chauffeur back in. When he left the house again, he had a large basket on his arm. Mrs Braidwood wanted the men out there to have food. 'Eudora doesn't get it,' said Braidwood. 'How can her home-cooking find its way into the right hands? Unless I dole it out myself,

239

I'll never know whose gizzard it's going down. She's crazy.' He put the basket on the seat beside Tannehill. 'You better see to it!'

'That's not why I'm here, E. W.,' the journalist protested.

'You've had a big heart all your life; you'll do it,' said Braidwood, beside his driver now. Up there, he gave off an aura of being in charge.

They soon reached the city limits, going by old slave quarters where forlorn barefoot families sat on porches. 'Pissed off being cooped inside those hutches, I'd say, rain rolling down their necks,' offered Tannehill. 'They'd sure appreciate our dropping this basket off, E. W.; they'd vote for you, if they could.' Tannehill laughed, then went on about the old belief, started doubtless at Jamestown, the day they bought the first niggers in 1619, that a man got rich using slaves. 'It took a machine – the cotton gin – before any slave owner made a penny profit out of them.'

'Is that a natural fact?' Braidwood was not convinced.

Out at the river's edge, Braidwood strode off to parley with his engineers and the police sergeant in charge of the prison guards. 'There's diddly-squat he can do,' said Tannehill, 'but he can't miss this; he's a need-your-votes go-getter. My job's to trump up the trip, loud and clear. Louisiana is too itty-bitty a pond for a fish to grow as big as he means to. Get a bridge named after him one day, or we'll see his statue someplace. He can charm the birds out the trees. He's so smart he can prove that water runs uphill. One of these nights, somebody will lie in wait and put a bullet in him.'

There were lanterns alight along the levee so that the

gangs working there could see to stack sandbags. Warders in oilskins stood around with rifles and dogs. Braidwood turned as Bellocq and the others caught up. 'They'll shoot to kill,' he said. 'These coloured boys are from prisons all around, some as far as Angola. You never know what a catastrophe like this might tempt a man to do.'

Tannehill told Bellocq that the slaves named the prison after their home in Africa.

Braidwood was angered. 'Well go on, you know so much about Angola!'

'Every inmate in chains there is guilty as sin, and who can say better than that?' replied Tannehill.

'I'd hate Mr Bellocq to go away thinking anything bad, Tannehill.'

'Bad what, E. W.? I thought you were out here with that crocodile smile to shake everybody's hand!'

'If I were that kind of operator, why Mr Bellocq would be taking his picture right here, where I'm doing the most good.'

Soon, Tannehill had his pad and pencil out, talking to a family that had come downriver on a raft. They stood by a brazier in the emergency kitchen. Each gust that struck the tent set the hurricane lamps swaying and brought fresh fear. The woman gave suck to a baby after it made a thin mewling cry. Her two girls had blankets over their naked bodies. They were no kin to the other two boys. The family had got them down off the roof of a cabin as they swept by. Braidwood said their parents had been washed away.

Time got a stranglehold on Bellocq again. His throat tightened; he heard the Jew's harp at Laudati's party. They were the same dream family.

'Where do we find real history?' Tannehill lit his pipe.

'We know the rain fell forty days and forty nights, that's what the Bible says; but things are trickier now with flood relief. Who's to know whose bank the cheques are in? Can I tell you? Why, neither I – nor any man drowning out there in the flood. Yet I'm come to witness and write it into history. And if I do find out the far end of things, then what can I do?'

There were steel shelves each side of the tent. Worn-out workers sat slumped with their heads on the zinc-topped trestle tables. An old man in his underwear went by, an overcoat hung on his shoulders. Braidwood made a show of tasting a mouthful of soup; he said how heartening it was. Bellocq went to look for Chenault and was directed to the hospital tent. He had been bitten by a moccasin. The doctor had had to amputate his left hand. 'That was one way to take the sting out of it,' Chenault said, with a rueful smile. He lay on an army camp bed, his face pale as the rain beat on the olive-green canvas above. 'It will cramp my style somewhat.' He held up a picture magazine. 'Maybe you should have kept on going, E. J., straight to Hollywood. Look at this now, Mary Pickford, Clara Bow – you could be doing pictures of these girls.'

'You are taking this very lightly. God knows how I'd get on if I lost a hand,' said Bellocq.

'What can I do about it?' Chenault shook the magazine. 'At least I have this one.'

Braidwood was there again, on tour, stopping briefly to ask each man how he was doing. He shook Chenault by the hand, then told Bellocq gruffly, 'Your friend can ride back with us, you know. He doesn't want to lose any more flesh to blood-poisoning.'

Chenault ran with the blanket over his head as the rain

fell heavier. 'There; wouldn't you know it?' Braidwood
cocked his head. 'I said it wasn't over yet.'

In the distance, a calf bellowed on the levee, another
orphan. A rain shroud hung on the horizon, lit by lightning. 'Unless it lets up, we're under,' said Braidwood.
A rat ran by; Braidwood threw a stone. 'Motherfucker!
They are the great survivors,' he said grimly, pointing.

Tannehill turned to Bellocq. 'Were you ever in
Mexico?'

Bellocq called to mind the badly lit picture of the
bandits; their faces lost now in the darker shadows that
cloaked his trip south. 'I was there at the wrong time –
I missed my date with history.'

'The heads on the coins are of Obregón and Plutarcus
Calles now, Madero's boys,' said Chenault. 'Would you
trust a man called Plutarcus?'

'*Con permisso, señors,*' said Braidwood. 'Sing out where
I can drop you!'

With Storyville long gone, Bellocq felt he was but passing
through, too. He tried to stay out of those streets, yet was
drawn back – usually on days when rain made them look
worse. The mansions had gone, torn down, fallen into
disrepair, or made over into lodging-houses. It struck him
that he had been old before his time all his life, now that
the real thing had begun to stalk him with swift stealth.

Something in the nature of a spring had gone inside,
and he could no longer stop and start the way he used
to. He was broken, but had to go on.

By now, even the steps of the public library took it
out of him. He went there often to avoid being alone.
He had seen the old man in the reading-room before, but
never paid much attention. Today, the man got up from

his chair and shuffled down the aisle between the tables. Hooking his glasses on, he said, 'I've seen you. It came to me just now. You're *Papá* Bellocq. You were around the District. When was it, now? I forget. You want a coffee? I got a place round the corner. Look it here, maybe a beer would go down better? I can sink one. Can't do a many, these days, you know,' he laughed, 'but they taste the sweeter. One thing about Storyville, you were never alone there for long. There was always some girl had time for you, if you had two dollars in your pocket, heh?'

They were on the stairs going up to the old man's room now. 'I get it all, here – spiders, beetles and roaches,' he said. 'You'll have trouble with those too, I guess, *Papá*. My floor is lousy with woodworm. One morning I'll open my eyes and find I'm in the room downstairs. Is there anywhere a body can live free of those in this city?

'On Canal and Bourbon you got "Bailey's Sure Injection" – it never failed. Or Dr Miles on Poydras would sell you a fine specific mixture for gonorrhoea and gleet. God bless Dr Ehrlich's "magic bullet", I say.' He laughed. 'I did time at the icehouse. Those were the days. A dime bought you a pitcher of beer, and a keg cost only a dollar. Jelly Roll Morton was running round living the fast life.

'I was there in 1914 to bury Josie Arlington at Metairie Cemetery. I was there with Tom Anderson. She was not the same woman after the fire at her place. I never knew how it got so bad, with the firehouse just down the road. I could not believe she paid thirty-five thousand dollars for that red marble tomb! It had those two big flambeaux on top and a girl knocking at a copper door – looking for a john, or what?' He laughed. 'You remember these?' He held up three copies of the *Blue Book*. 'They're a

244

collectors' item now. You got it free at the railway depot, coming right into the heart of it all, or you paid twenty-five cents in any bar or barbershop, if you didn't know where to go. Why am I telling you this, of all people? It's a cinch I'll forget it, else, that's why. Jesus Christ, sometimes I lose it. I was there twenty-four hours a day all those years – shit, how can I lose it? Fuck! Is that rain again?'

He went over to the window, fumbled in his vest pocket and took out a small comb to scrape at the few threads of hair he had left. 'Do you mind?' He crossed to the small basin to wash his hands, then stood still, staring as the water dripped from his fingers. 'I never knew all the ins and outs. You read it in the paper how the Mafia had killed Police Chief Hennessey. When was that? 1902, I guess. Nobody knew why. It was the same when the pony took sick, I remember, and couldn't get it up. If it couldn't get its dick stiff soon, it was going under the hammer. Emma Johnson was never noted for her magnanimity. Heh! Heh! You remember Olivia's dance when she was part of Emma's raree show? She'd clap that oyster on her brow, lean back and shimmy it all over her body until she got it down to her foot. Then she'd kick it up in the air, back to where it started, and do it all again.

'Judas priest, they had gold taps in those sinks and baths – but for all that fine furniture, curtains, pictures, none of those madams would shell out a fifth of what they made. Jesus Christ! Did they ever pay for street cleaners? Hell, no!'

Bellocq stared, not sure what he was supposed to say.

'Our trouble *Papá* is that all that's left for us to do now is die.'

245

12

In December 1949, Chenault wrote to Miriam Hecht.

Dear Miriam Hecht (I do not know your name now)

I found your address sorting E. J.'s papers. I heard
by accident, some time ago, you were married to
a salesman who sold farm machinery here until his
injury brought you both to Pittsburgh. I don't know
how you will take it, but I felt I had to let you know
that E. J. is dead.

It was rare that he would mention you in my
company of late, but he did have your address. Am
I right in assuming that you knew nothing of his life
after you left New Orleans?

He took pictures in Storyville until they closed
it down. After that, he did not have the same
feeling about photography. The war was on in
Europe, but he never wanted to hear about that.
He became morose, withdrawn. I went to see him at
818 Ursulines when he was ill. He had been solitary
all his life, and said he ought to have grown used to
that by now.

By then it was 1927, and everybody was over the
moon at the safe touchdown of the *Spirit of St Louis*
at Paris. You saw Lindbergh's picture everywhere.

My, my, they surely needed circuses in those days, our bosses. It was at that time they began to lay men off here, and I was one. I took work of all kinds after I lost my hand in the great flood.

The last time I saw him, July past, he asked me whether I knew that the first time syphilis got a mention in history was in a poem. We were going along Rampart to visit Anna Kjeld. She was in the isolation hospital. She had worked at Mrs Kite's, where E. J. took his best photographs. She hurt now in the spirit, too, frowned on by all, she said. The ward was such a dead place. She detested those snotty bitches coming round with their tracts, pleading with her to face her life. They made her feel as much a nigger as those other women, singing their never-ending spirituals. The doctor, too, was of a mind that she ought to give up what she had been doing, change what she was. She was afraid she had been in the game too long with Mrs Kite, and in other houses before hers. If her clients had had to show a medical certificate at the door she would not be in that fix. Her most fervent wish was that she had better caught the disease from a lover, and not in the flesh trade.

You will excuse my rambling on. We have only our memories to live with now.

I could never understand why E. J. used to say that he had not captured the real truth about the women in his pictures. To my mind, he had. He said he felt he did at the time; but later, looking back, was sure he had not. Life was but a series of decisive moments, he said, and some were easy to miss. People did that – they lived them, but missed the point, and they were gone. Unless he was working he did not feel alive. He was always stuck to find ways to put himself into life, he said. Nowadays people took their own photos, and he felt that was how it should be. Who needed a photographer?

E. J. could never get the hang of those Kodaks. That Bantam Special was a very slick machine when it hit the market: all black enamel with ridged metal strips around the casing. He would show me how the front opened, the double Ektar lens in its housing, the metal range finder, the rolls of film. He used to lie in wait at intersections to snap people unawares with that Bantam. Never could, though. He hated not being able to choose the light, he said – it was the right key in which to play the music. He had sought to stay true to his time and place; anything else he could not see his way clear to doing. I know how serious he was about his work. He studied the *American Almanac of Photography* every day. He left off trying to take pictures just before the start of Hitler's war. Old then, he sat outside the Eastman Kodak Company store. Unlike most of us, he had gone the other way and become more French as he aged. Did you know people in the District used to call him *Papá*? He fell at the corner of Common and Carondelet. Some men picked him up, but he was dead when they got him into his old chair by the water cooler. A little blood ran out of his nose, they said.

Did it ever occur to you that E. J. got stuck on you because, deep down, he knew that he could never have you? I think I realized that about you early. Not that I blamed you, nor am I seeking to blame you now. E. J. was not the easiest of men. His

248

portraits of those women bear witness to the truth of what I am saying. There was not one of them would be his; yet he left them all with us for ever.

I had to open the window; chrysanthemums can make the air dead and sickly in a room. The death certificate on the bedside table said he had died of cerebral sclerosis and uraemia. I looked for his old plates, but there was no sign of them. Maybe he did throw them out. I know that some of the plates were spoiled anyway. For myself, though, I do not believe he could bring himself to do it.

When the mayor closed Storyville down, there were auctions to sell the furniture, paintings and fixtures. E. J. bought an upright piano that Jelly Roll Morton used to play. I set the metronome going to ponder whether to sell his things to some rag-and-bone merchant.

Even as I said I ought to use the Bantam to take his photograph, that nobody made death masks any more – I had to go through with it. It was the first time I had done anything of that sort. I made up some plaster and tied a cloth around his head under his chin. When I had done, I brushed his best black suit and got him into it. It was no trouble to lift him into the coffin, never mind my hand; he weighed next to nothing. He had never said a word about that rose with your name on his arm. Did you know he had it? I picked a thread off his shirt collar, then folded his hands neatly and put a flower in his buttonhole; something he never did alive. I gave the rest of his clothes to the Salvation Army.

I enclose some prints of you. If you should visit

New Orleans you can find E. J. in No. 1 Cemetery in the family vault.

He would say that if you read Balzac, you had to give in to being 'mastered' by a master who had a viewpoint – who had dedicated his life to making sure you shared his vision of things. The great touch E. J. had was to be in the right place at the right time. But he was naturally desperate that he was about to miss something, or that it had gone already.